The
Soldier's
Letters

BOOKS BY SHARI J. RYAN

SHARI J. RYAN

The
Soldier's
Letters

bookouture

Published by Bookouture in 2022

An imprint of Storyfire Ltd.
Carmelite House
50 Victoria Embankment
London EC4Y 0DZ

www.bookouture.com

ISBN: 978-1-80314-612-6
eBook ISBN: 978-1-803146-119

To my family who I never got the chance to meet.

PREFACE

After *The Girl with the Diary* was written, I felt a longing to reconnect with the characters I had spent so much time with. At that point, I found a great storyline within Annie Baylin, a sub-character from *The Girl with the Diary*. *The Prison Child* then came to life. Spending another several months with these characters did nothing but create an even larger desire to stick with them. However, I came to a place where I had to decide if I would take the leap and write a point-of-view from the enemy's side.

If you aren't familiar with *The Girl with the Diary*, the story revolves around a Jewish prisoner, Amelia Baylin, held captive in a concentration camp during the Holocaust, and a Nazi, Charlie Crane, who wanted to run away from his position of power. The two found a friend in one another—a forbidden friendship that could have resulted in their untimely deaths.

Charlie Crane, the soldier—Nazi and SS guard—has a story much different from one of a typical Nazi.

I continuously paused at the end of that last statement, because in my mind, a Nazi shouldn't deserve a story worth being understood, never mind, heard.

As a Jewish woman, I grew up in the fear of hatred, anti-semitism, and the simple case of being a minority with religion. I hid the truth and kept quiet through my school years. Regardless of the times changing and improving (relatively speaking), there were times when a swastika was drawn on my school bus window, spray-painted on my driveway, and etched onto my school desk. These instances only added to my fear—a fear of being proud of who I am.

I have said many times throughout my writing journey that I enjoy writing what scares me the most. Those stories seem to evoke my deepest emotions, so I like to dig in that area.

A Nazi, though... the thought terrified me. How could I write about a Nazi and spin it in a positive direction?

The research was endless, and so were my questions. How did such a large population come to hate an entire religion? The answers were out there, and I found them: manipulation, propaganda, and unimaginable tactics that brainwashed many.

There were many Nazis who were against what they were forced to do. Just as the Jews were left without a choice, many Nazis were given threats that would leave them in the same life or death situation.

At a young age, Charlie Crane was left with the unthinkable decision to protect himself or an entire religion.

Through *The Soldier's Letters*, I provide insight on the internal battles Charlie endured and how he became a man with the power to kill. When the dust settled, Charlie did not move along in his life in contentment. As most would assume, his life was destined for a darkness that I dug into, understanding and realizing thoughts of a manipulated man more than I may have originally planned.

Now, reading back on *The Soldier's Letters*, I see how raw, dark, emotional, disturbing, and truthful the story came to be. In the mind of most, Charlie would not deserve a happy ending no matter how the story spun, but since I don't like to end a book with sadness, I had one heck of a time creating a realistic portrayal of Charlie's journey—one that he needed to endure to find his peace in the world.

My goal was to offer myself a better understanding of the "enemy," and though it pains me to understand how much hatred grew during the years of the holocaust, I now have a broader understanding of how life came to be.

I have poured my heart and soul into this taboo story, and I hope you enjoy the journey.

GLOSSARY

GERMAN

Ach du lieber Gott: Oh my God
ach nein: oh no
bäckerei: bakery
barbier shop: barber shop
danke: thank you
es wird am ende in ordnung sein: It will all be all right in
the end
Führer: leader (Hitler)
frau: Mrs
fräulein: Miss
Guten tag: good day
guten morgen: good morning
Hör zu: listen
hallo: hello
herr: Mr
ich liebe dich: I love you
ja: yes
juwelier: jeweler

mein: my
nein: no
Oberscharführer: Senior Squad Leader
Obergruppenführer: Three-Star Senior Squad Leader
rattengift: rat poison
sohn: son

FRENCH

Aidez-Moi: help me
j'ai besoin d'aide: I need help

PROLOGUE

The house in front of me was a vivid shade of blue—bluer than the sky, but not as dark as the ocean. The color reminded me of a blue-bird. The framed windows were a shade of forest green, and there were two small windows on each side of the matching door. The roof was old and tattered but supported the one lonesome dormer-window in the attic. The flower beds beneath the front windows were empty, but I imagine they were full of vibrant blossoms in the spring and summer. Trinkets clung to the windows from the inside where a fire illuminated a lonely table covered with a freshly prepared dinner.

I wasn't standing in front of that house to admire the unique colors and decor.

I had a task.

Sven shoved his elbow into my side as he walked past me, continuing down a line of Jews who were waiting for their next order. "Charlie, kill that woman. She is out of line," Sven asserted his command with an authoritative intonation.

I tried to step forward along the uneven cobblestones from where I was standing. The sight in front of me had me frozen. Through wisps of fog, I set my focus on the middle-aged woman.

With dark hair, tied in an unkempt knot at the base of her skull, and loose strands hanging in front of her eyes, she appeared forlorn while shouting for her children. She was wearing an apron, probably from the food she had just finished preparing for her family when a group of soldiers broke into her quaint blue house. "Let my children go!" The woman was trying to protect her family—her daughter and son. Sven told me to kill her because she was crying for her children, and we aren't supposed to tolerate such a disgusting display of emotion from a Jew.

Sven stopped walking when he noticed I wasn't following him. He stood, staring at me, waiting on me to fulfill his command. I still couldn't move. Rather than follow orders, I glanced back and forth between the woman's daughter, who was being pulled away by a comrade I didn't know, and then again at the distraught mother. She was reaching her arms out for her daughter, who was already so far away. At that moment, I knew the two would never reunite. The thought made me feel sick.

"Kill her," *Sven shouted*. "Do it now, Charlie."

I knew of the punishment I would receive for not following orders from a superior, but I couldn't move my arms, let alone handle a weapon.

Sven's hand pressed against the lapel of my coat as he pushed me away. "Coward," *he muttered, passing by me.*

Sven retrieved his rifle from the left side of his belt and aimed it at the mother's head, while the other comrade had the woman bent over in shame.

I couldn't do much else but watch her daughter grieve what would be an extraordinary loss in a matter of seconds. "I love you, Mama. Please don't hurt her!" *the girl shouted in a plea.*

"Amelia," *the woman countered.* "Fight and be strong. For me."

Amelia was the girl's name.

Amelia deserved a mother to face the horrors she was about to encounter.

"Mama, no," Amelia grunted. "Please, don't leave me!" Amelia pleaded as if her mother had a say in the matter. Though we all knew, only one person had the final decision, and Sven no longer had a heart in his chest.

Amelia's words buzzed over the blasting weapon. Her mother was taken down with one bullet. To the ground, she fell. Blood pooled instantly. The smell of gunpowder was potent, even through the thick air.

The world went silent for me even though screams were coming from all sides. The Jews were scared, especially while watching one of their own sacrificed as an example of what disrespect earns.

I watched that woman's daughter, Amelia; the pale complexion wash through her face as she stared doe-eyed at her mother's corpse. Amelia's head shook slightly with disbelief as she was pushed within a herded line, farther and farther away from her mother's body. Amelia couldn't have been older than sixteen or seventeen, and in an instant, her world had become darker than she likely ever could have imagined it would.

My chest felt as though it was caving in. No matter how many Jews I watched meet their ending as Amelia's mother had, the pain never lessened, and the heartache only grew stronger with the sight of every new-fallen body.

I was not meant to be a killer.

I refused to hate, no matter what I was supposed to believe.

* * *

Hello. I'm Charlie Crane.

Like many people who lived through World War II, I have spent years reminiscing about those years—the memories, decisions, losses, and gains. While I know plenty of older folk like myself who put the past behind them, I prefer to keep my past current to avoid letting anything I left behind, die.

My life has had many ups and downs, trials and tribulations, and enough death and destruction that has made me wonder if my birth was a mistake. Surely, I was not meant to live the way I have. Though beyond my dismay, I will carry the shadows from eradication within my heart.

I was born in the small town of Lindau within Bavaria, Germany—a place where houses and buildings replicate much of the fairy tales modern parents tell their children about today. Colored facades, in every hue, with gabled roofs, white-framed windows, cross-hatch decor lining the walls, stone-work adorned with deliciously pungent flowers; the world as I saw it was picturesque, and I was none the wiser that a place outside of Bavaria could look any different.

My mama and papa were Hans and Anja, a bread baker and a seamstress—both innocent and quiet.

My family didn't have a lot, but we made do to get by; always dreaming of a day when life might become more comfortable for us all. We weren't shy about our wishes and hopes, but as I became an older boy, I often wondered if we were too open about our desires. I began to think that by having enough and recognizing what we had, my family would someday have more than enough. Although, who was I to tell someone how to dream? Especially when that someone was Mama or Papa.

"He will change the world," I remember Mama saying, speaking of our country's new chancellor. "You watch, Charlie, he will make things better for us all. We will have an answer to our prayers."

There was no answer to our prayers. *Hitler* did not make life better for anyone. Instead, *he* stole everything from everyone.

"I don't like that man, Mama," I replied, speaking out of turn.

"Charlie, do not talk that way. That is pure blasphemy. Our

country needs change, and Adolf Hitler will do just that. You watch, he will." With a smart tap on my cheek, Mama pointed her finger, making her point clear, which only left me with more thoughts.

I was too young to understand the complexity and meaning of a country adopting a dictator as a leader. However, it might not have mattered how old I was, because Hitler's promises blinded many of us.

History was developing every single day. Life changed quickly for all: young and old, men and women. No one was safe with their thoughts and opinions because we were no longer allowed to think on our own.

Hitler's troops tried to mold us—me, but I was a strong boy and a stronger man.

I bent, but I did not break.

Adolf Hitler made laws against loving a different kind.

Then, I broke the law.

It was the best decision I have ever made.

CHAPTER 1

PRESENT DAY

I was sure this day would not come. After all, I have waited more than seventy years for this miracle.

My focus falls on the telephone—the one still connected to the wall by a cord. The ring is loud and high-pitched; foreign after how long it has been since the last time it rang. For a moment, I consider letting the old clunky black desk phone with thick buttons continue to chime. I'm sure it's just a tele-marketer.

I complied with society a few years ago and purchased a cellular phone, but after falling victim to this wireless world, I have found that the device has just one purpose: solitaire. The young man who sold me the phone was nice enough to down-load the game before I left the store, which promised to keep me entertained for hours.

With the small chance the call is not from a salesperson, I shift my tired body toward the edge of the seat. My recliner whines as I lower the footrest. The chair must be as old as I am by now. The three steps I take to my writing desk feel like a mile while wondering who might have taken the time to call an old man like me.

I lift the phone from the receiver and hold the cool plastic up to my ear. "Hello?"

The silence following my greeting forces a chill up my spine.

A young woman's voice starts and stops, but the sound is unfamiliar. I assume she must have dialed the wrong number until I hear *her* name.

Amelia.

Amelia Baylin.

I continue listening to the words coming from the other end of the phone. "She—she is alive, but not well. Her heart is failing—she's had two strokes. Charlie, sir, she's been asking for you."

While listening to who I now know to be Amelia's grand-daughter chatter with apprehension, I twist away from my desk, wrapping the coiled cord around my trembling hand.

A lump falls to the bottom of my stomach—a sensation I haven't experienced in such a long time.

Amelia needs me.

It has been seventy-four years since I have spoken to the love of my life. The only love of my life.

She remembers me.

My hand cups around my mouth as my eyes fill with tears... tears of joy. Then my gaze falls upon the matching leather recliner beside mine. *Amelia's chair.* She has never taken a seat in her chair, but having it beside mine all these years has made me feel like a part of her is with me when I sit here and contemplate the way life should have been.

Amelia should be by my side.

I have dreamt about her falling back into the chair with a sigh of relief after a long day. I have also dreamt about her easing carefully into the soft leather as her aging knees threaten to give out as mine do on rainy days.

With a sharp breath, I straighten my shoulders, turn back to the desk. "I will be on a train, first thing in the morning," I tell Emma, Amelia's granddaughter.

Amelia isn't well. She's in the hospital, but she is alive, and I'm going to see my girl.

I don't think I have moved this fast in years, but I know where my old leather suitcase is, and it's empty, ready to be filled with what I need to travel from New York to Boston. Before tossing clothes into my case, I slide the accordion closet door open in the hallway, inhaling the scent of dust and old books from the belongings I have stored in this small space. A cigar box from the top shelf contains everything I have ever wanted to give my Amelia.

I fold my hand around the soft wood, and it reminds me of all the times I placed a vast amount of love into this small enclosure.

I place my folded clothes neatly on top of the box and fill my shaving kit to the brim with incidentals.

One last thing: I open the top drawer to the bureau in my bedroom and collect the small yellow envelope that has taken up residence in my drawer for many years. I was sure I would never touch the contents during my lifetime. An estate sale would have been the last of it, but I'm still alive, and so is Amelia.

This changes everything.

CHAPTER 2

PRESENT DAY

I feel like the world is moving toward me in slow motion as I walk down the hall. I've been waiting so long for this day that I'm scared I may wake up from this dream again, and as usual, it won't be real.

I turn the corner, and in an instant, it feels as if time stood still. It doesn't matter how many years have passed. It doesn't matter that Amelia has white hair and that there are lines on her face. She is still the most beautiful woman I have ever seen.

"Amelia, my darling. You look as beautiful today as the last time I saw you," I say as I walk toward her. The surprised glimmer in her eyes tells me that Emma wanted to keep my arrival a secret, which makes me happy. I've wondered what the look on Amelia's face might be if we were to run into each other unexpectedly—the look I imagined.

"Charlie?" she says, recognizing me immediately. Her eyes are open wide, and tears trickle down her cheeks.

I take her hands in mine and immediately feel the undying connection between us. I remember the sensation running through my body as if it were only yesterday that I laid eyes on her for the first time.

I hadn't cried since the day they took her from me, but the tears are flowing freely from my eyes now. I'm not ashamed to cry because I've been holding it in, waiting for this day for seventy-four years.

* * *

How can two people find the right words to start with after so much time has passed?

Amelia found the words, and I'm trying to digest every one of them right now.

Amelia and I spoke until she fell asleep in her hospital bed. She told me things I never imagined, things that will forever change my life.

Now, all I can do is stare at her in awe.

Though a smile is still present on her face, I must wait until she wakes back up to continue our rendezvous—to continue learning about an entire lifetime I missed.

My attention has moved to Emma as I recognize that Amelia's beauty was passed down well to this young lady.

I would do anything to try and make up for so many lost years. I'm not sure where to start. Emma knows about me from reading Amelia's diary—that's how she found me.

Here we are, in a quiet room. Emma might think I don't have anything to say to her, but in truth, I have so much to say, and I'm not sure where to start.

Emma smiles the way Amelia does.

"Charlie, are you all right after taking that all in?" Emma asks.

"I'm not sure yet, dear. I need to digest your grandmother's words."

"I understand," Emma says.

"We should let your grandmother rest for a bit," I tell

Emma, who is slumped in a plastic bucket chair against the far wall of Amelia's hospital room.

"Oh," she speaks up, straightening her posture. "Here, I'll walk you out." Emma is very attentive and caring.

"Oh, sweetheart, I can find my way out and to the hotel next door. I might be old, but I have sharp navigational skills."

"I insist," Emma says, smiling lazily. Her eyes scream exhaustion, the poor thing.

"Very well," I tell her. I lift my arm, allowing her to walk through the open door first.

"I'll be right back, Grams," she whispers to Amelia. "Don't get into any trouble."

I chuckle, hearing the thought of Amelia causing trouble in her nineties. I guess some things never change.

We're halfway down the hall when Emma presses her palms against her cheeks, and then releases a hearty sigh. "What a few days this has been," she says. "The strokes were so unexpected. Grams has been very healthy, and we have been fortunate over the years. I was with her when it happened. It was awful."

"There is nothing fun about getting old, Miss Emma. Let me be the first to inform you," I tell her with a sigh.

"Oh, Grams has said this many times," she jests in return. "She makes it known every day."

"I'm sure she does," I tell Emma, staring at her profile, wishing I had been able to see it when she was a baby—wishing I had seen her mother as a baby, too. I wonder how many times her facial features have changed since then. "Well, I'm certainly glad you were there to take care of her. You very well could have saved her life, dear."

I get the feeling that Emma isn't looking for such praise as she shrugs off my comment. "So, I know it has been a long day, but would you like to get a cup of coffee with me down in the cafeteria?" she asks.

I drop my good hand into my pocket as we stop in front of the noisy elevator. "I will never turn down a cup of coffee, young lady." I suspect Emma might be foaming at the mouth with questions for me—another trait I believe runs through her DNA.

With heavy eyes, Emma stares at the circled numbers above the chrome elevator doors. I can't tell if she's avoiding eye contact, or if she is searching for her next thought. I'm a stranger to her, and I know well how strangers make people feel.

"My favorite color is green," I tell her, offering another small fact about myself.

"Green, huh?" she asks, keeping her focused pinned on the blinking number four.

"Not just any green, though... sea green. It's not as dark as forest green and not as wimpy as chartreuse. It's the perfect shade of green."

Emma smiles in response to my reasoning. "I like the way you think, Charlie Crane."

Once inside the elevator, I'm not surprised to see Emma's eyes flicker along with the descending numbers above the doors. I would do just about anything to find out what thoughts are racing through her head. "I'm upset that I didn't know about you until this past week," Emma says, biting down on her bottom lip as if the words she is speaking cause her pain.

I remove my hand from my pocket and hold it against my chest as I shift my weight from foot to foot. "Life unfolds at its own speed, darling."

Emma doesn't seem to have a response to my old-timer's saying, but the elevator doors have now opened. Emma steps out first, leading us down a short hallway that smells of chicken broth and cabbage. They aren't my favorite scents, but I haven't eaten since lunch and I'm famished.

"Are you hungry, Charlie?" The way she says my name is the way any young person talks to me when they aren't sure if

I'm borderline senile. Sometimes, I go with it. "It looks like they have soup and sandwiches over there." She points to a small buffet area beneath a glowing sign that says: "soups and sandwiches."

"Where are you looking, darling?" I ask, squinting my eyes off into the distance.

"Just over there," she says calmly, placing her hand on my back to guide me in the right direction.

"Those are soups and salads?" I ask her. "It just looks like a pile of rubbish to me."

Emma stops walking, and her cheeks brighten around her ears. "I'm so sorry. I can take you somewhere else. There are a few restaurants down the street. I should have known better. Hospital food is rotten."

I can't help the belly laugh rumbling through my gut. "My dear girl, I see the soups and salads. I smelled them long before we stepped into this cafeteria. The food here will do just fine. Don't you worry, okay?"

Emma looks mildly confused and a bit taken aback when she places her hand over her mouth. "I didn't mean to offend—"

"Nonsense. You didn't offend me. I was messing with you. This man may be in his nineties, but I assure you, I am still as sharp as a tack."

"Apparently," she says with a quirked eyebrow—a look I recognize from her grandmother. "Well then, help yourself. I'm going to grab a couple of coffees."

"Do you trust me to find an open seat?" I ask, holding my hand up above my eyes like a visor as I glance at the empty seats.

Emma's lips twist into a coy grin. "Very funny, Charlie."

I'm distracted by watching Emma's mannerisms as she puts together two cups of coffee in the corner of the large cafeteria. I take a tray and ladle the soup into a Styrofoam bowl. My stomach screams with added hunger from the variety of scents around me, and I take a wax paper wrapped sandwich too.

A young woman with a hairnet and tired eyes watches me as I make my way over to her with my tray so that she can ring me up. She takes a look at the food I have on my tray and punches her fingers slowly against the cash register. "Ten dollars and thirty cents," she drones.

"Wow, pricey soup," I joke as I place the tray down so I can retrieve my wallet.

"I get that a lot," the woman responds.

I hand her a twenty-dollar bill and lift my tray back up from the metal grate. She punches a few numbers into the register and the drawer pings open. She places the twenty-dollar bill under the bill flap and reaches for the small pile of tens. "No, no," I tell her. "That's for you."

"Sir, I can't accept—"

"Sure you can," I tell her. "Thank you for your help tonight."

The woman's eyes narrow as if my act is suspicious. "Did you receive good news tonight or something?"

It shouldn't be so hard to believe that a stranger wants to leave a woman a nice tip. *Maybe the tip will cheer her up.* In New York, it's a sign of respect. Or so, I think of it as so. "Not exactly, but I got to see the love of my life for the first time in seventy years. So, that's something, right?"

The woman looks more confused now than she did when I offered her a tip. "God bless you sir."

"Yes, we are all blessed to be here."

I spot Emma taking a seat at one of the empty tables just a few feet away from the buffet. She takes her phone out of her pocket and brushes her thumb up and down the screen. Gosh, I remember a time when people would take the opportunity to look around a room when sitting down for a breather. Now, all anyone ever does is tend to their mobile devices. It's as if there is an entire world happening behind the shiny screen.

As I take careful strides to the table, making sure my soup doesn't splatter out of the bowl, I notice Emma places her phone back in her pocket. "Anything interesting happening in the world?" I ask, taking a seat across from her at the table.

"What do you mean?" Emma responds.

"Your phone. Surely something interesting must be happening on that face journal program." I know the website is called Facebook, but I feel the need to act the part of the role I'm playing.

"Facebook," she corrects.

"Yes, that program."

"It's just a website," she says, chuckling softly.

"Oh, what's the difference, right?"

Emma takes a sip of her coffee and presses the other cup over toward me. "I'm curious to hear your story," she says.

I nearly choke on my first sip of soup, hearing her statement. It's not that I wasn't expecting her to ask me about who I am. I would be inquisitive too if I were her. "My story," I say after swallowing the mouthful of broth.

"Yes, I mean, I read my grandmother's version of your story, but I'm smart enough to know there are two sides to every story. Isn't that right?"

Emma mentioned she had read Amelia's diary, but I don't know what Amelia wrote about me or didn't write about me, which means there is a chance she doesn't know the full breadth of my past.

I take a deep breath and straighten my posture. "Well, what would you like to know first?"

Emma takes another long drawn out sip of the steaming joe, unblinkingly staring at me. "What's your beginning?"

"My beginning?" I repeat, stalling to answer, because there isn't a simple response.

"Yes, where did you come from, Charlie Crane?"

CHAPTER 3

1935 — BAVARIA, GERMANY

12 YEARS OLD

It was a Sunday morning, and Mama was preparing breakfast made up of fresh Dutch apple pancakes with a heaping dollop of whipped cream. The house smelled sweet, like confectionery sugar and roasted coffee beans.

Sunday breakfast was my favorite time of the week. It was the only morning no one had to rush around before six a.m. There was time to rest, while we sat as a family and ate until we were full to our hearts' desire. "Charlie, sohn, how was school this week?" Papa asked.

Being a bread baker, Papa had to be at the shop around three in the morning and sometimes wouldn't make it home until nineteen hundred hours. He was responsible for baking, cleaning, and prepping the kitchen for the next day. Despite the hours he worked, Papa never showed his exhaustion. Instead, he would come home with a fresh loaf or two and a smile from ear to ear. As a child, I sometimes asked if he was having fun baking all day. He said he was living his dream.

However, there were times when I would walk by his and Mama's bedroom at night, spotting Papa rubbing his sore heels and Mama cleaning up the aftermath from a burn he acquired from one of the ovens. I never knew Papa to be without swollen veins across both of his temples.

"School was fine," I answered. In truth, school was getting the best of me. Our academics had seen a change in focus. We were learning more about war, politics, and economics; none of which I had an interest in learning. It was much of what Mama was talking about at home, but more pointed and direct.

Things were changing in the world, and no one was shy about the matter.

There was talk about a new school program correlating with efforts to help the suffering economy, but the teachers didn't seem to have much information on the subject. The only information shared was that if the school opened, only the boys would move to the new school. I debated having a discussion on the matter with my parents because I didn't know how they would feel about what might have been no more than a rumor. Although, I also wondered if Mama and Papa had already known, but chose not to discuss the possibility with me for the same reason.

"How is Claude doing? Is his leg healing up all right?" Papa asked while running his fingers through his light blonde hair that mirrored my own.

Claude had been my closest friend since we started grade school. He lived two houses down the road. We were sometimes referred to as double trouble—not because we were mischievous, but because we were curious, and our curiosity often led us to adventures that would land us on our behinds in a ditch. Claude was the one who fell in the ditch that time. We had been lucky before, but this last adventure led him to a broken fibula. Now his leg was in traction. Claude couldn't even leave the first floor of his house, so our adventures had come to a pause.

"He's still stuck in bed for another two weeks," I told Papa.

Papa made a double tsk sound with his tongue. "Well, I

have something for you. Maybe you could bring it to Claude's house and keep him company for a bit, later," Papa said, reaching into his deep pocket before pulling out a palm-size pouch.

I took the black suede pouch from Papa's hand and tugged on the thin cord that held the opening together. I poured the loose contents into my hand. "I've seen these before. Jacks, right? They're nice, Papa. Where did you get these?" We never went hungry, but extras didn't come around often. Mama always said we lived within our means.

I rolled the round nubs in my palm, swiveling them around the small rubber ball. "A man, Jacque, came into the shop yesterday. He was raving about the oatmeal raisin loaf he had picked up the night before. He was so pleased with the measly bread that he requested to speak directly to the baker... me."

"No one ever asks to speak to you, you've said that before," I reminded him of his own words.

"No one *has* ever asked to speak to me before yesterday, sohn. I was thrilled to receive such a compliment. Paul called me out into the storefront and the man, Jacque, was dressed in a nice pair of slacks and a long, forest green coat. It was obvious he's an affluent man. Imagine, a man like that telling me my bread tastes good—it was unreal." Papa paused a moment, and his icy blue eyes stared through the wall behind me. "It was wonderful. He took my hands and shook them both at the same time, asking if I had any children. When I mentioned your name, he reached into his pocket and pulled out this pouch, and then told me to give it to my sohn."

"That was very nice of the man," I told Papa.

"He said to me, 'Any man who can make my family smile on account of food, deserves praise. I hope you are teaching your son to bake as well as you.' His smile was endearing, and it was so nice to be spoken to the way I was, Charlie."

I didn't know what to say to Papa. It made me sad to hear

how happy he was from one mere compliment. "That is wonderful, Papa."

"I spoke to the man for a bit longer and found out he was new to the area, brought in for government business. It was a nice talk."

The mention of government business made me feel skittish. Our town was small, and other than the newspapers, and household chatter, all happenings within the government seemed too far away to affect us.

"Let's eat. Shall we?" Mama said, placing down a pitcher of freshly squeezed orange juice. Mama looked between Papa and me, squinting her eyes as if she was trying to figure out what we were discussing. Her eyes settled on my hands, and the bag I was holding. "You told him, Elias?"

That was the moment when I started looking back and forth between the two of them, wondering what Papa supposedly told me.

Papa cleared his throat. "I just gave him the Jacks, so he could take them to Claude's later."

Mama closed her eyes, her lashes casting shadows over her cheeks. "Charlie, starting this coming fall, you are enlisting in a new school for boys your age." Part of me wanted to ask her to repeat what she had said, but I heard her clearly.

My eyes went wide, staring at Mama with wonder. I couldn't think of a good reason for Mama and Papa to pull me out of my school. I had friends. For the most part, I liked my class.

"Soon, your other classmates will be joining you, as well, Charlie."

It made no sense. There was nothing wrong with our school. "But why?"

"It's what's best for you. Plus, you were offered a spot and we should be considered lucky that you have been chosen and admitted at this time."

I didn't understand a word of what she was saying, because it was as if they were leaving some critical information out of the explanation.

"Why me?" I asked. "Why was I lucky to be offered a spot in this new school?"

"Well, Charlie, according to society, you are perfect. Blonde hair, blue eyes—you have what it takes. So, we are fortunate for that, ja?"

"What does my hair or eye color have to do with this school?" I questioned.

Mama smiled at me with kindness. "Let's not focus on the questions that will surely be answered for you when you start class. Consider yourself lucky."

All I could focus on was my question about the importance of being blonde and having blue eyes. How did that equal luck?

"What if I don't want to go?" Normally, I wouldn't speak out of turn to my parents, but I didn't want my life to change. I suspected most boys my age would have felt the same.

"Charlie Crane, how dare you speak to us that way!" Mama scolded me.

I placed the bag of Jacks down onto my worn corduroy pants, crossed my hands, and lowered my head with shame. Everyone was silent for a long moment. "Charlie, we only want what is best for you," Papa added.

I couldn't respond because at that moment I wondered if he knew what was truly best for me.

When breakfast was over, I quietly excused myself from the table and exited through the front door. With the bag of Jacks secured in my hand, I made my way down the cobblestone path to Claude's house. I was sure if anyone were to understand how I was feeling, it would be Claude.

* * *

Rose bushes and cornflowers decorated the stone walkway to Claude's house—the sweet scent was strong, and the bees were buzzing loudly. I lightly tapped on the front wooden door of their white and black Tudor-style house, waiting patiently to be welcomed inside. I heard the chatter from within, but couldn't make out what they were saying. Claude's sister, Annika, opened the door. She was six years older than Claude and me, and she was training to be a nurse at the nearby infirmary.

Annika was becoming a spitting image of their mother, too. She was only a few inches taller than me, but her nose stuck up an additional two inches. I never liked her because she looked down at me in the non-literal way too. Most often, when I would visit their house, Annika would stare at me for a long minute and then curl her lip with a look of disgust. I didn't understand why she despised me. After all, she had hopes of becoming a nurse, and as far as I knew, nurses were supposed to be kind to all people.

"What do you want, Charlie Crane?" Despite her natural hatred for me, she seemed more bitter than usual that day.

"I was hoping to spend some time with Claude," I told her.

"He can't play," she said. "You dips did it this time. Why can't you be more careful?"

"I know," I responded. "I'm sorry Claude got hurt. I just wanted to come and visit him."

"Annika, who is at the door?" Mr. Taylor called out from the family room.

"It's no one important," Annika replied in a similar shout.

I heard Mr. Taylor's chair moan and groan, hinting he might be coming toward us. "Is that the famous Charlie Crane?"

"Famous?" Annika mocked him. "He's nothing but a trouble maker who landed Claude in traction."

She blamed me for Claude's accident even though I warned him against trying to make his bicycle skip over the ditch.

"Yes, sir," I replied.

"Come on in, Charlie. Annika, get the boy a glass of milk, will you?"

Annika grumbled as she rushed off into the kitchen.

"I'm in here, Charlie," I heard Claude shouting from the next room over.

"The boy is getting restless," Mr. Taylor said, following me into the dark room, decorated from top to bottom with brown fixtures.

"How are you feeling?" I asked Claude. He was still in the same position I left him in a few days ago in his makeshift bed, with his leg hanging from a sling.

"I want to get out of this bed. That's how I feel," Claude replied. "But you know what, Charlie? When I'm better, I get to go to a new school. I received an invitation just last week. I bet we can get you in too if you like. Would you like that?"

The new school. Was Claude excited about the new school? He must have heard more information about the place than I had.

"Claude, take it easy, sohn. I don't know if Charlie would be interested in this type of school. We should leave that up to him and his parents to decide."

My world felt like it was being torn out from below my feet. Something felt awry, and I had already lost Claude as an ally.

"I was also invited to attend. Mama and Papa told me this morning."

"That is fantastic," Claude shouted with excitement. "We can go together."

The walls felt as though they were caving in on me, and for reasons I couldn't quite put my finger on.

It must have been a sixth sense I was feeling.

CHAPTER 4

1935—BAVARIA, GERMANY

12 YEARS OLD

I hardly slept the night I found out I would be going to a new school. I had never enjoyed the action of change, which was probably the real reason for my lack of sleep, since it was impossible to know what changes were coming toward us as a country.

My mattress squealed as I rolled out of bed, which informed Mama that I was awake.

"Charlie, breakfast will be ready soon," she shouted from the kitchen.

I slipped on my knickers from the previous day. The suspenders were still attached, making the act of dressing a bit simpler. Knowing Mama would not take kindly to filth, I took a pressed collared shirt from my wardrobe, buttoned and tucked where appropriate. I had plans for the day, and I couldn't have Mama stopping me for a clothing issue. I even combed my hair to the right as she preferred. With my knee socks pulled up and outdoor shoes secured, I scurried down the short hallway, finding the savory and salty aroma of pretzels and sausage.

"You are already dressed as if you have somewhere to be," Mama said, speculating rather than asking if I had such plans.

"Yes, Mama. I plan to visit Papa at the shop. I was going to see if he needed help with any of the cleaning duties."

Mama narrowed an eye at me, ready to call my bluff. I was not a good liar. "Charlie, you have never asked to help clean the bäckerei."

I tented my fingertips in front of my waist, thinking of a way to sound more convincing. "Well, Claude can't do much, and I have been bored. That is all."

"Ja, I see," Mama said, still obviously questioning my intention by the intense stare she was giving me. Mama took the dishrag that was draped over her shoulder and wiped down the wooden board she had floured to prepare the pretzels. "Are you still upset about the new school, Charlie?"

She knew me all too well. "No, Mama. I'm not upset. But I like my current school, and I don't understand why I need to go elsewhere. I'd much prefer to stay put."

Mama wiped her floured hands on the bottom of her apron and strode toward me. As she leaned down to close the height gap between us, I peered into her ocean blue eyes that looked like mine. Except her eyes were full of hope while mine felt full of despair. "This change is for the best. I know you are comfortable at your current school, but you are receiving a wonderful opportunity, and we would be foolish not to accept the invitation. You must understand."

I didn't understand. My grades were fair, nothing to brag about, and I didn't stand out as an overachiever, so I couldn't see a reason anyone would send me an invitation to a new school. In any case, Mama was not about to budge on the matter. Papa was my only hope.

Mama offered me a dimpled smile and pressed her warm hands against my cheeks. "*Mein Charlie, es wird am ende in ordnung sein,*" she would often say.

It will be all right in the end.

I wondered how she could know such a thing. Though, I

was not one to query Mama or Papa. They knew best, but my questions continued to grow, and the answers did not satisfy my concerns.

I stared through the four-paned window across from the dining table as I devoured my breakfast. Mama stared at me all the while. "How is Claude feeling?" she asked as I took my final bite of sausage.

"He is getting well," I answered with a mouthful.

"Good, send him my best," she said, resting her arm on the table, holding her chin up by her fist. "You are still heading down to the village, ja?"

"Yes, Mama. I want to visit Papa."

"Very well, Charlie. Please don't find any trouble along the way."

"I won't," I agreed.

I took my cleared plate and brought it over to the sink basin. "I will see to your dish, Charlie. Run along, sohn."

The floorboards bounced as I ran out the front door and onto the damp cobblestone road.

Frau[4] Agnes, from next door, was watering the red poppies she had planted in the flower box outside of her front windows. "Guten morgen, Charlie," she hollered with a quick wave. "Where are you off to so early in the day?"

"Papa's bäckerei," I replied.

"Ah, very well. Charlie, come over here a moment," she said, waving me toward her flower beds. I did as Frau Agnes asked, wondering what she could want with me. She was an older woman, firm, but sweet. She often had her nose in our business, or so Mama would speak of at supper time. She was also known to be a bored housewife with too much time on her hands. Her gray eyes stared at me coldly as I came closer. Then her dark bushy eyebrows arched. "I would like to ask you to bring me back a small loaf of bread, ja?" Frau Agnes reached into the pocket of her apron and retrieved a five-cent coin. "I was going to make my way into town today, but if you are already on your way, I would be most grateful for the delivery," she continued, handing over the money.

"Of course, Frau Agnes."

"Good boy, Charlie. Don't find any trouble on your way, now." Ever since Claude's accident, Mama and Papa, as well as all the neighbors, think I'm one to look for trouble wherever I go. It isn't true, however.

I waved goodbye to Frau Agnes and continued down the road, passing a few shops along the way. The barbier shop was closed, and there was no usual line of men wrapped around the street corner awaiting their turn. I peeked into the window of the next shop. The cobbler, Herr Franc was in his usual position, hovering over a tattered wooden table while hammering a nail against a shoe's sole. The pungent scent of herring stung my nose just as I spotted a line spilling out of the small seafood market. I swooped around the line, bringing myself back to a parallel spot to the shop windows that I enjoyed observing on the way to the bäckerei.

Just as I was coming closer to Papa's bäckerei, the clouds formed a thick mist. It wasn't quite raining yet, but by the look of the darkening sky, a downpour was imminent. I snuck under the awning in front of the juwelier's shop. Herr Herwitz had run the place for more than fifteen years, but the storefront was dark that day. In place of the window displays were lines of newspaper, covering the glass from the inside. The store wasn't just dark, it was closed, but writing scrolled across the window. The main headline on all pieces of newspaper read: 'Die jüdischen Angreifer' (The Jewish Attackers).

I wasn't sure what the article meant by the 'Jewish Attackers', but I knew Herr Herwitz was a Jewish man. There was a chance I didn't understand what was I reading, but I pieced together the facts well enough. Thinking of the situation more,

Herr Belson, the barber who ran the shop just a few stores away was also Jewish. What was happening?

The black painted writing across the last storefront window blended in against the newspaper, but on the outside of the window, the words, 'NO JEWS HERE', were written in large letters. It pained me to think of Herr Herwitz, his position, and the business he spent his life managing.

I stormed into the bäckerei, letting the bronze bell hanging from the door's spring announce my entrance.

"Charlie, hallo!" Herr Paul greeted me from behind the front counter. "What brings you in today?"

"I thought I might help around the store a bit," I offered.

"Go on back and see your papa. I'm sure he could use a hand," Herr Paul replied, moving down the side of the glass showcases containing baked goods. The store smelled like heaven—a combination of surgery sweets and fresh loaves of bread. My stomach knew nothing but hunger when I stepped into the bäckerei.

Papa was in the back, pounding on a heap of dough. Flour was flying through the air like snow, and the thumping sound bounced off the nearby walls. "Charlie, what are you doing here?"

I slipped my hands into my back pocket and rolled onto my heels. "I came to help, Papa."

"Help?" he questioned.

I didn't offer to help often enough, I guess.

"Yes, Papa. Put me to work."

Papa nodded his head to a broom in the corner near the lavatory. "Go on," he said. I rushed to the broom, swiftly taking it between my hands.

"Thank you," I offered.

A short time passed when Papa called my bluff on just wanting to help out in the shop.

"What is it that you want to talk about, sohn?"

Papa also knew me better than I figured. "I just wanted to keep busy," I lied again.

"Nonsense. I can see by the look on your face that there is something you would like to say. Plus, no one truly wants to sweep a bread shop. Tell me what's on your mind, sohn."

I glanced up at Papa. His sky-blue eyes glistened beneath the light hanging overhead. He had flour on his right cheek, and his toque-hat was hanging crookedly to the side of his head. I could only see some straggly overgrown brown hair poking out beneath the hat's rim. I hadn't noticed Papa was overdue for a haircut.

"Why aren't Herr Herwitz or Herr Belson in the shops today?" I asked, feeling concerned about the answer. Papa didn't like me inquiring about adult knowledge, but I was curious as I was sure many people were.

Papa's gaze dropped from mine, and he took his battered wooden rolling pin and took his emotions out on the dough. "I don't have an answer to your question, sohn."

"It's because they are Jewish, ja?" I asked.

Papa closed his eyes and nodded his head ever so slightly. "Charlie, there's a mess over there that needs a sweeping." Papa brushed his arm across his forehead and pointed to the other side of the back area.

"Is the new school because we are separating from the Jewish people?"

Papa dropped the rolling pin down to the center of the dough and strode around the table to where I was standing. "Listen to me, Charlie," he said. "I know you think we have a choice in what is happening in our country, but we do not. We don't get to control our leaders or the decisions made from people above our heads. We either follow the rules, or we pay consequences, ja?"

I shrugged because some of what he was saying was confusing. "You are to go to the new school, and we do not have the choice you think we do. It is for your own good, despite the nature of our reality. We must believe that everything happening today is for our best interest, Charlie. You need a promising future, and the new school will offer that to you. Do you understand me?"

I understood clearly at that moment. Mama and Papa didn't want to scare me into realizing that they had no say over where I went to school. We were to follow protocol, and if we didn't follow, a consequence could arise—whatever that might have been.

"Yes, Papa."

"Charlie, go on home, sohn. Go help your mama around the house."

There was evident pain in Papa's eyes when I looked up at him—a type of pain I was sure he did not want to discuss. "Yes, Papa."

"Good boy, Charlie."

I placed the broom back in the corner. "Oh, I need to bring home some bread for Frau Agnes. She gave me some money," I said, handing Papa the five-cent coin.

"Very well, sohn. Take a loaf from the rack over there," he said, pointing to the cooling area. "Here is some paper to wrap it with." Papa handed me a sheet of brown paper, and I tended to the hot bread.

"Go straight home, Charlie. Say hallo to Frau Agnes for me and kiss your mama."

"Yes, Papa."

"Everything will be all right, sohn."

After spending a short life believing every word Mama and Papa spoke, it was in that moment that I first questioned... What if Papa was wrong?

CHAPTER 5

PRESENT DAY

Emma is stirring the broth in her bowl with a spoon, taking in my words, likely trying to digest them with the same amount of confusion I felt back then.

"Why were you so concerned about going to a better school?" she asks. It's the same question I was asking myself over and over. *Why was I concerned?*

"I don't know why I was worried before starting the new school, but I later found out there was more than enough reasons to feel the way I was."

"It's just school, right? What could have been so bad?" Emma continues. Her eyes squint at me as if she might understand better if she can see more clearly. It's a lot to take in, I know. There are still days when I question what I lived through.

I take a sip of my steaming coffee and focus on the warmth running down the back of my throat as I recall those days. It was so long ago, but at the same time, it feels like it was just yesterday.

"It was not just a school. It was Hitler's Youth Program, designed to raise boys into Nazis. *That* is what everyone was feeling so honored to have their children join. Of course, we didn't know the fine details right away, but even when more information came about, people seemed to enjoy the concept, or at least, agree with Hitler's plans."

Emma clears her throat and takes a sip from her coffee cup. "I'm sorry... what is Hitler's Youth Program? I've never heard of such a thing."

"Many haven't, darling. It isn't a part of history people are proud to share."

CHAPTER 6

1935 — BELGIUM, GERMANY

12 YEARS OLD

Summer ended quicker than I would have liked, which meant the dreaded day of starting a new school had arrived.

"I'm proud of you, Charlie. You are going to learn so many wonderful subjects. This school is going to prepare you for your future." Mama pinched my cheek as I left the house that day.

I didn't think there was much of a reason to be so concerned with my future at only twelve years old.

There were classrooms in my new school, yes. The desks we sat at were nothing fancy, as the founders of the new school promised to offer. Elite Boys—that was how we were supposed to be perceived—the best of the best. But, our desks were old; the wooden tops etched with names, some with vulgar sayings. The rusty-brown linoleum floors were peeling and clashed against the pale-yellow walls. The windows, stained by the sun on the outside, were covered by a film of dust and cobwebs on the inside. The classroom smelled of mildew, chalk-dust, and bleach. What was worse was that the teachers we had didn't seem confident in what they were teaching, not even to a twelve-year-old child.

At least I was with Claude. We both started in the fall after he was well enough to be out of bed. I did my best to hide my lack of desire to attend this school because Claude couldn't contain his excitement.

The school was made up of all boys as warned, but it was instantly apparent that gender wasn't the only singularity the school idealized. It didn't take long before I noticed that all of us boys had a striking resemblance with our varying shades of blonde hair and hues of blue eyes. I still couldn't understand why those attributes would be favored.

I recall one of the first days of classes and the teacher I had. Herr Leon, he was a self-proclaimed politician of sorts. Of course, I didn't know what that meant then, but what I gathered was that he had no actual background in education.

Herr Leon wore a similar uniform to the students: taupe corduroy shorts, a mustard yellow button-down shirt, a black tie, and a tawny leather cross-chest belt that connected to a waist belt, finished with silver emblems. Then we also had our black ankle-high boots, intended for the marches we would take. Herr Leon was a tall man, his ashy blonde hair was greased and comb-slicked to the side. His face was clean-shaven, and his dark eyebrows were permanently in downward turned angles pointing in toward his nose. Without speaking, he emanated a sense of misery.

My feeling of distaste for Herr Leon was solidified shortly after watching him write a string of words along the green chalkboard. We watched attentively, waiting to see what was written while listening to the thin piece of chalk scrape, crumble, and ping off the board, while a boy two seats down coughed through the sound of a barking dog. Another boy sneezed, and Claude, who was sitting next to me, cleared his throat. The room was full of nervous sounds. Then, for a moment when Herr Leon stepped away from his written words, the classroom became silent, still, and I slowly read the words to myself: 'Jews are the devil!'

I felt deflated, as though the air was draining from my lungs. During my short life, I had seen the words but had never heard anyone speak so much hatred about another. No one had to ask why the teacher wrote those words on the chalkboard because he continued to draw pictures beneath his words. He outlined four faces, two profile angles, and two point-blank angles. One profile picture displayed the eyeballs set inward, and a nose jagged and long. The front-view showed eyes too close together, and a nose that took up too much space along the center. The other two pictures had symmetrical features on both the profile and front-view.

Herr Leon held his piece of chalk up to the unsymmetrical drawings. "These are Jews. They are biologically defective, and we must stay away," he explained. "However, those of us here, right at this second, are the start of a new race to outlaw anything bred beyond perfection. We are Aryans, a race superior to all others."

The coughing boy from two seats down raised his hand, and then spoke before being called. "I thought God made us all look different for a reason, ja?" he suggested.

Mama had preached this to me, as well. Her reason was to keep me from staring or pointing at a person who didn't look like me.

Herr Leon's eyes went dark, and he walked toward the boy with his chalk outstretched. "Nein. Nonsense! We are one kind, and we must unite to continue our race. We must not let the demons in, for they want to abolish our kind. They want to kill us. They are monsters, those Jews. You understand, boy?"

My heart stopped beating, or so it seemed. I questioned why the Jews would want us dead. What had we done to be on the receiving hand of so much hatred?

Herr Leon continued: "They are awful people. They don't believe in the same kindness we do. We must stay away. We have to keep them out. It is the only way to survive."

Survive.

Claude peered over at me with a lost gaze. It seemed as though he was silently thinking the same questions as me, probably wondering if I was as lost as he. I shook my head slightly, enough for him to see I felt the same. Something was not right.

It seemed like hours before class ended, but when we left, there was nothing more than silence among many of us. We strode through the hallway toward the exit, all of us in formation.

A group of boys gathered outside of the school doors, huddled in discussion. I stood just outside of the cluster, listening to what they had to say.

"I heard they're going to train us to become soldiers so we can fight off the Jews," one boy said.

"My papa told me we might be lucky enough to meet the Führer."

"We might meet Adolf Hitler?" another boy responded with a sound of delight and excitement.

"We are part of his youth program. That is what this is, ja?"

Claude wrapped his hand around my arm and yanked me away from the crowd. He hobbled in front of me through his limp and then glanced over his shoulder to offer me his sound advice. "Charlie, you can't listen to them. No one knows the facts. We have to do as told, and everything will be fine." I couldn't see how anything would be fine. "Let's go into town for a snack, ja? Mama gave me some money."

"Okay," I told him. Claude and I walked to town as we had often done, but from Bavaria rather than Belgium where we currently boarded. The village wasn't a far walk, but it took us a while with the pace Claude moved. He was still in pain but did his best to hide what he was feeling. However, I knew his expressions well.

Just before we made it across the road to the cafe, we

noticed a crowd of German soldiers huddled in a circle. "What do you think is going on?" I asked Claude.

Claude stood on his good foot, pressing up to his toes with hopes to see over the heads of the tall soldiers. "There's smoke," he said.

Claude, in all his curiosity, walked toward the men, jumping up and down on his left foot. I walked around the side in search of a peephole, which I quickly found. "There's a fire," I told Claude.

Right as I spotted the flames, the crowd of soldiers dispersed into a direction away from us. We were able to see quite clearly now. A rusted metal barrel with flames licking the rim is what we were seeing. Claude and I walked up to the fiery blaze, finding the barrel full of books. The leather-bound covers were burning as the pages curled into the spine, one by one, burning from the outside. Hebrew letters covered the charred pages. The books belonged to the Jewish people, and the German soldiers were burning them all. Why such a disgrace to books?

I kicked the barrel as hard as I could, hoping to knock over the contents. Maybe some of the books could be saved. "Charlie!" Claude shouted. "Nein, Charlie. Nein."

"We must save the books. They are just books, Claude," I argued back.

"They *are* just books. It isn't worth finding trouble over, Charlie. Stop." Claude wrenched his hand around my wrist and pulled me with all his might. "Let's go, now, Charlie. You're going to get us into trouble."

"Is this who we are to become?" I yelled at Claude as if it was his fault that the books were on fire.

"I don't know," Claude responded. "But if it is who we are supposed to become, there must be a good reason for it all."

CHAPTER 7

1937—BELGIUM, GERMANY

14 YEARS OLD

It wasn't long before our classroom discussions about our pointed hatred for the Jewish people turned into battlegrounds where we were trained to fight and protect our kind from the enemies who wanted us eradicated... or so said our teachers.

"Crane, to the ring," I heard. I was being summoned to fight, to prove my capabilities, maybe even my worth.

Sven was my battling opponent. He was one of the top-ranked students in our school, often chosen to be a teaching assistant in the lower level classes with the younger students. Our paths had crossed many times throughout the previous two years, but not in this type of setting. With round, beady eyes, a rigid nose, and a defined jaw, he stood before me waiting to take me down with one swing. Sven was much more blonde and fairer than I, and he had at least a foot on me. Though Sven was sixteen and I was fourteen, we were still matched up to fight each other.

The superiors said it was for training.

Mama told me fighting was not the answer to anything. "We must not do to others as we wouldn't want done to

ourselves," she would say. "Always help, never hurt, Charlie."
Her words replayed over and over as I slipped on my boxing
gloves. I agree with Mama, and I don't believe in hurting other
beings, but the school was teaching the opposite—I was fighting
to protect myself. My scrawny fourteen-year-old body stood
before Sven with only a pair of oversized maroon boxing gloves
to offer protection. I let my hands dangle by my sides. My gloves
should have been protecting my face.

Sven narrowed his eyes at me and as we were taught, held
his closed fists up. "What's the matter, are you a stupid little
Jew?" His words were just words to me. They didn't cause
enragement as he likely intended. "This poor boy wants to be a
part of the Jewry," Sven continued. He was pointing his fist at
me while observing the watchful eyes that circled us. The attention he was encouraging was not necessary, but Sven enjoyed
acting as a showman.

I wanted to cry, but not out of fear, just out of pure sadness
that life had taken this despairing turn.

Sven's gloved hand made contact with the side of my nose. I
was knocked out in less than a second. I didn't defend myself as
I should have. A part of me wanted to feel the surface pain more
than what I was suffering with inside.

I regretted my decision while enduring the pain that was
comparable to being hit by a swinging metal boulder. Within a
blink's time, I was flat on my back, trying to tune out the hoots
and laughter that surrounded me.

We started school together as boys, and within months, it
became clear we were all there to worry about only ourselves.

"Charlie, you need to get up," I heard from above my body. I
didn't want to open my eyes. I knew what I would see—the
crowd encircling my body, wondering if Sven had killed me. I
focused on the grass beneath my flattened palms, the way the
soft blades tickled my skin. Some of the grass was touching the

backside of my right ear too. It was nice. When I was a small boy, I would run barefoot in the patch of grass we had behind our home. Mama would tell me to protect my feet, but I enjoyed the sensation too much to listen. "Charlie." I heard my name again. I opened my eyes, afraid of staying still any longer.

Claude was the only person in view. "Come on. I'll help you up," he whispered.

Through the thick of the militaristic school and training, we were going through, Claude and I remained friends, just as we had been. Our superiors didn't admire friendships, so we kept a slight distance and were casual when we spoke.

Claude helped me up to my feet, and we moved off to the side and away from the crowd. "Charlie, brother, you have to pull it together. You can't keep taking those kinds of hits from the older boys. You have to train like the rest of us."

I shook my head, feeling a wave of nausea surface. "I want to run away," I told him.

"You know we can't leave, Charlie. There is only one option, and it's to look forward. We are training for protection. Someday, we'll appreciate what we are becoming, you know this, ja?"

There wasn't a day I wanted to be in training for whatever reason our country was in preparation mode. I understood very little because nothing made sense. I was digesting what I was supposed to acknowledge, but I didn't want to believe half of what I was learning. I don't know if I was alone, thinking this way, or if all boys around my age had gotten good at hiding their feelings. It was clear that some of the boys seemed to have taken a liking to their studies and training. They had a different look in their eye, in a competitive sense. Sven, for one, had wanted to knock me out. I could see the desire growing as he stared me down. We were being built to hate, and it was getting the best of many.

"Come on, Charlie. Let's go get changed and ready for our next class." Claude continued to follow the advice he had given me. We were to look forward and not back on what we once had.

It seemed impossible.

CHAPTER 8

PRESENT DAY

"There was a school to build Nazis..." Emma states, but also questions. "I have wondered how and why so many people came to hate the Jews in such a short period. It hasn't always made sense or added up for me, but this clarifies a lot."

Emma's eyes haven't blinked in some time. She seems shocked and taken aback by my story, and I wonder if this changes her initial opinion about me. She seemed happy to meet me at first, but I'm familiar with the way people truly see me once they find out what I have done. "Some of the men I grew up with whole-heartedly believed the lies we were taught," I tell her. "The 1930s were a dark time in history, darling."

Emma stands up from the cafeteria table and collects my empty bowl and coffee cup. "I'll be right back. I'm just going to toss this in the trash."

"Thank you," I tell her. I believe she needs a moment to breathe and digest my words.

Emma walks toward the garbage can almost as if in a trance. I don't share my stories often anymore, mostly due to these types of reactions. It isn't that I can't handle the response—

because I feel like it is my obligation to teach about hate crimes to prevent the act, but at the same time, I feel as though I'm stealing a person's innocence when I offer the truth.

When Emma returns, I can see the questions igniting within her bright young eyes. "So, if you were trained to hate Jews—my kind—why did you choose my grandmother to love? Of all the people in the world?" Emma asks, scratching the back of her head.

Emma isn't looking at me in the eyes anymore. I'm afraid my story has already offended her, and like so many others, I will have to prove my innocence in whatever way I can.

"The day I met your grandmother was one of the worst days of my life," I begin, knowing how my words might sound to Emma. "If I had the chance to meet your grandmother in any other way than how I did, I would die for that opportunity."

Emma brushes a strand of hair behind her ear and then wraps her arm around her opposite shoulder. She's uncomfortable. "I think I remember reading about that day," Emma says.

I almost forgot Emma read Amelia's journal. However, I don't know what she wrote in that journal. In fact, if she were to give me the opportunity, I'm not sure I am strong enough to read what she might have written about me. "It was the day your great-grandmother was killed," I say, speaking softly and less clearly than I had been.

Emma pauses for a beat and clasps her fingers together in front of her waist. "That's right," she says. "The guilt you felt after watching my great-grandmother get shot was what urged you to help my grandmother, right?"

I can't argue her question. I want to say our love branched from pure intentions, but my only pursuit was to make sure young Amelia was okay. "Yes," I answer simply.

"What did you do after they shot my great-grandmother in front of their house?" Emma asks. "Did you have a drink with your buddies after? Did you steal goods from their house, or did you squeeze into one of the freight cars on the train with the Jewish prisoners?"

I was not expecting these questions or the anger sprouting from within Emma. She seemed stoic up until now.

"I wasn't—I couldn't..." I can't think of the right words to begin.

"It doesn't seem like a hard question, Charlie. What did you do after you watched my great-grandmother die on the street?"

"I can explain it to you," I tell her. I'm just not sure there is a good way to explain what happened that day.

Emma begins to amble slowly so I can keep up, but it's obvious she's done having a sit-down chat. "I'm listening," she says, trying to sound complacent, but the edginess she has suddenly found is loud and clear.

"Even after the crowd carried Amelia away toward her destination, I still hadn't found a way to make my feet move from their frozen stance outside of your great-grandmother's house."

CHAPTER 9

1942—TEREZIN, CZECHOSLOVAKIA

19 YEARS OLD

Amelia was heading to the train that would bring her to Theresienstadt, a camp for the Jews to reside. Our raid swept several streets in the surrounding area, resulting in a long line of scared Jewish men and women, waiting to learn more of their next destination.

The people lined up before me all had similar expressions written across their faces. They weren't wondering where they were going next like the rest of the line. They were trying to figure out why a woman was lying dead in the middle of the road.

My comrades were no longer nearby as they were still raiding other houses, which left me to tend to the woman's remains.

It had been no more than ten minutes since she was shot down. No one checked her pulse to make sure she was gone, because no one had cared enough to do so.

The weight from my feet finally lifted since Sven told me to kill the woman. I took the ten steps over to the body, wanting to close my eyes and become blind to the reality of this woman's fate.

The woman was on the smaller side, thin and frail—possibly from hunger. Her skin appeared young as I studied her up close, but the loose strands of her hair covering her face made her look aged. She might have been in her late thirties or early forties. My gaze fell upon the bottom hem of her apron, where I spotted two embroidered names. "Jakob and Amelia."

I placed my fingers against the side of her neck, checking for a pulse, but her skin was already cold, and there was no sign of life. I glanced around the street for signs of the other soldiers, but there was still only a line of Jews. I was the person on guard to keep the people in line, but they were not of my concern at that moment.

I scooped my arms beneath the woman's body and cradled her into my chest, standing back up with her. I didn't want to see the looks on the faces from the people watching me, so I held my focus on the woman's complacent face—the face that was no longer suffering, but rather, at peace. The line of Jews parted for me as I walked toward them, cutting through toward the woman's house. The door was still open, and the food was still untouched on the table. I made my way through the small living area, finding a bedroom decorated with floral linen and gold-plated frames with captured black & white stills. I spotted a rag on the vanity table in the corner and snagged it with my fingers.

I settled the woman down on her bed, pulling the linens away as I did so. While holding her head up, I covered the pillow-case with the rag, then rested her head on top. I don't know why I was so concerned about ruining the linen with blood stains, but there was a part of me that prayed Amelia would see her home again someday, and though her mother most likely wouldn't be there then, I didn't want to leave her blood behind as a reminder. My thoughts were unclear, and my actions weren't justified, but it was the only way I could move on from that moment. It was the best I could do for the woman —for Amelia.

Once I placed the bed linens over the woman's chest, I was able to breathe a little more. I wondered if I was considered a murderer just for the reason that I watched this woman lose her life.

I lifted one of the framed photos from her nightstand and studied it for a moment, admiring a smiling girl with short dark hair that was parted to one side and held together with a bow. Her small grin showed mischief, but also sweetness. Her eyes showed the life of a carefree girl, one who was ready to conquer the world. The photo couldn't have been too old, maybe a few years at most. I believe the girl was Amelia. She may have been fourteen or fifteen in the photo. It was hard to assume she would never resume that gleeful, young look again.

Once the frame was set back on the nightstand, I said a silent prayer over the woman's body, wishing for eternal peace. The lump in my throat grew as I walked away, feeling as though a shadow of death was following in my creaking footsteps. I passed a bedroom with a bureau on its side, and I stepped inside to set it upright.

The next bedroom had clothes scattered outside of a makeshift closet. I assumed someone was hiding behind the draped curtains, concealing the storage space.

I swept the scattered clothes back into the closet and pulled the drapes shut. The bed was made up of white linens, pulled tightly around the sides except for the bottom right corner that was furled into a pile at the edge. I tugged the corner, allowing it to hang neatly once again. As I turned for the door, I found a stack of paintings by the doorway.

I knew I should have no longer been inside of that house, but my curiosity was piqued, and my heart was hurting. I felt the need to learn all I could about the family—the family that was torn apart forever.

Each painting was a display of flowers, red and yellow, mostly. The artist had a lot of talent. I assumed who the artist was by the fact that the room had dolls perched on the bureau. This bedroom must have been Amelia's, and these paintings were by a girl who would have made an incredible artist. Instead, she was on her way to confinement.

I closed the green door to the house as I left, feeling the burning stares against my back. When I turned to face the line of Jewish people who were still waiting for their next direction, their gazes fell, making sure to avoid eye contact. I was a monster to them, just as we were taught they were to us Germans.

There was no other choice but to walk alongside the line to find the other soldiers. They were likely at the train, preparing for departure, but I knew it would take some time to load all the people.

My heart hurt with each step I took past the Jewish people. They were terrified of me. They were terrified of everything. No one moved a muscle as I passed. They were scared to blink, except for one little girl. She had big brown eyes, a small pug nose, and rosy cheeks. She was watching me with question. I don't know if my presence scared or distracted her, but she dropped her cloth doll. It fell off the curb, but her mother gripped her fingers tightly against the girl's shoulder, keeping her from retrieving the doll. The girl's lip quivered, and my chest ached.

I stopped walking, leaned over, and lifted the doll for the little girl, handing it back. "There you go, sweetheart," I said, forcing a smile that would make her less afraid. I shouldn't have been making her less afraid. I was only teaching her to trust a man dressed as I was, and that was the last thing she should have been doing.

"Thank you," she offered in a squeaky voice.

Her father pulled the little girl away, hiding her to his side.

When I saw the train in the distance, I considered boarding, calling myself a Jew to endure the punishment my kind was dispensing. In fact, I did try to board the train, but another soldier caught me by the back of the jacket and called me a jokester.

There was nothing funny about shoving hundreds of people into a freight cart without circulating air.

I rode on a buggy beside the train, listening to the other men poke fun at what they had seen over the previous few hours. I had thoughts of jumping from the buggy with hopes of sparing myself from the darker kind of hell I was heading toward, but I was pinned between several others.

The ride seemed to drag on forever, and though I did my best not to look at the slow-moving train, I couldn't help but look and wonder what the scene looked like inside. We had trouble closing the metal doors as it was like stuffing sausages into a casing.

I'm not sure if I was imagining the sounds, but I could swear there were suffocating screams and cries pouring out of the cracks between the metal slats.

I was beginning to feel dead inside—like a ghoul using the body I once used to feel alive, to then, only betray me while portraying a life that was no longer one of my own.

Three weeks after that dreadful day, I was assigned guard duty at Theresienstadt, a ghetto for the displaced Jews. The ghettos were a place to contain our so-called enemy, making it easier for Hitler to decide their future.

We were told to provide the bare essentials, use whom we could for work, and the others would meet their fate as the universe intended. My hope was that there was enough work for all the Jews, leaving none of them behind. However, I knew very well that there were elderly and sick Jews among the groups we were bringing in daily.

When our buggy came to a halt outside of the ghetto, my

stomach buckled. I felt sick each time we withdrew the crowds from the trains. The smells, screams, the horror written in the eyes of our prisoners—it was too much.

Many of the Jews were split up from their friends and families. Then they became frenzied while scanning the area for a familiar face. It was like watching a small child searching for their missing parent. In fact, that was actually the case for some children.

"Charlie, report to intake," Sven shouted to me.

Of all the men I have spent time around throughout the previous years, I hated Sven the most. Therefore, the irony of becoming Sven's subordinate bothered me greatly. He was cut from the same cloth as Hitler; that much was apparent. Sven was working toward acceptance into Hitler's high-ranking positions of the SS army—the most elite of soldiers, bred from the Aryan race back to the 1800s.

Sven would get there.

I strode to the table, where we were registering each Jew who walked through the arches of Theresienstadt. The lines were endless, and each person who stopped in front of me was terrified of what I might say.

"Oh, Charlie," Sven called out again. "Here." I walked toward Sven's outstretched hand that was holding a note. "Assignments."

I took the paper and scanned down the center.

- Women with children: Cell Block GVI 21
- Healthy women without children: Small Fortress Block B
- Women between the ages of twelve and eighteen: Cell Block GIV 5
- Men between the ages of twelve and eighteen: Cell Block DVI 6
- Men above the ages of eighteen: Cell Block DVI 5

- Elderly women above the age of sixty-five: Cell Block GV 16
- Disfigured women: Cell Block GV 3
- Disfigured men: Cell Block DV 4

Questions to be asked:

- Name
- Prisoner Number
- Age
- City of Origin
- Profession

I took a seat at the table, lifted my pencil, and waved over the first prisoner. Despite that I was doing something against my desire, being forced to work in a toxic environment for illogical reasons, I couldn't compare myself to those in front of me.

"Listen up, listen up. Men to the left, women and children to the right. Make two lines now, come on," Sven yelled. "Men over here. Let's go. Let's go."

I wasn't sure why I was instructed to send the men if they were then being led to a different check-in point. I could only assume nothing was preplanned, and rules were created as we went along. That's how things had gone in the past few years. Changes were implemented with hardly any notice, and we were expected to follow at the same speed.

As I registered the women in my line, I did my best to avoid eye contact. I didn't think many would have looked me in the eye anyway.

"Amelia Baylin," I heard. I couldn't help but lift my eyes at the mention of the name Amelia. There she was; the woman whose world was stolen just hours earlier. I felt frozen as I stared up at her. At first, her eyes were closed, and she seemed to be channeling her anger; understandably so. When she opened her eyes, though, it was like seeing the ocean for the first time. There was a world inside of her that I yearned to know, in just that one second I made eye contact. The emotion and the feelings I had were a reminder as to why I was not looking others in the eyes.

Amelia and her sapphire blue eyes did something to me that day. I felt connected to her after being inside her house and doing what I could for her poor mother. Still, she would not understand that there was good in my heart—not while I was wearing a swastika on my arm. The more I looked at Amelia, the more I noticed—a gloss, marking the tears she must have cried. Her cheeks were red and chapped, and her beautiful auburn hair was in knots. Still, she held her nose up to the sky and refused to blink her long dark lashes.

"Your age, Fräulein?" I asked.

"Seventeen," she spoke.

I spotted her assigned number scribbled on her yellow Jude patch and notated it in the registrar.

"Do you have a profession?" I countered.

"I'm seventeen," she responded again. "I don't have a profession."

I had a job to do, and standing from my seat, and taking this woman by the arm was not part of that job. However, if any Jew were to talk out of turn, we were instructed to handle the situation as we saw fit. Therefore, I deemed it necessary to escort Amelia to her given block. It was quite stupid, but I needed to tell her I was sorry about her mother.

Only a select group of the women were being taken further into the small fortress, where we were conducting our intake. Other women would be sent to the housing development on the other side of the ghetto. Amelia was to stay within the confine of our imprisoned area as she was a prime candidate for administrative or medical work. She would be considered one of the lucky women.

Amelia tried to yank her arm from my grip, but I needed to make a show of the fact that I had control over her. "Where are you taking me?" she snapped.

I wanted to tell her to watch her tongue as it would earn her nothing but trouble or much worse, but I didn't have the heart to speak to her in that way.

"To your assigned block," I answered.

I brought Amelia into the main entrance of Block B, feeling the stone walls caving in on us as I escorted her to what would look like a prison cell. The blocks where we kept the prisoners appeared much like the catacombs in Paris, and in some cases, worse. We were to treat the Jews as if they were animals. In fact, horses and cows lived in better circumstances.

Amelia cleared her throat as she continued to comply with our pace. "What's going to happen to us here?" I could tell she was trying to sound brave through the firmness of her question, but her voice shook, admitting to fear.

I took in her question, trying to summon a good response, but I heard voices of comrades in the nearby vicinity, and I couldn't risk the chance of any of them hearing a civilized conversation between Amelia and me. They would punish her to punish me.

"Why would you ask such a stupid question?" I announced, feeling the words catch in my throat.

"Why are we here?" she continued. At that moment, I realized what I was dealing with; Amelia was no ordinary woman. She was brave, strong, and resilient. She struck me as the type to die trying, and maybe that was what she was attempting to do at that moment. I felt as though she was testing her boundaries.

"To offer you shelter, of course. Just as you were told." I don't know what Amelia was told. I know she was torn from her home, forced to watch her mother meet her death, and then shoved onto a train. However, we were told to inform the Jews that we were going to be replacing their homes with new shelter. It was supposed to prevent mass chaos.

"One of you killed my mother—" I didn't hear the rest of what she said because my head began to spin. I don't know if she witnessed me standing there when her mother was shot, or what she may have seen, for that matter.

The first response that came to mind was: "I'm not one of them." I would be shamed and punished if anyone heard me say such a thing. Though, I was not one of them, and that was the truth. "We are all different, just like every one of you."

Her response was instant and did not require much thought. "You're a Nazi, so you are no different from the rest."

I was a Nazi. I represented hatred, antisemitism, and murder. I served the Führer, Adolf Hitler, and his disgust for Jews.

"You don't know what you're talking about," I told her. I shouldn't have responded. I should have let her have the last word because she was right. I was a Nazi, just like the Nazi who shot her mother, and the one who frisked her body as she stepped off the train. We were a united front, left with only our internal thoughts to separate us as beings.

We reached the door to her cell block, and I pressed on the rusted metal to wave her inside. "This is where you will be staying," I told her, taking a look at the conditions from within the room. The bodily capacity was almost at max. The air wasn't circulating, and the smell was volatile—a mixture of urine and vomit. The women, already settled on their wooden bunks, were glowing with a faint look of sickness. They stared at me with drooping eyes and parted lips. They were starving for both food and answers, neither of which I could supply.

"This is where I will be living?" Amelia asked, needing confirmation.

"Yes," is all I could say. My last meal was gurgling in my stomach, and my head was throbbing. I couldn't answer any more questions, and I couldn't bear the thought of forcing another innocent woman into the barren cell.

As soon as Amelia was inside the block, I closed the door behind her, nearly falling against the opposite wall while feeling disgusted with morbid affliction.

I told myself I could not go through with my tasks any longer. I wanted to run away and escape my duties. I needed to find a way out. I would run away that night; that was my plan.

However, before I made my way back out into the courtyard again, I began to realize what I would be leaving for only the selfish act of escaping.

Maybe I could escape, but Amelia and the others, they could not escape without being summoned to death. Running from the prisoners would be just as selfish as the tasks I was completing.

CHAPTER 10

1942—TEREZIN, CZECHOSLOVAKIA

My body was heavy as I marched out of the last barrack hallway for the evening. The Jewish people were released from the train. More than half were then sent to their next destination, and the others were given assignments to their appropriate blocks.

People were crying, and the sounds of those cries echoed around me. They were suffering and scared, and I was walking out of the building freely. It was getting late and I knew I had a long night ahead. Most of that time would be spent staring at a wall, trying to remove the sights and sounds from my head.

"Charlie," a voice called from the distance. At first, I kept walking, not wanting to be bothered with conversation. Claude caught up to me, though, and placed his hand on my shoulder. "Charlie, I'm worried about you, brother."

Claude had been worried about me for the last seven years. I knew I shouldn't have been his problem. Our friendship was still intact, but he had adapted better than I. It was hard to tell if he had accepted our fate or if he had gotten good at masking his feelings. "I'm all right," I lied.

"Nonsense. Let's go down to the village for a beer, ja?"

I shrugged. A beer would not fix what had happened in the daylight. "I'm tired," I told him.

"You need a beer, and so do I. I need my friend right now, Charlie." I assumed Claude was saying what he thought might convince me to comply with his offer. He was right. If Claude needed to talk, I wouldn't turn him down.

"Okay, one beer," I told him.

Claude slapped my shoulder twice and grinned. "Good man," he said.

Neither of us spoke much on our walk to town, and the silence highlighted the scene two blocks away from the pub we were heading toward. A door slammed, boots clomped, the clanking metal of pistols sounded loudly between the alleyway's stone walls. "Halt!" The shouts were in German. Our people were chasing down more Jews.

Claude and I stopped walking to watch what was happening, but it was over just as fast as it began. Two gunshots, and I assume two more Jews were dead.

It was only a short minute before we watched the Jewish bodies tossed to the street from the building they had just infiltrated. The soldiers responsible for the deaths came out in a fit of laughter as if they felt joy after pulling a trigger two times.

"Let's go, Charlie," Claude said, walking ahead.

Every time I saw another lifeless body, a part of me died with them. I couldn't allow the acknowledgment to become a numbing feeling or I would be as heartless as those shooting the pistols. I didn't move when Claude had, and when he noticed my frozen stance, he turned back for me and grabbed my arm to pull me along. "Tune it out, Charlie."

Claude was often telling me to tune it all out. "Don't you feel anything?" I asked.

Claude pulled me away from the glow of the streetlamp and toward a wall of shops. He dropped his hands on my shoulders and lowered his head a couple of inches to look me in the eyes.

"If a Jew was standing right here with a gun pointed to your head, would you let him shoot you, or would you shoot him first?"

At the point we were at, I would have let the man shoot me, but I couldn't tell Claude how I felt. He wouldn't understand. "The Jews don't have weapons," I answered instead.

"We don't know that," Claude replied.

The Jewish people were required to forfeit their weapons, along with any other valuables. These procedures were not new and had been in place for years. It was unlikely that a Jewish person would still have ownership over a weapon. Therefore, the playing field was not fair, and we were out to kill.

"You cannot think this way, Charlie. You're going to land yourself in trouble one of these days, do you understand?"

"Why is this so easy for you?" I asked my best friend. Claude and I were no longer seeing eye to eye. It hurt to think I was alone with my thoughts, but I had seen it coming for years.

"You think this is easy for me?" he questioned as a spark of anger lit up his dark eyes.

"It just seems—"

"I am not a murderer, Charlie. Nor do I have plans to become one. However, if it is them or us, I choose us. It's simple. We are in a time of war, and we cannot forget this."

Claude didn't have much else to say as he spun on his heels and continued toward the pub. He didn't seem to care if I was following this time. Though, I did follow in his footsteps as I didn't want to see any more bodies tossed onto the worn cobblestone road.

We sat a small table off to the back corner of the pub staring at two steins of beer—one for each of us, both sweating with condensation. Neither Claude nor I spoke a word before he took the first swig. "This pains me," he said. "I wanted to be a businessman, you know." I didn't know Claude had dreams of becoming a businessman. Our future goals didn't mean much after we joined the German regiment. After eighteen years old, the military was our only future.

"I wanted to be a baker like Papa," I replied.

"It doesn't matter now, and it hurts to think that way, so I choose not to think about it, Charlie."

"I understand." I did.

"You think it doesn't pain me to see dead bodies? I had to lift a child out of a gutter last week. He was shot, Charlie. Someone shot a child. When he was in my arms, I thought about how I would feel if *he* was my son, and my heart—" Claude paused and pinched the bridge of his nose. He inhaled sharply. "Charlie, if I let the thoughts overwhelm me, they will kill my soul. I will give up. I will put a pistol to my head. However, I still have hope for the future, and I am doing what I must to see that future." *Our futures might eat us alive after watching the world burn to dust*, I thought to myself.

I had come to learn that Claude and I were, in fact, still on the same page. I wasn't as alone as I thought. It was just that I wasn't hiding my feelings as well as Claude.

"I spoke to Annika last week," Claude continued. "She told me they bring the sick Jews to a different wing of the hospital where she works. They are euthanizing them even if they have a chance to get better. Annika isn't doing well, Charlie. She was a mess, crying, and telling me to keep strong because this is only going to get worse. Annika wanted me to tell you the same."

Claude's sister was never very nice to me, but we were all on the same side now, fighting against what we were fighting against.

"Men," someone called out from behind. A hand slapped my back. The chair at the edge of the table was pulled out, and another soldier we had gone to school with sat down with us.

"Jonas," Claude greeted him. "Hallo, how are you?"

Jonas placed his stein down beside mine and rested his elbows on the tabletop. "It's been a long day," he said. "I have to be back for guard duty in two hours. I'm on overnight watch this week."

"I had that last week," Claude mentioned. "The cries—"

"Ja, it's bad," Jonas agreed. "I heard they transported over five hundred prisoners to Auschwitz today."

"That ghetto must have more space," Claude added.

Jonas's eyes grew wide and his blonde brows furrowed. "Ach nein. Auschwitz is no ghetto. It's a killing center. Those transported to that location will be—" Jonas sliced his finger along his throat. "The Jews are being eradicated—some gassed, some executed, then cremated."

Claude and I stared blankly at Jonas, taking in the information I hoped was misinterpreted. It wasn't that we weren't aware how freely they were murdering the Jewish people, but hearing of a killing center was a much larger type of organization when it came to murder. "Why?" It's the only word that came to mind.

"Don't you know the Führer wants to rid all the Jews?" Jonas's statement was matter-of-fact, but I don't think he could have understood the meaning of his words.

"*The Führer... Hitler wants to rid the world of Jewish people...*" I muttered to myself.

"You were one of Hitler's men, correct?" Emma continues. I feel like I'm on trial once again. These particular trials are never-ending in my life. How do I explain or prove my innocence when there is no such label for a Nazi? I am an enemy and a killer by association. In all technicality, I assisted Hitler in his plan to achieve the annihilation of the Jewish race. I have spent the last seventy-four years of my life staring back at my reflection in the mirror, calling myself a murderer, even though I did not murder anyone. I was an accomplice, and that makes me just as guilty. After all the years of forcing myself to hear the truth out loud, the pain has not lessened. I should have been murdered too, and yet here I am, walking around freely.

"You see," I tell her, leaning forward to rest my elbows on my knees. "Once I was a part of Hitler's youth program, I was taught and bred to believe that I was being trained to protect Germany against a religious force that almost demolished our country during World War I. I was to become one of the 'elite' men protecting our country against another depression. If I did not continue, I was told I would be letting my family down. I would be a 'nothing' for the rest of my life. Essentially, I would forever be a failure. Manipulation affected me in so many ways," I try to explain.

Emma is pacing the small area in front of me, holding her fingers against her temples as if she has a headache. She may very well have a headache after hearing this confusing story. "How—but how can one man convince an entire country of lies? I don't understand."

The answer is simple. "Power. It took Hitler ten years to gain the trust of the German people, and once he had their trust, the rest became simple for him."

Emma looks furious, but I don't think it's with me anymore. It's the face of a person learning how awful this world had once been.

"So, then, when did you realize things weren't as you were led to believe?"

I close my eyes, bringing my mind to settle on just one occasion. "It's hard to pinpoint a specific time when I realized the world was falling apart, because I was being manipulated to think we were doing good for the world, but when I started to experience the result of all the lies, it was too late. I had absolutely no control."

CHAPTER 12

1942—TEREZIN, CZECHOSLOVAKIA

Each morning, I woke up in a daze, wondering how I had gotten to be where I was. One thing was certain; I was not waking up in the comfort of my home. Since moving away from Mama and Papa, I had been moved around along with the fleet of soldiers. I was already feeling lost when I was assigned an apartment unit in the center of Terezín.

The morning I was to move into my apartment, I crossed the uneven cobblestone toward the yellowed-stone facade and walked through the double set of raised panel doors into a narrow hallway. The hickory plank flooring and white and blue peacock-feathered wallpaper offered a homey feel, though the space smelled of damp must and soiled laundry. My superior said I wouldn't be spending much time in the apartment. Therefore, reading between the lines meant I should ignore the sights and odors from my new living quarters.

I creaked up the old, thin stairwell, hearing a clamor of thuds echoing from the floor above. The thuds became booms, and then a sudden crash warned me to move away from the stairwell. As I made it to the top step, two soldiers swept through, both linking arms with a young couple. The man was fighting his way from the hold, and the woman was in tears. A sparkling wedding band was the last of what I saw of them. They were either Jewish or rebellions of the war—it was hard to tell.

As I had been doing, I shut my eyes and closed out the scene, forcing myself to move forward despite the ache in my chest. I knew all too well the future of that couple. The wedding band would be all that was left until it was taken from her.

Apartment number four would be mine.

Mine.

The apartment was not mine, which was apparent by the warm decor of the unit's interior, the scent of fresh tea wafting from the tea kettle on the stove's burner, and a tobacco filled pipe still smoking from an ashtray across the room. I also noticed a ball of cream-colored yarn and a pair of knitting needles that must have fallen to the wooden floor in front of a blue suede sofa.

I took a seat, finding comfort in the worn upholstery until I noticed that the seat was warm. The couple from the hallway—this was their home, and now I was to live there.

More guilt.

The loose ball of yarn fell apart in my hand as I retrieved it from the floor, trying to carefully place the mass on top of the iron and oak coffee table. The yarn reminded me of the days Mama would sit in her armchair, facing the small wood-stove while knitting sweaters, scarves, and hats in preparation for the upcoming frigid days.

How did I get here? I wished Mama had taught me how to knit.

The apartment may have been warm with finishings, but I was cold with dread. I stood from the sofa and circled the two areas from within the unit. The living area attached to the kitchen, where a teapot was still burning on the stove. I lifted the pot and poured the water down the drain. Two China plates were resting in the sink's basin, so I took the rag from the countertop and cleaned each plate and then placed them where I found the other matching plates. I moved onto the burning pipe as it also needed to be cleaned. It didn't take long before all of the household items were in their correct spots. Maybe if the couple returned someday, they would be happy to find out that someone tended to their belongings. It was the least I could do.

I brought my belongings into the bedroom, finding cream-colored linens draped over the bed. A hand-carved walnut frame encased the mattress. Picture frames rested upon the matching nightstands—most portraits were of the couple looking elated in their marital bliss, while others were pictures of the pair at a younger age. They must have been together awhile.

I couldn't bear the thought of sleeping in their bed; it was *their* bed, not mine. I planned to sleep on the floor.

The camps were overfilling with prisoners, and I was given someone's home.

There wasn't much time to unpack my bags, nor did I want to begin. I carefully placed my two trunks down on the bedroom floor, promising to tend to them when I return from duty.

The walk to the ghetto camp was short, the air reeked of sewage and felt thick beneath the low-bearing clouds. Beyond the gated arch, the lines still spilled around the buildings. Intake of the Jews from the last import appeared never-ending, and nightfall was arriving. Watching the same expressions day after day—the fear, turmoil, hunger, and pain, were causing me phantom sensations. There were days I was hoping to fall ill, and even worse, fall so ill I might end up bedridden in a hospital where I wouldn't have to follow the repetitive death-marching orders.

With a heavy breath, I glanced at my watch, finding myself a few minutes early for a meeting I was to attend.

I recall thinking: *the day could not get worse.*

I later promised to never entertain that thought again in my lifetime.

There was a vacant block within the small fortress of Theresienstadt where we were told to assemble that night. Typically, we would meet in the administration building, but this meeting appeared more exclusive to the guards working in my section.

The dirt ground within the walls served as a cushion to my tired feet. I had been on guard duty since the sun rose and only given a two-hour break to move my belongings from the hotel I had been staying in with four others to the seized apartment. They needed space at the hotels to pack in more prisoners beyond the capacity that the camps could hold.

"Hör zu!" The Oberscharführer called out as he stepped into the block where the few of us guards were congregated and awaiting orders. He was our senior squad leader, and we took most of our orders from him. "As you know, we have been transporting many of the incoming prisoners," he said, folding his hands behind his back. "However, the space is thinning out faster than we can transport. With this problem escalating, we have decided to take additional measures to manage the issue. With that said, we have added a trace of rattengift to the food." He paused the informative speech, allowing his words to sink into our heads. *Rat poison.* They were about to feed the Jews rat poison. "As you may assume, this process will help us eliminate some bodies. Therefore, it is imperative that all prisoners ingest their food tonight." The Oberscharführer cleared his throat, and I wondered if the sound was a tick from nerves, or for emphasis on what he was saying. "The strongest will merely fall ill, but the effects will be temporary. Tomorrow, we will begin recruiting the newest Jews for labor work. Those who are well enough will receive assignments."

He left out the fact that the weak bodies would likely perish. If not, they would be on the transport list.

It wasn't that I didn't see what we had been doing to the prisoners, it was that I was beginning to take a closer look. I was becoming familiar with faces, I was seeing the life within eyes, and I was notating the consequences of our actions.

I stood quietly in the back of the dirt-ridden area, taking in the scent of sweat among the heavy air. The Oberscharführer stared above our heads as if he was lost in thought. I stared back, wondering what thoughts were going through his head, but his eyes reminded me of two pieces of coal, his skin was pale, and the sheen on his forehead made him appear ill. Maybe he was feeling nothing inside. *Was I the only one feeling the detriments of murder?*

"Rest assured, men, your supper is rattengift free," the Oberscharführer said with laughter, an evil sound that over-filled the space around us.

Mama taught me that those who caused pain would at some point be reunited with a mirrored revenge. Her lecture was intended to teach me how to walk away from conflict. Everything Mama had taught me was beginning to feel irrelevant now. Had Mama known what she and Papa were signing me up for with Hitler's Youth program, she might have eaten her words.

At some point within the last few minutes, Oberscharführer must have dismissed us, but I was lost in thought because the others were dispersing through the chestnut wooden door. I placed my hand around the edge of the wood while passing through, my fingers tracing along the dents and divots. I had my orders to carry out, which felt more of punishment than a task, but my footsteps felt heavy as I left my weighted tracks in the dirt and rubble.

When I stepped outside into the setting sun, I noticed a paint splash of pinks and blues. The beautiful colors were being swallowed by the darkness, much like the prisoners. The foreshadowing of the evening was overwhelming.

Before I reported to my assigned block, I stopped at the administration building for my nightly supper. I had been rationing myself to cabbage soup and bread after paying close attention to how little we were feeding the prisoners. Why should I feast on meats and rare cheeses when the Jews were starving? I realized my thoughts were of my own and not common among the other soldiers, but to me, it felt like a parent devouring a roast while watching their children starve. The Jews were helpless like children, waiting at the mercy of our giving hands. It was too painful to take much more than what they had.

By the time I reached my assigned hallway of barrack units, sounds were echoing along the narrow hallway. The retching throats, gasping breaths, and bodies expelling poison was all I could hear.

I placed my hand against the stucco finish on the wall, steadying my dizzying thoughts. The first cell to check on contained Amelia, a lone Jew I felt responsible for after watching her mother meet her fate within this war.

The door gave way with a tug, and the foul odors spilled out of the confines. Vomit, excrement, urine, and body sweat were a combination of aromas that could make a healthy man fall sick.

At least half of the women in the cell were unconscious, some laying in the secretions of their waste, other's flopped over their wooden bunks like rag dolls.

Look what we have done, was all I could think.

I stood in the doorway, staring with disbelief, never seeing such a sight. The prisoners who were not unconscious were doubled in half, clenching their midsections, crying out for help. One woman had an arm reaching out to me. She believed I would offer my hand in return, and I called myself a monster when I didn't walk forward.

"Aidez-moi!" the woman cried out. "J'ai besoin d'aide!" I was almost glad that I did not speak a word of French. It was easier not knowing what she was crying for considering I wouldn't normally ever ignore a cry for help, but I wasn't allowed to respond.

It took a moment before my eyes fell upon Amelia, her small body crumpled on the floor beside a puddle of vomit. Her sunken eyes met mine, and my heart shattered. Amelia was not reaching for me, but her eyes—they were crying for help. Her skin was ashen, not the complexion of an ordinary living being. I considered she might be moments from meeting her death, and I wanted to scream out loud for the madness to stop. *How could I just stand there?*

My feet moved faster than my mind was working. I was stepping into the confines of our prisoners' abode. The stench was becoming increasingly more vile, and I feared becoming sick too, so I retrieved a handkerchief from my back left pocket and pinched it over the bridge of my nose.

CHAPTER 13

1942—TEREZIN, CZECHOSLOVAKIA

The sun hadn't risen, but there were slivers of gold illuminating the horizon, warning me that I didn't have much time. The Magdeburg Barracks, a close walk from the apartment, would hold the roster of job assignments. I needed to see Amelia's job placement. I was worried that she might have been on the transport list since the reasons for who got sent away were becoming blurrier by the day.

The yellow building sprawled out in front of a courtyard, the landscape was no longer flourishing, but instead, filled with dead grass. It wasn't uncommon for the soldiers to be walking in and out of this building since we utilized it for administrative tasks. A soldier greeted me at the front archway, his head tipped in my direction, followed by "Heil Hitler," and a solute. There were many sectioned areas of office space, but I was familiar with the layout. I was also familiar with where particular lists were devised. I would find this list on the third floor.

Some of the Jewish prisoners had been assigned roles in this building and would often be in control of the various lists. I believed this to be the case for the work order placements.

An older Jewish woman was working at one of the small

tables. Her gaze was stuck on a stack of papers, and her fingers tapped wildly against the keys of a typewriter. When she noticed my presence, she stood at attention. "Guten morgen, Herr. What can I do for you?"

"You can take a seat," I told her. I wasn't like the others, getting a rush out of controlling these poor timid women.

The woman reclaimed her seat instantly, abiding by what she heard as a command. "May I see what you're working on, fräulein?"

The papers were scooped into her hands and offered to me without another thought. My rank, due to my length of service, was high enough to allow me a touch of freedom and to act as I wanted without being questioned. It was the only benefit of keeping my mouth shut long enough to earn my stripes. Most often, I chose to know as little as possible because the truth destroyed me most days.

The list was, in fact, a display of which prisoners were to be sent off to the death camps. Peering at the list offered me more insight; there were multiple death camps, rather than just one as I thought.

I had written Amelia's prisoner number on a napkin, and then studied it before entering the building.

24225. 24225.

It was at least five long minutes before I spotted the numbers. Amelia was placed with a job to work manual labor on the administration grounds behind this very building. She would freeze to death in the cold winter months, as would the others stationed to work outside performing construction tasks.

Though guilt ate at me for switching Amelia's position for another prisoner's, I felt it was my obligation to keep her safe. We had connected, and the look in her eye, questioning my reasons for locking her up, had settled deep inside my brain. I was sure Amelia had been assigned a position to work with her hands due to her noticeable feisty behavior, but construction was not the job for her. Amelia would be placed in the medical unit, performing tasks to help the other nurses. I took the pen from the woman's desk and crossed out the jobs and wrote them in as I saw fit.

Forgive me, 342355.

"There was an error on the paperwork that needed to be corrected. Everything is fine now," I said to the woman, handing the stack of papers back.

"Very well, Herr. I will see to it that I type up your changes right away."

"Danke, Fräulein."

I tipped my head toward the woman and walked away, feeling a slight sense of relief. Amelia would not be placed on the transport list or in an unthinkable task. She might survive longer now.

Being focused on helping Amelia was giving me a false sense of relief. While I knew I should have been trying to help more people, I also knew if I helped too many, I would be spotted and reported. Therefore, even though I was doing something that felt right, it didn't seem like enough.

I made it back to the Small Fortress, outside of the cells just in time to hear the shouting of orders, assigning the prisoners their jobs. It was my job to stand guard, make sure there were no wanderers after the prisoners received their directions. Still, I stood, watching over the confused prisoners, some dragging their feet, other's shuffling along.

It wasn't long before I spotted Amelia. She was holding her black, knee-length coat shut tightly over her chest. At first, she appeared lost while looking in every direction of the area that was enclosed by block units, but then there was a look of certainty within her eyes when she spotted the medical block. I don't know if it was relief she was feeling, but she didn't appear as terrified as she had been the last few times I had seen her. What was more important was that she didn't look ravished by the poisoned bread she was fed the night before. It was a miracle she was on her feet, moving forward.

"Crane, what are you staring at?" Sven, my nightmare in the daylight, shouted. "Don't go falling for one of those mongrels, you hear?"

His words scared me more than switching information on administration papers. If he were serious and thought I had eyes for one of the prisoners, Sven would be the first in line to do away with Amelia as an act to punish me. "You must be out of your mind," I shouted back.

"I was joking with you, fool. Don't worry so much. You'll die at a young age." There was no irony or humor behind his words. Everyone in this camp aside from us soldiers was likely to die at a young age—because of us.

CHAPTER 14

PRESENT DAY

The waiting room door opens, and Dr. Beck, Amelia's doctor, is standing at the door. "Amelia is through with her pre-op tests, and she is asking for you, Mr. Crane. She'd like to speak to you alone," he says, settling his gaze on Emma as if he's wondering if she'll be okay with me being alone with her grandmother.

After all, it appears as if Amelia and I are still strangers.

"How did the testing go, Dr. Beck?" I ask.

"Well," Dr. Beck says as he walks into the room, allowing the door to close him inside. "Everything went as well as to be expected with pre-op testing, but as I had mentioned to Emma before you arrived, being that Amelia is in her nineties, there is a chance the surgery will cause complications—possibly fatal complications. I need everyone to understand the risks involved."

The doctor's words feel like hands around my throat. I have come this far, and I have promised myself that if I could see Amelia just one more time, I would be a happy man.

That was a lie.

I want to see her every day for the rest of my life. How could I not?

"Thank you for your honesty," I tell Dr. Beck, standing to shake his hand.

"Of course, sir."

"I'll be right back, Emma. Thank you for allowing me to have some time with your grandmother," I tell her.

Emma smiles nervously and quickly resets her focus on Dr. Beck, likely about to ask more questions.

I don't need to hear anything more from the doctor at this moment, however. I need to see Amelia.

The walk to Amelia's hospital room isn't long enough for me to collect my unruly thoughts, so I close my eyes and take a deep breath before entering her room. It's the third time I have walked in to see her today, and the third time my eyes have had to adjust. It's like I'm in a dream, walking toward my love with nothing in the way.

Nothing except for a broken heart.

Amelia has her eyes set on the television hanging from the corner wall. I tap my knuckles gently on the oak door. "May I come in?" I ask.

"Well, I asked for you, so obviously," she says with a choky laugh. "I thought you might have left to get some sleep for the night?"

"I have decided I'm sleeping here, or in the waiting area, rather. I'm not leaving you Amelia." My words sound ridiculous. Amelia has only been mine within my mind.

"Charlie, are you all right?" She is asking me if I'm okay when she is the one in a hospital bed with a heart condition that could end her life tomorrow.

"Amelia, I am fine."

Except, I'm not okay. Not only am I worried about losing her again, but I am also trying to understand everything Amelia said to me before falling asleep earlier.

"We have a daughter," Amelia said. "Her name is Clara. We have a granddaughter, too—Emma, who you have met."

Emma—my granddaughter.

I have a daughter.

My whole life, I have wanted a family.

I didn't know I had one.

"Just two hours ago, I informed you you are a father. Most people don't say they are fine after receiving such earth-shattering news."

I would be lying if I said I wasn't thinking a million little thoughts. "I feel guilty," I tell Amelia.

"I figured you might need a little time to digest the news," Amelia says.

"You fell asleep on purpose?" I question.

Amelia grins. "Charlie, we can't fix the past, and I know for a fact that there is no time for guilt."

Amelia is as strong today as she was all those years ago. "I should have been there for them. I'm so sorry, Amelia." Tears break through the corners of my eyes.

"Charlie," Amelia hushes me with a smile. "It was out of our control."

My chest is heavy with pain. "Life could have been different."

"Yes," Amelia says. "Sure. But Charlie, let me explain something to you." She pats the guest chair next to her bedside. "Sit." I do as Amelia asks, except I fall into the chair rather heavily—the pain weakening my body. "This is hard for me to say, but for years after I last saw you, I went through some tough times. I was—traumatized, Charlie. I couldn't sleep. I couldn't eat normal portions of food. I could hardly focus on where my attention was needed. My thoughts were full of nightmares, but there was one thing that always saved me from those thoughts eating me alive."

I can hardly stand to look her in the eyes, hearing these words, but I take her frail hand in mine and enclose it with the warmth I can offer. "What was that?"

Amelia sniffles and her lips curl downward. A tear trickles down her cheek. "It was you, Charlie. You were the sun peeking through the clouds, the fire on a frigid day, the food when I was starving. You were my hero. You made me hold on. You gave me strength when I was so fragile. I didn't think I needed someone to pull me out of the rings of hell, but Charlie, I did. I needed you, and you saved me. You gave me a life. You might not have been living beside us all, but you are the reason we are here."

"Oh, Amelia," I cry out. "I would have been a good father. I would have been a good husband. I would have given you the world if I could."

Amelia smiles through her tears. "I knew it then, and I know it now. I see you in Emma. You and your soul have traveled, Charlie. You have traveled generations. You are here, living within us."

"I missed out on our life," I tell her. It hurts me more than anything has hurt me in longer than I can remember. "I could have had a life with you."

"Look at me," Amelia says, her voice stern and brave. "I'll be damned if I die on that table tomorrow, Charlie."

"As will I," I tell her. "I wrote you letters. I wrote you so many letters, Amelia. I didn't send them because I didn't know where to send them."

"Bring them to me, Charlie. After my surgery, I want you to read me every single letter. Please. We have time to relive the past and to move forward into the future. We have time. Tomorrow is not my last day."

I shake my head, understanding, and listening. "I will have those letters waiting for you tomorrow."

"Before you go, Charlie, can I ask you something I never had the chance to ask?"

"Anything, sweetheart." I can't imagine what she could have been wondering all these years.

"Why did you choose me to save?"

CHAPTER 15

1942—TEREZIN, CZECHOSLOVAKIA

Amelia was assigned to her new job three days ago. She caught on to her role quicker than I would have, and she's a natural at helping others. Her assignment was to keep a log of all sick prisoners and mark down their ailment.

My post for guard duty was within viewing distance of where Amelia stood, which allowed me to watch her with a clipboard in hand most of the day. I shouldn't have been gazing so intently, but she intrigued me with her strength, courage, and determination. Amelia stood straight, her shoulders back and her nose to the sky. When beaten and weak people didn't typically have the motivation to remain upright, Amelia was anything but typical.

The air was arctic as we saw the middle days of February. The only benefit to the cold was the freeze of repulsive scents surrounding the camp. It hurt to inhale that type of cold.

The line in front of Amelia was made up of meek people wearing single layers of clothing. They huddled together for warmth, which wasn't ideal with diseases running rampant. Amelia kept a scarf over her mouth. It was a smart move to keep out the cold and to keep her safe from contracting an illness.

Patches of snow surrounded everyone's feet, and the brown dirt was frozen. The sky was white, and the clouds were low enough to feel the fog. Still, Amelia kept her line moving fluidly, knowing she could be scolded if the pace was not acceptable. Nevertheless, she offered attention to each person in line.

I also noticed she kept tissues in her coat pocket. They were hidden inconspicuously since the Jews were not entitled to such things as a tissue, but on more than one occasion, I watched Amelia lean down in front of a child and wipe their nose. She even offered a smile that I know she couldn't feel anywhere inside.

The people in line weren't there for a small colds or minor wounds—those issues were handled privately with whatever means the Jews could find. The medical line was strictly for those who may face death as a result of their illness. Every child in that line affected Amelia's expressions. It was as if she saw an x written on their foreheads. *It was the truth.*

Amelia was sweet to every person, often placing her hand on a cheek or a shoulder for comfort. Through her pain and misery, she was trying to be kind to others.

Maybe she was unaware of the life lessons she was teaching me each day, but I began to take more food, and I was dropping rations into pockets of prisoners walking by. I was worried about being caught, but I was more concerned about children starving, mothers who were desperately trying to keep their children alive, and the men who were worked to the bone. I knew in my heart, no one had a good chance of survival, but suffering every day was not something I could bear to watch.

It was almost sundown when I stepped away from my post and strode toward Amelia, which I had been doing more and more often at the same time each day. She saw me coming, and I could tell by the look on her face, she knew why I was approaching.

Amelia glanced around, nervous as always. "Fräulein, a

word please." I used an authoritative tone while speaking to her in front of others. The worst thing I could do was make anyone aware of the help I had been offering Amelia, especially Sven, who was always on the lookout for suspicious behavior.

I took Amelia by the elbow and led her to an enclosed area in front of an unused block. "Charlie, we're going to be caught," she said.

"Take this," I told her. I had been taking bread as it was the easiest to pocket, but I was able to take a little more that day since no one was around during my late lunch. I reached into my pocket and retrieved a slice of sweet cake as well as a couple of bread rolls wrapped in papers. "Eat."

Amelia stared down at the bread. "Charlie," she sighed.

"Eat it, Amelia. You need sustenance."

"Why are you doing this for me?" she asked.

"Why have you been helping some of the women in your cell?" I didn't mean for my question to frighten her, but her face became pale. I had walked by one night, watching Amelia bandage a wound on the arm of a cellmate.

"I was wrong," Amelia said, swallowing hard. "Forgive me. It won't happen again."

I felt my head shaking from side to side. "Nein. Do not apologize." Amelia's eyes grew wide. She was terrified of me.

"It was a punishable act," she stated.

"I will not report you, Amelia. You are a good person."

Her eyes relaxed and narrowed. "And you?"

I felt my stomach churn as I continued to stare into her gaze. "I am a monster."

Amelia shook her head. "No, I see kindness in you."

"Nein," I argue. "I am one of them."

Amelia reached her hand up to my cheek as she had done to the ill people in line. "Charlie, I see something more in you." Her hand was soft, her touch was gentle, and the warmth—it was something I shouldn't have felt from a Jewish woman. It could have cost us both of our lives. "Thank you for the bread." Amelia took the paper-wrapped goods from my hand and smiled. It was the first time I had seen a genuine smile from her. Even in the grimmest of times, she was beautiful inside and out.

"I don't want to be here," I admitted.

"Neither do I," she replied. We both released a soft laugh. A laugh within a prison—it seemed impossible.

"Charlie?" Amelia's voice was soft like a passing breeze. "Why *are* you here?"

"I have been bred since I was a twelve-year-old boy, molded into one of the Führer's men. If I walk away or disobey, the punishment would affect more than just me—my family's well-being could be affected. I am stuck."

I wasn't sure if Amelia truly understood or believed my words to be the truth, but it was the only explanation I could offer.

"Charlie, family is everything," she said as a hitched sound lodged in her throat. "Everything. I miss my mama, papa, and my Jakob. It hurts."

I glanced from side to side, ensuring we were alone, and I wrapped my arms around her. "You needed a hug that day you lost your family, and now too. I am so sorry about your mama. She didn't deserve what happened." Our hug was short-lived, due to the fear of being seen, but she needed a human touch for comfort.

"No, she didn't." Amelia's dark eyes stared through me, appearing to be lost within the horrors she may have been replaying in her head.

"I will try to find your papa and Jakob," I offered. It might not have meant much; they both could have been sent to a death camp, but I would look for them.

Amelia nodded her head, and a tear threatened to fall from her eye, but she pressed it away with the back of her fist. "I would appreciate that."

"What was your favorite past-time?" I asked her, wondering about the artwork I spotted in her bedroom after I placed her mother down.

The corners of Amelia's lips curled slightly. "I'm a painter. Though I planned to attend a nursing school like many of the girls I grew up with, I promised myself if it didn't work out, I would happily live as a painter—an artist. I want my paintings to be on display in a gallery window for the world to see. I know it's a silly dream."

"It's not silly at all. It's a beautiful dream," I said, enamored by the way her eyes widened at the thought. "Were you aware that Bohemia is known for producing some of the most incredible artists in the world?"

Flutters erupted in my chest while listening to her excitement. "You will someday become a famous painter too." It was not a promise I could make, but it was a prayer I would make. I knew her chance of surviving in those living conditions was unlikely.

"Maybe," she said as her smile faded. "At least I'm getting experience with nursing, right?"

I didn't feel any better about helping that situation work out, but it could have been worse.

"Ja."

Amelia took the bread from my hand and unwrapped the paper, taking one roll into her other hand. She pocketed the remainder. Amelia fed herself the bread fairly quickly, holding her hand up to her mouth to catch any fallen crumbs. She was starving, and I was not.

The Jews were all starving, and we were not. The idealism made us savages.

"Thank you for the bread," Amelia said once she had finished the small ration.

"Don't thank me. You deserve food," I told Amelia.

I should have been worried about another soldier finding

out what I had done. I should have asked her to keep the bread a secret, but I couldn't.

"Yes, but so do the others."

"They do," I agreed.

"Come, I must bring you back to your line."

Amelia had grown to understand the appearance we needed to portray. She should be fearful of me, and I must handle her as if I was disgusted by her presence. I wrapped my black-gloved hand around her arm and walked in front of her, leading the way back to the main square.

"Let us not have this conversation again, ja?" I say as I release her to the line. My throat tightened against the words I was forced to speak. We were a picture of realism, but if someone were to take a closer look at the details within the mixed colors, they might see the truth.

CHAPTER 16

1942—TEREZIN, CZECHOSLOVAKIA

It was the first day of spring, though it didn't feel as such. There was a brisk wind, and the sky-covering clouds were ominous. I was on duty to intake another import of Jewish prisoners, and it was my task to transport as many people as possible to their next destination. We were to keep only a certain number of elderly, wealthy, women, and children. The men were to go. I didn't understand the reason, but surely there was an illogical reason blooming from behind the Führer's desk.

Sven walked by me with a clipboard in hand. Fog was pluming at his lips from the cold, and for a moment I thought I might have escaped an unwanted chat. Sven considered us comrades, dare I say friends, but I had never given him a reason to assume such a thing.

"Crane, what are your numbers?" Sven asked without turning to face me. I reached toward him with my clipboard, handing over the list. "Send the next group directly to the Auschwitz killing center." He was free with his choice of words, whether or not it be the truth. The prisoners could hear him clearly, and by the ghostly looks sweeping across each of their faces, the panic was palpable. Mothers were grabbing hold of their children, cradling them against their warmth. Men were doing the same with their wives. All I could do was stare down the line of families who would never be together again. I recalled the days when I was taught that the Jewish people wanted us—the Germans—eradicated. *Is this irony? I think not. Now, I'm here, watching these Jewish children try to hide their tears.*

"Move," Sven yelled at the line of Jews. As the year progressed, the incoming prisoners were showing up in worse conditions. Stores and markets were no longer selling goods to Jewish people because Germany had invaded so many countries with our rules and laws that we took away hope for survivors. Once the Final Solution was put into place two years prior, there was only one end goal—kill the Jews.

"Women and children to the right," I said. My voice wasn't loud. Each word burned in my throat. "Men to the left." I closed my eyes, because bearing witness to the prisoners' expressions after they comprehended my statement was too much to see. The sounds of cries and pleas escalated, followed by Sven picking the offenders off with his pistol. Hands were covering mouths, and eyes were bulging. Smoke was filling the air. I wanted to tell each one of them how I sorry I was.

"To the train," I said, pointing to the left. Only one out of five would stay in Theresienstadt. "To the train." *To your death,* is what I was saying.

My words were on repeat until the sun had set. I was ill when I walked away. I needed someone to talk to, but what would I say? I just sent a thousand people off to their death today. The lucky ones would still get tortured here.

I was on my way to the gates, leaving freely for the evening. Even that felt like a sin when so many people were sleeping on wooden planks against one another.

The open square between the blocks was on my way, and I spotted Amelia registering her last three patients.

She knew not to call out to me, but her gaze found mine for a split second before glancing back down at her list. "There's a mess over there, you know," I spoke out, marching toward her. "Why haven't you cleaned it?"

"I—" she mumbled.

I took her by the arm and tugged her back behind the dark block. "Are you okay?" she asked. *Was I okay?* Amelia was always worried about me when *she* was the prisoner. "You look ill, Charlie."

"I'll be all right," I told her. "I sent a lot of people... away. I'm a murderer, Amelia."

Amelia placed her clipboard down and squeezed her hands around my shoulders. She shouldn't have been touching me. If anyone saw...

"You are not a murderer, Charlie. We're both following orders, yes?"

"Ja," I replied. "But I still do not feel better. I sent people to die."

I wasn't sure if Amelia knew where other prisoners were ending up, and I hadn't found information on her brother or father yet. The lists were not accessible to me, though I had looked.

"To die?"

"I have been told this, ja," I said.

"You wouldn't have been able to stop it, just as you wouldn't have been able to prevent it if you were on the other side."

I lost myself in her caring gaze. Amelia's bewitching eyes sang me a lullaby and could calm me even in the most horrendous of circumstances. It shouldn't have been possible. "How can you have so much forgiveness for me?" I questioned. I couldn't understand why she didn't hate me.

She should hate me.

Amelia shrugged her shoulders. "Because it looks like you

need a hug. A person who needs a hug can't be all that bad, right?"

I did need a hug, and I needed to cry too. Amelia looped her arms beneath my elbows and rested her head on my chest. She offered me whatever warmth she had, and she hardly had any to start.

"Thank you," I offered.

"Feel better?" she asked, stepping away.

Nothing in the world could make me feel better after what I had spent my day doing. "Your kindness is appreciated." Then, I did something I shouldn't have done. I kissed that beautiful woman on the cheek.

Amelia placed her hand on the part of her cheek I kissed, gazing up at me with her breathtaking stare. "Charlie," she sighed with shock.

"I'm so sorry, Amelia."

I ran off without thinking that another soldier could find Amelia behind the block where she shouldn't have been. By the time I reached the front gate, I had thought enough to turn around and make sure she returned to her assigned spot in front of the medical door.

"Charlie, wait up," I heard as another guard allowed me to walk out through the gate. "I'm leaving now too. Let's grab some supper." It was Claude. We hadn't had a lot of time to spend together in a while, and the idea of company sounded better than sitting in a couple's apartment alone.

"Ja, that sounds good." We were forced to walk farther into town then since much of the area had been blocked off for a place to hold prisoners.

The pub where we ended up at was dark and dismal inside. The crowd was not lively, and was mostly made up of other SS officers like ourselves. It wasn't hard to find a table that night. Claude looked as exhausted as I felt, but who were we to complain? "I didn't think things could get worse," Claude said with a heavy sigh.

"Things can always get worse," I countered.

"Some of the men are losing their minds, Charlie. I can see this look in their eyes like they believe killing Jews is the only answer."

"What other way are we allowed to think?" I asked him. It was a rhetorical question because I knew the answer.

A server greeted us and took our simple orders. All the while, I noticed Claude was not able to look me in the eyes. Something was wrong, more so than what we had been watching in the ghetto camp.

"You are keeping something from me," I told him, waiting for his gaze to lift from the battered chestnut table where he drummed his fingertips.

"Brother, I received a letter from Annika last night." Annika was good at writing Claude letters. She kept him in the loop of what was happening with their family and in our hometown of Lindau.

"How is everyone—everything?" I asked, assuming there was terrible news brewing.

Claude shook his head, and his blue eyes lifted from his downward stare. "Your papa—he's ill, Charlie. Very ill."

A lump formed in my throat, and my neck became stiff. I had received a letter two weeks ago from them, and everything sounded well and fine at home. However, my letters to them had been scarce and most without much detail because I didn't want to concern them. Now, I'm wondering if they were doing the same with me. "What is the matter with him?" I managed to choke out.

"Annika admitted him to the hospital last week. He was having trouble breathing. She believes he has influenza. I'm not sure of his current condition. According to the date on the postmark, Annika sent the letter almost a week ago."

"I must leave," I told Claude without thinking about if that was even possible.

"How?" Claude asked.

"I'll request leave. I have to get home." I knew it could have already been too late. Papa could have died, but if there was a chance he was still alive, I needed to be with him. Influenza was sweeping through the nation and killing thousands. The odds were not in his favor.

"Maybe there's an officer in the administration building, ja?" Claude suggested.

Our food arrived while I was planning a way home. I had enough money to take the train, and it would be the fastest form of transportation. I could make it home by morning.

I ate my ordered schnitzel in less than a few bites, forcing the food down my throat. Poor Mama must have been a wreck.

"I'll walk you to the administration building. I'll help in any way I can," Claude offered.

"Danke."

"Charlie," Claude said as I stood from my seat. He placed his hand on my arm. "I'm sorry."

I bit the inside of my cheek, feeling pain surface from every inch of my body. This war had kept me from my family, from following in Papa's footsteps, and from taking care of Mama while he worked. *Damn this war*, I thought.

Luck shouldn't have been on my side. I didn't deserve any luck after what I had been participating in day in and day out, but there was a Gruppenführer working late in the administration office, and he granted me temporary leave.

I even managed to snag a train ticket just minutes before departure. I thought God wanted me to be with Papa, but I was having trouble believing in God then. God wouldn't have wanted all those prisoners murdered daily.

"Send my best to your folks," Claude said. He reached

forward and gave me a quick hug. "Stay strong, Charlie. Let me know when you're back."

* * *

It was six in the morning when I arrived home in Bavaria, and it was seven before I made it to the hospital where I hoped to find Papa. I waited at the Admissions desk for someone to assist me. The hospital was packed. People were coughing, and it was the only sound I could focus on, even when a young woman asked if she could help me.

When I noticed her voice, I turned and found a familiar face among the sick. "Charlie Crane?"

Shoulder-length curled blonde hair, bright indigo eyes, and a smile that matched Claude's. Annika was not very likable in our earlier days, but age and war will soften a person, and whatever she had gone through these last few years had changed the girl she once was. Annika dropped her clipboard and ran around the side of the desk she stood behind. A nurse's uniform looked right on her; it was where she was meant to be and where she wanted to be. She threw her arms around my neck as if we were once as close as Claude and I are. "How are you?" She pushed me away, looking me up and down, maybe checking to see if I was still in one piece. Of course, there wasn't much of a reason to be concerned since I was on the side of the war that was causing the damage.

"I'm worried," I told her. "Claude told me about your letter."

"I didn't know how else to find Claude. You boys are never around much, are you?"

"We're on the move a lot," I confirmed.

Annika placed her hand on my back, leading me down the adjacent hall, which felt promising. I hoped it meant Papa was still alive.

"Charlie, your papa isn't well. I'm afraid he doesn't have much time. Influenza spread to his lungs quickly," she said, still pushing us forward as if we were running out of time.

Before we walked into a small room, Annika handed me a medical mask. "Place this over your nose and mouth for protection."

I did as she asked and entered Papa's room. The sun was rising above the horizon, pouring light in through the room's dark curtains. Papa looked peaceful in the bed, partially covered by a white sheet. Mama sat by his side with a mask secured over her face, as well. She was startled when she turned around, spotting me in the doorway.

Her hand cupped over the mask and her eyes clenched. "My Charlie," she cried, her words muffled and hardly decipherable. "You're here. You're home."

"Mama," I said, reaching my arms out for her. I'm not sure when it happened, but at some point in the last few years, I became at least a foot taller than Mama. I had been surpassing her height since the age of thirteen, but the difference had become dramatic. I was tall like Papa. "Look at you, my sohn."

Mama had aged. Her hair was still pinned up, not a strand out of place. Her eye makeup was perfect without so much as a smudge, and her clothes looked freshly pressed. Always a seamstress. "Papa isn't going to make it, Charlie. He has been asking for his sohn, but I couldn't reach you. I even called the SS headquarters, and they said they would get a message to you, but I was not at home to receive a return call if you tried."

"No one told me, Mama. Claude received a letter from Annika last night. I took the first train home."

Mama looked past me, over to Annika and her eyes welled. "Annika has been amazing, Charlie. She has hardly left your father's side," she said, reaching for Annika's hand. "You are such a good girl."

"Charlie," a groan forms from beside me. "Charlie, my sohn. Is that you?"

The only words that came to mind when I twisted my head to look at Papa were: *This is it.*

"I came as soon as I heard," I told him, kneeling before him. I took Papa's hand within mine and squeezed. "It's too soon, Papa."

Papa smiled weakly. "Charlie, we all have a time. I have lived an extraordinary life." His life, as far as I had known, had been anything but extraordinary. He spent most of his days slaving in a bakeshop to provide for us. How could that make for a good life? All that work for what? So he could die before the age he could sit down and relax.

"I want more time with you, Papa." My words were as selfish as they sounded out loud, but it was true. I had been away for so long, training for the war, and I had missed being with my family.

"Every second we have is a blessing. Every second is worth remembering. If you add up all those seconds, Charlie, you will have a lifetime of memories to live with."

I tried my best to contain my composure, but my heart was breaking so violently. "I love you, Papa."

"And I love you, Charlie. Listen to me, sohn. After the war is over, find yourself a nice wife and give her the life I tried to give you and your mama. That is my dying wish, ja?"

"Ja, Papa. I will do my best." I was already busy imagining a life I could never have with a woman who shouldn't have wanted to know me. "I hope someday I can give my son or daughter what you have given me. You are the best papa a boy could have. The best."

Papa's lips pressed together, and he closed his eyes. His head shook slightly from side to side. "That's my boy."

Annika placed her hand on my shoulder. I knew it was time

to give Papa some space, so I took my seat beside Mama and held her hand throughout the morning.

In Papa's final moments, Mama rested her head on his chest and cried quietly, "es wird am ende in ordnung sein."

It will all be all right in the end.

"You are right, my sweetheart," he said, taking his last breath.

Papa passed away at noon, and we sat by his side for the next six hours, watching and waiting for the angels above to collect his soul.

Losing Papa was one of the many punishments to come.

CHAPTER 17

1942—TEREZIN, CZECHOSLOVAKIA

The train ride back to Terezín was unfathomable. I had never felt such unrelenting pain. Worse than losing Papa was leaving Mama, brokenhearted and alone. My leave was only for a short three days, which meant I had to leave Mama in her fragile state. She promised to be all right, but I knew better. Annika offered to stay with Mama until she would be well enough to be on her own, but I wasn't sure there would come a time when Mama would be okay without Papa.

Despite my sorrow, this train ride couldn't possibly compare to the ones the Jewish men and women were enduring.

The world sped by the train's window—a blur of greenery and morning fog accompanied by the sound of steam whistling from the engine.

As a young boy, I dreamt about riding trains as often as I could, because I wanted to see every corner of the world, learn every language, see every species of flowers, smell the ocean's air, and taste foreign cuisines. There was a world out there waiting to be discovered by a young boy, but now, the world was at war, and I was afraid what I had once wanted to experience was being destroyed little by little every day.

It wasn't until I was older and nearly at the end of my schooling that I was able to ride a train for the first time. It was as great as I hoped it to be. Though, the times following the initial trip were less than desirable. Today, however, had been the worst train ride to date. Every time the cart swayed, my stomach lurched, and I considered what would happen if I became sicker.

I closed my eyes, wishing away the feeling of nausea. Papa wouldn't want me suffering this way, but there was not much I could do.

Sleep took up much of the ride, and when I woke to a hollering announcement of the next stop, Terezín, I felt as though I could continue sleeping for another ten hours.

The walk from the train station felt like miles, when in reality it was only just a few blocks to my apartment. The night was rolling in fast, giving me a good reason to sleep more of the agony away. I hiked up the stairs to the apartment and let myself inside. Just as the first day I moved in, my gaze fell upon the ball of yarn resting on the floor.

I had not touched anything other than the dirty dishes and the smoking pipe to clean. This home was not my home, which was why I removed my boots at the door and hung my jacket on the guest's coat hook.

My wool socks caught on the splintered floors, reminding me of our floors at home. Mama would hand-make rugs to place over the bad spots, but they were pesky, and the cause of many of my bruised knees.

The bedroom was as I left it a few days earlier. The guest linens were laid out on the cot I found in the closet, and the extra blanket was folded neatly over the white cloth. I still refused to sleep in the bed—the sacred place of a happily married man and woman. If by some miracle they were to return, a bed with someone else's imprint would only add to their sadness. Furniture was never just furniture; they were objects used as a foundation for memories. Just as their furniture didn't belong to me, neither did their memories.

Sleep did not find me that night. The grooves within the ceiling's paint grew a judgmental face; the shape of a down-turned grimace judged me until I broke out into tears—tears so heavy the backs of my eyes ached.

When morning came, there was a pounding in my head, and my tear-soaked skin burned. "I should have fought harder, Papa. The war has stolen so much from so many, and now it has stolen from me too. My grief is stronger than I, and I don't know how much longer I will last in the conditions, watching the suffrage—the condemning brutalities. My nightmares follow me like a shadow." A grown man shouldn't wish for his mama to stroke the side of his face or for her warm kiss on the forehead. He should be comforting her instead. I don't know when I turned from a child to a man, but the transition was not seamless, and I don't feel as though I was ready to close the door on my childhood. The scars in my mind would be with me for life, and my innocence will never return. I felt deprived, but it could be worse. I could be a Jewish man in line, waiting for my death to arrive in the most unthinkable way.

With slow, lazy steps, I made my way to the guard post where I would stand for hours, watching death find many. The sun was high in the sky, bright as ever, but I felt the weight of the spring air, damp, heavy, and foreboding.

Amelia was within viewing distance, standing before her line while checking in the ill. Still, she wore a smile across her sullen face. I could assume Amelia wouldn't survive much longer, and the days of watching a beautiful girl wither away would soon come to an end. Along with the change in temperature, I could sense a new way of life creeping upon us.

The sick lines were becoming shorter. People were not waiting for medical care as they once were... because most had died. When a short break offered Amelia a moment to place down her clipboard, so she could wring the tension from her wrists, I made my way over. The apprehension I once felt before approaching a prisoner was no longer as jarring as it should have been.

Upon my arrival, Amelia clasped her hands together and stared down at her feet—the torn black boots with frayed laces. Her shoes were proof of the wear and tear she was experiencing. "I am so sorry to hear your papa is sick. The others were talking, and I overheard your name," Amelia said, beneath her breath.

I gritted my teeth and clenched my jaw as I was not expecting to hear those words from her mouth. "He is gone now. I deserve it, but he did not," I tell her.

Amelia's eyes closed, and I placed my hands behind my back, clasping my fingers around my right hand. I had almost forgotten that I must look as though I was speaking to her with authority.

"You are not a bad person," she whispered. "No one should lose their mama or papa."

Not only had Amelia's mother been murdered, but her father perished in the last month. His body was found in a supply closet. Then, like the other lifeless bodies in the camp, he was sent to the crematory. Even death was not enough of a punishment for the Jewish people.

"How did you get through it?" My words were not much more than air, and it was a question that should not have earned me an answer.

How had she gotten through any of what she had been through thus far?

"Prayer," she uttered. "Life here on earth is far worse than what is next for us all, Charlie. We are the unlucky ones." My throat felt swollen with pain, my jaw tensed, and my face became hot. The pain was unreal, but her words gave me freedom—something I could not offer in return. "I'll say a prayer for you and your papa."

A Jewish woman, being tortured day in and day out, was offering *me* a prayer. Amelia was the good the world should be.

At that moment, when a hand clamped down on my shoulder, I debated never speaking to Amelia again.

CHAPTER 18

PRESENT DAY

"You looked beyond the nature of our reality, seeing through the uniform, recognizing a warm heart, and separated me from the cold. I didn't deserve your faith or prayers, yet, you still offered them," I tell Amelia, staring into her endearing eyes. "That was why I chose you, darling. That is why I have always chosen you."

Amelia squeezes my hand. "You could have been killed so many times, Charlie. I wondered why you thought I was worth your life. Whatever the case may have been, my feelings did grow for you, and I questioned my sanity many times. However, not once did you give me a reason to feel ashamed for the way I felt, and I appreciated that."

Amelia struggles to shift her body. She is clearly uncomfortable in the hospital bed, with wires tangled around her arms and torso. After one last tug on the sheet, she folds her hands and rests them peacefully on her chest.

Life has had its way with us both.

"Why are you having surgery tomorrow? We're old, Amelia. We shouldn't be going under the knife at this age."

Amelia unclasps her hands and taps my knuckles. "Charlie,

when I saw you walk into my room earlier, I knew my life was not over. I have gotten this far in life from trusting my gut. Therefore, I will make it through the surgery tomorrow, and then I'm going to ask you never to leave me again."

After Emma called me the other day, I prayed Amelia would not hate me after having a lifetime to consider who I was to her, but I didn't expect her to still care for me the way I do for her.

"I never gave up hope that we would reunite."

"Never?" Amelia questions.

My head sways from side to side. "Amelia, I bought his and hers sofa chairs more than a half-century ago. Your chair has been waiting for you beside mine all this time, never sat in, never used. I knew someday you would find your chair to grow old in next to me."

Amelia presses herself up into a more upright position on the bed, pushing through her evident discomfort. "A chair?" she questions, inquisitively.

"Your chair," I correct her.

Amelia smiles—that smile that hasn't changed, the one where her eyes tilt in the corners, following the curve of her upturned lip. Age has nothing on her beauty. "I look forward to sitting in my chair," she says, her head resting softly into her pillow.

"You need sleep, darling." I lean forward and place a kiss on Amelia's forehead, letting my lips linger for a second longer than necessary. "Tomorrow is the first day of the rest of our lives."

"I'm going to hold you to that, Charlie Crane."

My legs feel heavy and tired as I walk out of Amelia's room, down the hall, and back into the waiting room where I plan to wait for the rest of my life to begin.

"How is she?" Emma asks as I take a seat on one of the blue padded chairs. Emma must have put lotion on her hands because the small area smells of lilac and vanilla. It smelled like newspaper when I left. "Is she all right?"

"She is Amelia. Of course, she is all right, dear."

Emma stands up and moves two seats down to sit next to me. "Reading Grams's journal has changed so much for me, Charlie. She was so secretive about it all." Emma wraps her long hair behind her back and straightens her posture while staring tiredly through the wall.

"It was a way of blocking out the pain," I explain without knowing the truth, but I can only imagine her reasons were similar.

"Yeah, speaking of pain, what happened to your arm?" Emma asks. "The journal didn't say much about that."

I glance down at the prosthetic arm I wear as a Band-Aid—the kind of bandage that hides pain rather than assisting in the healing process.

CHAPTER 19

1942—TEREZIN, CZECHOSLOVAKIA

A routine is what we had for the first two months of spring: a steady onslaught of murders, death by sickness, and deportations to the killing camps. All along, I felt like a bomb was about to drop on us all.

"Crane!" A commander was shouting my name from a distance. I recognized the voice, as did the hairs on my neck. Any time Sven called my name, it was an awful sound. "All of my men are to meet at headquarters at thirteen hundred hours. Understood, ja?"

"Ja, Herr," I responded, holding my flat palm straight out in front of me. "Heil Hitler."

"Heil Hitler," he responded before walking off, staring longingly at Amelia as he passed by her. I hated the way he looked at her. It wasn't long ago that he confessed his desire for Amelia.

"Jewish woman or not, she is a beauty. What a waste," he said. It was the day I was caught speaking to her, but the conversation appeared to be appropriate between a soldier and a Jewish prisoner because I had been careful not to be caught in any other situation. However, Sven wanted to be the one

controlling Amelia. Since then, he had kept an eye on her. He had also given her unnecessary orders, causing me to fear what else he had in mind.

My guilty conscience didn't know if his attraction to Amelia had something to do with me, or if he still would have spotted her if we weren't caught conversing that day. I knew of men barging into the women's cells at night, and then taking advantage. I prayed Sven wouldn't hunt Amelia down for that same reason.

I lifted my arm, allowing my sleeve to scrunch at the elbow so that I could see the time on my wristwatch. There was an hour before I needed to be at the administration building. We had meetings often, but they were pre-scheduled and at the same time each week. Something was different about the upcoming meeting. We were going to receive news about that hypothetical atomic bomb falling from the sky.

We all saw it coming.

I paced my area, overhearing Amelia tell another prisoner she would be right back. Often, she would run out of paper, or a pencil would break. Amelia would tend to the supply closet and return promptly as I had watched many times over the last five months.

The coast was clear, so I took a different route to the supply closet, meeting Amelia there. She gasped when I stepped into sight. Most of the prisoners were on edge, waiting to hear they stepped out of line for breathing the wrong way. People had been killed for that too.

"Charlie, you frightened me," she said, clutching her chest.

"Something is happening, Amelia. I don't know what it is, but I have a bad feeling."

"What is it?" she asked, retrieving another two pencils from a small box in the closet.

"An unplanned meeting," I whispered. "Be alert." I had nothing else to offer as a warning, but she should know to keep her eyes open for something coming. "If I must leave... I will come back for you, Amelia."

"Leave?" she questioned.

"The orders I receive, they don't always offer me much warning." I took her hand in mine and gently kissed her knuckles.

She inhaled sharply and straightened her frail shoulders. "Well, I have survived this long here. Surely, I will be okay."

I didn't understand how she could remain so calm. Maybe it was a front, but Amelia was undoubtedly stronger than I.

"Amelia," I spoke in a hush.

"Yes, Charlie," she responded with a raised brow.

"You look beautiful today." I attempted to tell Amelia she looked beautiful every day. I could only imagine how she must have felt without access to proper hygiene, food, and other bare necessities of life.

I had fallen for this woman.

Two weeks prior, Amelia referred to us as friends, and I realized in that instant that there was something other than a friendship brewing. Our hiding spot for that moment had been within one of the non-working shower rooms. Amelia had threatened to run away from the camp. When she spoke those words, my heart shattered. The thought of what would happen to her if she tried such a thing was incomprehensible.

"You can't leave me," I told her.

I was not trying to appear selfish. I knew Amelia would die if she left.

"Charlie, we are just friends," she told me.

Just friends. We were no longer just friends. My stomach hurt with the thought of not seeing her again. My heart pounded, and my knees were weak. Because of her.

"You're not my friend, Amelia," I told her. My voice sounded broken, but I tried to remain firm. I was determined to make her understand.

Amelia's eyes grew wide as she gazed at me. I couldn't tell if she was confused, upset, angry, or feeling the same way I was. Her sullen response was, "I understand," which made me realize she didn't know what I meant.

"No, you don't," I told her, squeezing my hands around her shoulders. I didn't know what I was doing at that moment, but my heart was steering the wheel.

"Charlie," Amelia whispered as she pulled herself free of my grip. I was scaring her, and it was the last of my intentions.

My gaze locked upon on her lips. I couldn't look anywhere else. My breaths were heavy, and I placed my hand on the plastered wall above her head, leaning toward her with hunger.

"Are you okay?" she asked, her voice quiet and unsure.

I allowed my forehead to fall softly against hers. My other hand looped around Amelia's small frame, and I pulled her into me, claiming her lips as if I needed them to survive. Oxygen didn't seem necessary at that moment, though I was becoming breathless quicker than anticipated. The air was tight within the broken shower room, and sweat was trickling down the back of my neck. I was committing a crime, but at the same time, confessing the feelings my heart was screaming out loud.

Amelia kissed me back with the strength she had, uncaring of what might happen next. For that blissful minute, there was no war, there were no prisoners, I was not a monster, and she was not walking a plank toward her death. We were just Charlie and Amelia, and she was my girl. I was falling in love with a woman I knew I couldn't hold onto, and there was nothing I wanted to do to stop it.

Long drawn-out delicious minutes passed as we stared into each other's eyes searching for a future we could only conjure in our dreams. "Amelia, I—I am in love with you. I love you." My words were not thought out, but they were the truth. For months I had watched that beautiful woman overcome the most treacherous situations. I questioned her strength—if it was even human. She, who could put a smile upon her cupid-bow lips to ease the worry of a child and his mother, had to be an angel on this hell of an earth. There was no other explanation, and I was enamored and fascinated by her strength. I would do anything to save her. Anything.

Of the parts I loved most about Amelia was the reason behind the response that awaited me. "Charlie, if I tell you I love you, you'll leave me, just like everyone else I have ever loved, so I'm sorry I can't offer you the same affirmation in return."

I didn't offer Amelia my love in exchange for hers. "I don't care if you love me. I don't care if you do and never tell me, but I needed you to know that I love you, and I will do whatever I can to protect you."

It was the truth she needed to hear.

"Oh, Charlie," she uttered. "You must stop calling me beautiful. It's absurd. I'm just glad there aren't mirrors here to see the truth."

"Whatever truth you believe is merely a reflection of how you feel, rather than what is real. Do not forget that."

A door opened and closed in an adjacent corridor, so I took the free second I had left and kissed the woman I yearned to be with, in any other situation than this. Amelia dropped her pencil amid the moment.

Boots were thudding closer.

"Pick up the pencil, ja?" I scolded her. "Let's go, let's go." I tried to convince myself that my dictating words were for play, but to everyone else, they were real. I wondered if Amelia felt that way, as well.

I took her by the elbow and tugged her down the hallway, nodding at the soldier passing by us. "I love you," I whispered in her ear as I gently flung her out the door.

* * *

Soldiers stood around a meeting table in a pea-green painted
room, waiting for orders. It was thirteen hundred hours on the
dot, but it was another five minutes before the Obergruppenführer greeted us.

"Heil Hitler," the officer greeted us.

"Heil Hitler," echoed in response.

"Men, everything you hear in this room is to be confidential,
ja?"

"Ja, Herr," again, everyone spoke at once.

"One of our commanders has been assassinated by the
Czechoslovakian Army in Prague. We need men on the front
lines immediately. You are all deploying first thing in the morning. We have trained long and hard, preparing for this situation,
and I have faith you will all come out on top. As of now, your
guard posts will be manned and covered while you are gone. All
questions may be directed to your superior. Otherwise, we will
meet at the train tomorrow morning at five. Go on home and get
some sleep."

"Heil Hitler," the men roared again on the way out of the
meeting room.

My eyes locked with Claude's. He was standing across the
room. The look we shared was full of child-like fear. Toy guns
and pretend war battles as children are things we will only be
able to reminisce of now.

My first thoughts should have been fear of stepping into a
combat zone, but I was more afraid of leaving Amelia alone
after I pleaded with her not to run away. The new orders felt
like the last chapter of a bad book.

Some of the other men were full of excitement. The cama-
raderie was shockingly high. This war had been nothing but a
blood bath, and we were walking directly into the line of fire.
What reason was there to be excited? A few of the soldiers were
off in the corner, making a mockery of shooting a weapon,
sound effects included. Did they not understand? War means

life or death. We have been watching the Jewish prisoners lose their battle, and now we might lose ours.

I ran back to my apartment, grabbing the telephone from the entryway table. I dialed home, praying Mama was in the house and would answer.

The call was thankfully connected. "Crane residence," Mama answered.

"Mama," I sighed with relief.

"Charlie, my sohn. Is everything all right?"

"Mama, I'm being deployed to Prague in the morning. There is a battle, and they want me to fight."

"Charlie," Mama said, her voice cracking with fear. "No."

I swept the back of my hand across my forehead, wiping away the sweat. "I don't have a say in the matter, Mama. I don't want to go, believe me."

"Charlie, I can't lose you too," she cried. Mama was crying. She was so strong, always, even when Papa died. The pain was written across her face when I had to leave, but she promised she would be well enough to carry on. "My baby. This is all my fault, Charlie. I should never have agreed to that stupid school. This is all my fault, and now I might lose you too."

My back slid down the wall of the foyer in the apartment until I hit the floor. I ran my fingers through my hair and then rested my hand on my cheek. "Mama, this is not your fault. We are in a war and have no control. You were right to have me trained properly. I might be dead now if not." My words were not true. I wished more than anything that I didn't attend Hitler's school, but if there is anything I had learned over the last several years, it was that we could not change what had already happened.

"No, Charlie. Do not say that. I was wrong, and I was a bad mother for making you go to that terrible school. I see it all so clearly now, sohn. You must never forgive me. Never."

"Mama, enough," I scolded her. "It doesn't matter how I got here. I'm here, and I will fight until I can come home to you."

"I love you my Charlie. You are a good man, and I don't think I had much to do with that, but I am proud of who you are and what you believe."

"I love you, Mama. You had everything to do with me being a good man. You and Papa, both. I know how to love, and that's more important than all else in the world. Take care, Mama."

"Es wird am ende in ordnung sein... *It will all be all right in the end*, my sohn."

I dropped the receiver and threw my head against the wall. Why did this world have to be such a cold and dark place? It didn't have to be this way. I was not confident that I would make it through this alive. I had so little left to offer.

CHAPTER 20

1942—TEREZIN TO PRAGUE, CZECHOSLOVAKIA

We had been in Prague just over two weeks now, marching the streets, looking for answers about two assassins responsible for one of our commander's deaths. The story had many gray areas, but our mission was to find the two men responsible. Rumor had it that they were hiding somewhere within the borders of Prague.

In reality, we were there to battle until we collected our answers. I should not have been nervous since I had been preparing for a time like this since I was twelve. My rifle was in my hand, and we were marching over stone streets, eyeing the people of Prague with suspicion. Most of the people who remained in the area were trying to carry on with a normal life, as normal as possible after their Jewish neighbors were sent away. Sven had me by his side, as usual, and he was the last person I wanted to be around while raiding another city.

"You," he shouted to a lone man walking down the street with a loaf of bread wrapped in paper. The man's face drained of color as Sven approached. I trailed behind, looking elsewhere, not feeling the need to add more stress to the current situation. Sven got a kick out of terrorizing innocent people. It offered him more power than he needed. "Where are you off to?" Sven continued to scrutinize the man.

"Home, sir. My wife is unwell, and I am out collecting a few items for her."

Sven stood in the man's way, tilting his head to the side, studying the poor man. "How long has your wife been ill?"

The man swallowed loudly enough for us to hear. His nerves were evident by the sweat on his face and the redness of his cheeks. "About a week, sir."

"Do you work?" Sven continued.

"Sir, I have a cattle farm."

"Very well," Sven said, peering over the man's shoulder. "You best get home to your wife, ja?"

"Thank you, sir."

I held back a sigh. I knew better than to question Sven's way of conducting business, but much of his efforts seemed unwarranted.

As I looked around the area we had been marching, I noticed other soldiers questioning locals at every corner. In my mind, I wondered what resident of Prague would rat out one of their own and tell us, the enemy, whether or not they know of the assassin. Their attempt at murder was against a man who stripped this region of all Jewish people. I can't say I blame the assassins. However, I kept that bit of information private.

A whistle blew from down the street where Astor, a soldier of rank parallel to Sven, was waving him over. "Crane, come here," Sven called for me to follow as if I was a dog.

With our rifles pressed against our chests, we crossed the road meeting Astor at the corner. Another resident of Prague was pinned against the brick wall by Astor's subordinate who pressed the end of his rifle against the local's head. The man had dark greasy hair, long enough to cover his right eye, and his face was sunken, pale, and covered in sweat. His white under-shirt had yellow stains, and his brown pants had tears at the knees. The man smelled foul, as if he had been living on the streets for some time. The nervous glint covering his face did not show a look of being trustworthy, but I knew we had no other leads yet. Therefore, he would become a puppet for Astor and Sven. "Name?" Astor asked the man.

"Callum," he replied, sounding breathless from just the simple answer.

"You must take us to the location, ja?"

Callum's eyes were wide as his gaze darted back and forth between us all. Sweat percolated on his forehead and ran down the side of his temples. "One million marks," Callum requested through his shaky voice.

"You show us the home first," Astor told him. "If you are correct, we will pay the bounty." Astor turned to face Sven. "He claims to know where the assassins are hiding."

"Take us there," Sven told the man.

Callum responded with only a quick nod of his head, leading us several miles down the long roads. All the while, the rifle's mouth was against the base of Callum's neck. I wouldn't necessarily trust the man, but if he was willing to help, I would not threaten his life with every step, but I wasn't one to make that call.

In the center of town, we spotted a building of flats. The units looked vacant, as there was no sign of life around us. I would not have thought a family was still occupying the space, but we would soon find out if that were true. We gathered into the building, marching up several flights of stairs until we stopped in front of a beaten wooden door.

"Here," Callum said. "In there."

We had gathered several of our soldiers before barging into this home that could contain none other than poor residents of this region.

Sven was the first to pound his fist against the door. The greatness of his thrusting booms should have warned whoever was inside. I prayed the homeowners were not an old couple sitting in their chairs, watching the trees sway outside their windows. Surely, Sven's incoming announcement would frighten them to their death.

A young man answered the door, holding it open no more than a crack, but there was enough space to see his nose and mouth. "C—can I help you?"

"We must search your home," Sven announced. "You must all vacate."

"This is not a good time," the young man responded. "You see, I have elderly parents."

I knew any form of negative response would lead to Sven knocking a door down. "Move aside, young man," Astor shouted over Sven's shoulder.

It was no more than a few seconds before Sven threw the door to the ground. We piled into the small flat, though I stood by the open doorway as I didn't plan to be the questioner.

A family of three occupied the home. Though dark from the navy blue papered walls and small windows, candle flames were not present, nor were there lamps to light the way. We could see just what the dull rays of sunlight offered: three terrified faces.

I imagined this was what Amelia's face must have looked like when the soldiers pulled her from her home, and it pained me to the core. I wanted to be done scaring people, torturing, and fighting the innocent. It was unnecessary, and I was sure those three people knew nothing of the assassins.

"We are conducting searches in the area, looking for the men responsible for our commander's death. Do you have any information that might be helpful to us?" Astor asked the three of them.

The woman, who I assumed to be the young man's mother, sat in a hand-carved wooden chair in front of a cut tree stump being used as a small table. She was toying with a small ball of yarn, weaving the threads around her fingers. Her white hair was a mess even pinned up, and her dress was torn at the hem and covered with a stained apron. Poverty was becoming an epidemic; that much was clear.

The man did not look much better, though he was on two feet with his arms crossed over his chest. "We know nothing that could be of help to you," he offered.

Their son, however, was showing signs of nerves. It could have been because German soldiers were standing in his house, but he had a similar disposition to Callum. I didn't want to accuse this family of a war crime, but I could not control what Sven and Astor would do next.

"Boy, you look like you know something," Sven said directly to the young man. "You all must leave so we can conduct our search."

"We are not hiding a thing," the father spoke. "You must be mistaken."

"Then surely you won't mind if we take a look," Sven replied, removing his cap while walking farther inside.

"Come along," the father told his wife and son. However, the young man refused to stand. Instead, he shook his head as he took a seat on the floor in the corner of the room. I was sure at that moment he was guilty, and Sven and Astor were also sure. Sven moved quickly across the small living area, cornering the son. "You do have information for us," Sven told him, grabbing his arm and lifting the boy to his feet. Sven dragged him out the door, throwing him against the wall in the hallway.

The rest of us stared silently at the man and woman who could not be bothered to make eye contact with us. The man and woman stood silently in the hallway, doing as we told them. All the while, their son was being questioned by Sven and Astor.

However, the boy was not cooperating. Therefore, we were

no closer to locating the assassins. It seemed as though it was a wasted effort.

"I must use the washroom," the woman spoke up. "Please."

One of the other soldiers escorted the woman back into her flat and stood outside the door, waiting for her to finish.

Except, after nearly an hour, the soldier reappeared in the doorway alone. "Astor, a word, please." Astor and his subordinate spoke privately, but I overheard the words: "cyanide capsule" and "she's dead."

Astor disappeared into the flat, almost as if he had preplanned what was happening. The son and father were taken to another area of the building by Sven, leaving Callum and myself alone in the hallway. I glanced over, wondering what thoughts were going through the young man's head.

"We grew up together," Callum spoke from beside me. "Daniel and I, we were once close friends." Callum turned in his friend for money.

An hour had passed when Astor appeared in the doorway with the unthinkable- the mother's head contained in a glass bowl. My stomach lurched. "This should get the boy talking, ja?" Astor said with a smirk. "We should be on our way soon."

There were no words to speak. My mind felt darker than it had before, and I was starting to believe I would never see a purpose for daylight again.

When I remembered I was not alone, I peered over at Callum, who now understood the repercussions of his actions. His eyes were not blinking. He appeared dead, staring through the wall before us; he was in shock. I took the boy outside and sat him on the curb.

"You have been starving, ja?" I asked him.

Callum shook his head. "I—I was desperate. My wife is pregnant, and she can't move. My father is dying. We're all in the same house, and everyone is hungry," Callum cried out. He's young to have a wife, but age was not a factor any longer.

Lives were cut short, and the age of death was far younger than it had been.

I reached into my pocket and pulled out a handful of marks. "I don't know if they will pay you the money you requested. In case they don't, feed your family tonight." I closed his hand over the money. "We are all trying to survive. It's all for one, Callum. I understand."

I didn't truly understand, but it was the words he needed to hear because desperation in a time of poverty means people are forced to choose between loved ones.

The day carried on for what seemed like forever. If only I could convince myself I had seen the worst of my reasons for being in Prague.

CHAPTER 21

JUNE 1942—PRAGUE, CZECHOSLOVAKIA

We found the assassins beneath floorboards on the bottom floor of the apartment building. The beheaded mother and her son were hiding the convicts. The father knew nothing of the act. Regardless, the son and father would be left to face the repercussions of protecting the assassins. Death would soon find them.

We should have all been able to go back to our guard duties since we found the perpetrators, but no such luck.

We continued pacing the streets through the night. Under the dark sky, the street lamps illuminated the wet puddles left behind from a small passing rainstorm. The world around me looked much like a Van Gough oil painting. I was unsteady from a lack of sleep, and the roads were swirling beneath the flickering stars.

I didn't feel much better as the sun crept over the horizon, reminding me that summer was on its way. My daze broke at the sound of marching boots in the distance. The sound was not steady like a parade of soldiers, but rather an unruly group of men running toward us.

My eyes were slow to blink as a herd of Czechoslovakian soldiers rushed toward the church we were standing before. They were after us for finding their assassins; it was the only thing that made sense. This was the battle our commanding officers saw coming. We were playing pieces in their game of chess.

Weapons were firing. A hand-to-hand combat fight was imminent, and I stood frozen in the square. My instinct led me toward the church. If I could find a gully near an underground door, I could sit with my rifle and protect myself. I had no desire to kill for the sake of winning this battle. I only wanted to stay alive. I knew I was a poor representation of the German soldiers, but I no longer cared.

I found a hole next to the basement entrance of the church. I could see most of what was happening, and the rest of my men were in the thick.

I was a coward.

"Charlie," a whisper sounded like a scream while under fire. I turned in every direction, seeking the source. Claude appeared from behind me, crunching down on the stone step above mine. "What are you doing over here, brother?"

"Hiding," I told him truthfully.

"We should be fighting, ja?" Claude was covered in dirt as if he had been in a trench. He reeked of gunpowder, and I was afraid to ask where he had been.

"What are we fighting for?" I asked him in return.

"Our lives," Claude said.

"Our lives don't matter anymore. Can't you see?"

A look of defeat swam through Claude's crestfallen eyes. "You're right, brother."

"Just stay here until things cool down," I told him. My advice was not sound. We could both end up in trouble, as this was the equivalent of turning our backs on the others.

"I cannot do that," Claude said. "We're here to do a job,

Charlie. If we are caught hiding, we will be treated much like the enemy."

I wanted to grab onto Claude's arm and pull him deeper into the hole I was situated within. The thought of a time when we were young kids came to mind.

Our mothers were shouting for us. It was supper time, but Claude and I were hiding, hoping we could prolong our playtime. We were giggling behind a tree, our forefingers pressed against our lips while we peeked around the trunk. "They're coming," Claude whispered as our mothers walked into sight.

"Shh, maybe they won't see us here."

"You boys are about to be in a lot of trouble," Claude's mother shouted at us.

Claude moved first, more fearful of his mother than I was of mine. "We're here, mother," he called.

"Claude Louis Taylor, we talked about this, sohn," she continued shouting.

"I'll see you tomorrow, brother," Claude said while waving goodbye.

Claude's blonde hair flew above his ears as he ran through the tall grass toward his mother. It felt like it might be an eternity before I would see Claude again.

Just as I couldn't hold Claude back while we were children, I couldn't keep him back from defending our country at that moment. "I'll see you in a bit, brother," he said, waving me off.

Claude's blonde hair flapped against his cap as he ran toward the gunfight.

Don't go, Claude.

A cold sweat covered every inch of my body, clothed or not. There were so many bullets flying in the near vicinity, but I couldn't see where they were coming from. I sat still, watching smoke billow as the air filled with the smell of powdery smoke.

Claude didn't make it more than thirty feet.

A bullet struck him, but I didn't know where. All I knew

was my best friend, my brother, was taken down. I had to help him. My heart felt like the heaviest part of my body as I moved toward Claude, watching in every direction. There was no possibility of keeping myself out of the firing range, but that didn't matter at the moment. I needed to save Claude—if it wasn't too late.

I threw myself beside Claude, lying face down, keeping my hands beneath my chest. "Brother," I whispered. "Open your eyes." Claude's eyes slowly peeled open. He looked tired, as if he had just woken up out of a deep slumber. "Where were you hit?"

He didn't answer. I pushed myself up to inspect him for a gunshot wound, finding blood pooling out from beneath him. It appeared to be his chest.

I wrapped my arm around his body and held him tightly. "You're going to be okay, brother. You hear me?"

"Charlie," he whispered.

"Shh," I hushed him. I didn't want him to talk.

"Charlie," he said again. "Go back to where you were. You are the smart one."

I grit my teeth so hard my jaw hurt. "I will not leave you."

"I'm not going to make it, Charlie. Tell Mama I said I'm sorry. Tell Papa I tried to be like him. And tell Annika to be strong for me. Tell them I love them, Charlie."

"Claude, stop talking nonsense, you hear me?"

"I love you too, brother."

I squeezed him tighter, praying that God spared him. He was a good man, not like so many of the others. We all deserved to die, but selfishly, I didn't want to lose Claude, and I didn't want to die either.

Claude had no more words. His eyes were open, staring directly at me, but I didn't know if he was still there. I reached for his neck to search for a pulse, but another round of gunshots rang out around us.

I began to crawl away in an attempt to reclaim my hideout.

Just as I was about to make it back to safety, the ground shook.

A muffled thud stole all forms of sound.

Black smoke filled the air around me.

I couldn't move.

An ice-cold searing pain drove through my spine.

A feeling of numbness took over.

Death felt imminent.

CHAPTER 22

JUNE 1942—BEELITZ, GERMANY

I saw baby blue tiles framed by white cement lines. Cream-colored linens and medical equipment surround my body. "Claude?" I tried to ask anyone who might be nearby. "Is Claude okay?"

Padded footsteps closed in on me, but when I tried to lift my head, I found my body stiff and weighted down.

Panic set in.

"Herr Crane." The woman's voice was soft, unrecognizable, and foreign. "You're awake." Her words came out as a statement rather than a question. However, I didn't know when I had fallen asleep or ended up wherever I was. "Are you in much pain?"

It was then that I began to take inventory of my body parts, but I wasn't feeling much of anything. "No, no pain."

"Good. We have given you medication to help." A nurse—she is the one speaking to me. "I am nurse Geni." The woman placed her hand on my right shoulder. "We almost lost you, Herr."

"Claude. Have you seen my friend, Claude Taylor?" I asked her.

The nurse had kind eyes, almost too kind to see the horrors a nurse in her position must see. She was peering at me with sadness and sympathy, rather than empathy. Her lips pressed together as she forced a small smile. "We should focus on you right now, ja?"

"I am quite all right as you can see," I told her. "It's Claude that I'm worried about." Nurse Geni took a chair from the side of the room, lifted it and brought it over beside me. She was about to say something awful. People always take a seat when they must deliver bad news. "He's gone, isn't he?"

"I'm afraid I don't know anything about your friend, Claude," she began. "Herr, you have been sedated and unconscious for nearly a week. You were hit with shrapnel from an explosive. Your arm was severed very badly, and the surgeons were forced to amputate what was left. It was the only way to save your life."

My heart must have stalled as she was talking because I wasn't sure I was even breathing. Instinctively, I glanced to my right arm, noting it was where it should be. With a slow movement, I twisted my head to the left, finding the sleeve of the hospital gown I was wearing flattened against the bedding.

My left arm was gone.

As a child, I feared the thought of death, wondering how someone could understand the meaning of being gone for eternity. I would lie awake, wondering if we would come back to earth someday in a new body, or if our souls traveled infinitely through space. I could never wrap my head around the meaning of forever, but I could block out the thoughts knowing I would be dead and therefore would not have to worry about those thoughts.

This was different. I was alive and would have to live on forever without a left arm. It was a part of my body that had been with me all my life. I didn't know how to live with only one arm.

The war had stolen my arm.

"Charlie," the nurse whispered, forgetting about the manners or respect for authority I was owed but didn't want. "This isn't going to be easy, but you are alive, and that is what matters."

"I can still feel my arm, and it doesn't hurt," I tried to explain.

Nurse Geni smiled kindly, her red lips glistening beneath the orange light. "Our minds are capable of a lot, Charlie." The nurse righted the sheets and pulled them taut across my chest, carefully avoiding my left shoulder. "Your mother has been here, but she left to freshen up. I'm sure she'll be thrilled to find out you have awoken." I don't know how Mama has dealt with the news. I promised her I would be careful. I never wanted to put her through more pain than what she had already endured. "Rest, Charlie. I'll let you know when your mother has returned."

Nurse Geni walked out of the room, each of her movements slow and agile. The environment was likely made to be a calm and restful place, but I felt anything but peaceful. I looked over at my left shoulder again, feeling the need to apologize to my body.

How could I keep moving? I wasn't sure if I was even out of danger. Still, my biggest concern was Claude.

"Nurse!" I shouted.

Nurse Geni was quick to return. "Yes, Herr."

"Please, could you do a little research and find out about Claude Taylor. He was with me in the battle. He was shot. I need to know, Fräulein. It is most important."

"Very well," she said with another soothing smile. "I will see about finding information on your friend."

* * *

I had fallen back to sleep after the nurse left my room, but now a soft hand was sweeping alongside my cheek. The familiar scent of soap told me who was sitting beside me. "Mama," I called out before opening my eyes.

"My Charlie," she replied, sounding heartbroken and despondent.

"I am so sorry, Mama," I groaned. "I am so sorry."

Mama shook her head, and her eyes filled with tears. "You are alive, my sohn. You have no reason to be sorry."

"I was trying to help Claude," I told her. My voice was hoarse and must have been hard to understand, but by the look on her face—the puzzlement, I knew she comprehended my words.

"What is wrong with Claude?" I thought Frau Taylor would have notified Mama.

"He was shot, Mama. I was sure he was not going to make it."

Mama's eyes grew wide, the whites covered with red veins. "No," she whispered. "No, not Claude."

"I don't know where he is, Mama."

"Surely if he were dead, Frau Taylor would have been notified by now, ja?"

I wanted to shrug my shoulders, but trying to move my body seemed useless. I didn't know if I could even shrug my left shoulder anymore. "We will find Claude, dead, or alive. We will find him."

"I wonder when I'll be allowed to go back to my guard duty," I mentioned. It was a passing thought—much more than a passing thought. Since I had left Theresienstadt, I had been fearful of Amelia being transported to a killing center. So many thoughts were going through my mind at once.

"Oh, Charlie. You won't be going back to any type of duty. You have lost your arm. Surely they can't expect you to work any longer."

Losing my arm was my free ticket home, away from the battles, and the war.

And also, away from Amelia. I couldn't do that.

"Mama, I met a woman," I told her, fearful of what she might say after finding out the following details.

She smiled, quaintly at first. "You did? Where did you meet her? What is her name?"

I swallowed hard, feeling the lump travel down to my stomach. "Her name is Amelia."

"How lovely," Mom responded with a bright look in her eyes.

"She's Jewish, Mama."

Mama jolted from her seat as if she was sitting on a loose spring. Her hand folded over her mouth, and she paced the small room for a long moment. "A Jewish woman?" she said through an exasperated sigh.

"Ja. She's a prisoner at the camp where I was stationed."

"Charlie," she huffed. "You could be put away if you were caught with a Jewish woman, or worse. You must not continue to see her."

"I'm not like the rest of them, Mama. I don't hate others for what they believe."

"I know, Charlie, but you are putting yourself in danger, sohn."

"I need to protect her, Mama."

Mama returned to her seat and rested her hand on my knee. "I am proud of the man you have become, Charlie. I will always be proud of you. Make sure you think this through, though. You are alive and have the rest of your life ahead of you. We are living in a time when rationality is no longer relevant. We aren't allowed to choose who we love—" Mama cupped her hands over her eyes and pressed her lips together. "Nein. Nein. I am wrong, sohn. I am wrong. You are the one who has always been right. Listen to me, and listen to me good, Charlie." She leaned forward and took my chin within her hand. "I will support you in whatever you do, and whomever you love, but you be careful. Do you understand me? I will not lose you. I will not, Charlie Crane. Do not do anything that will get you killed. That is my only plea as your mother."

I tried to smile, but even the muscles in my face were weak. "I will not get killed, Mama. I was meant to save this woman, though, and if it isn't too late, I intend to do that for her."

"I'm proud of you, Charlie. However, you have a long road of recovery before you start saving another person, ja?"

I had hope. It might have been false hope, but I was alive, and I had a plan.

CHAPTER 23

MAY, 1943—TEREZIN, CZECHOSLOVAKIA

ELEVEN MONTHS LATER

I did not think I would need to plead for permission to return to Theresienstadt. In my wildest dreams, I wouldn't have imagined asking to go back to the concentration camp, but I had one reason to return, and it could have been for nothing. The chances of Amelia still working as a medical assistant were beyond slim, but if there was a chance, I needed to go back.

I remained in the hospital for a month and was sent home with Mama to recover. It was nice to be home for a bit, but the thoughts of what I left behind, of what I saw, gave me a different outlook for the future. I was not returning to Hitler's playground to be the bad guy. If God kept me alive after blasting my arm off, then I was meant to do something more with my life.

In the year I was gone, the town of Terezín had taken to the war, showing the side effects of death, ashes, and smoke. The once beautiful area was discolored and gray. I didn't know what to expect when walking back in through those gates of hell.

"Welcome back, soldier!" My comrade greeted me with a smile. I had forgotten his name, but he knew of me. More fellow soldiers welcomed me with open arms and pats on the back. It was wrong. Why be happy while people were dying all around us, because of us?

My gaze was wildly searching the area for a familiar face, but everyone was staring at me, and then the tied-off sleeve of my left shoulder.

Then, through an opening, I spotted the beautiful woman.

She was alive.

Amelia was still alive.

She looked frail, skin and bones, and pale. She had been even more brutally starved than before I left. Despite the condition she was in, my heart pounded heavily within my chest. I wanted to cry, fall to my knees, and thank God for this tiny miracle. However, I couldn't even make eye contact with Amelia or others would know where I was looking. Through the corner of my eye, I noticed her gaze sweep over me. She then departed her post and fled into the medical block.

Something had changed.

My heart dropped, wondering what had happened while I was gone.

Was she okay? Did she learn to hate me?

I walked through the cheering crowd of soldiers, noticing the stares from passing Jewish prisoners who were all emaciated, getting closer to their promised death. I wondered how they were still alive.

"Brother." The uttering of the word, his voice—my body froze. "You're here."

I stopped walking and turned toward the sound—the best sound. I had to bite my bottom lip to contain my emotions as I saw Claude standing before me, in one piece.

For a while, no one knew if Claude was alive. It took months to find out he was in a military hospital outside of Prague. The bullet missed his vital organs by a hair, and though the damage was severe and took a great deal of time to heal, he had survived. Claude was looking for me while I was looking for him, but it wasn't until Frau Taylor nearly knocked down our door one hot morning at the end of July, that we found out Claude was alive and sent back to Theresienstadt.

Claude threw his arms around my neck and slapped his hand against my back. He sniffled and buried his face in my right shoulder.

"I thought you were dead," he told me.

"I thought you were dead," I replied.

We walked side by side around the building toward the newly assigned guard post. "When I arrived back here at the ghetto, you weren't here. The battle was over, and everyone who survived came back."

"I'm sorry to have worried you," I offered.

"You tried to help me," Claude said, "and you lost your arm because of it, didn't you?"

"I would give up all my limbs to help you, brother," I told him.

"You were the smart one to take cover, Charlie. This war is ugly, and it's every man for himself now."

"Claude, I need to tell you something, and I need you to try and understand."

Claude's eyebrows knitted together, a look of question and confusion tugged at the corners of his mouth. "What is it?"

"I wasn't cut out to be the bad guy." I leaned forward, keeping my voice quiet. "My stay here is temporary. There is a woman—"

Claude backed away with a hearty smile. "Who is she?" His excitement would fade when I released the truth.

"You will think less of me," I told him.

"Never. I would not think less of you no matter what you do, Charlie."

My gaze dropped to the dirt below our feet. "I need to save someone from this camp."

Claude's head pulled back, recoiling from my statement. "You could be put into prison, or worse, Charlie."

"I am aware," I told him.

"Who is she?" Claude asked again.

I closed my eyes and pulled in a short breath, seeking courage. "The woman who is checking in the ill prisoners."

Claude crossed his arms over his chest—something I could no longer do. "She is a beautiful woman," Claude agreed. "I wasn't aware you two knew each other."

"I came back because of her, Claude. They didn't want me back—not with a missing arm."

I didn't know what thoughts were going through Claude's head, but his eyes narrowed as if he couldn't find a proper response. "Charlie, that woman, among many others, are on the transit list. She is going to be sent to Auschwitz within the next two days. I'm so sorry, brother."

The odds of Amelia being transported when I returned seemed unlikely. "The special project," I commented. I assumed Claude was aware of what was about to take place in the camp. "The special project" was the only reason my superiors agreed to let me return. We were about to begin beautifying Theresienstadt to fool the Red Cross into thinking Theresienstadt was not a prison. We were to make them believe that this ghetto was created to support the arts and talent of a Jewish community. Propaganda at its finest.

"Ja, brother. They must get rid of anyone who appears emaciated. That woman does not look well, nor do most of the others she arrived with."

I swallowed hard, knowing what I would have to do much sooner than anticipated. "I was about to ask you if you wanted to get some supper tonight, but I have a feeling you might have other plans now," Claude suggested.

"Ja. I have to save her."

"You love her," Claude stated.

"I do love her. Thoughts of her kept me going this past year, and I didn't even know if she survived the terrible odds here. She is alive though, and I'm going to do what I promised myself I would do if I found her to be here still."

Claude placed his hand on my shoulder. "What about you, Charlie? What about your life?"

"I believe I was given a second chance so I would not have to die with guilt. Therefore, if I die trying to save this woman, I know I will have died doing something right."

Claude nodded his head. "You are on to something, brother. You are a smart man."

I don't know if I could refer to myself as intelligent for the decisions I was making, but in my mind, the outcome was better than being a puppet for an evil dictator. "Take care of yourself," I told Claude. "When we all get out of this place, we must find each other, ja?"

"We're brothers, Charlie. We'll always find each other."

It was a proper goodbye—one I once thought I would never have. I didn't know if my actions would result in death or the ability to never to see Claude again, but he was alive and well, and that was enough satisfaction.

I spent the next several hours deciphering a plan. There was a chance Amelia wouldn't trust me or want to leave. There was no telling where her thoughts were at, but she was unaware of her imminent future, and she needed to know her options.

It was later that night—the prisoners were confined, and the only soldiers left on the grounds were the night guards. I made my way into the cell Amelia was assigned, finding her frail body asleep between several other lifeless women. She was so much smaller now than she was when I left. I was able to scoop her up with one arm and take her out of the cell. She was startled by my presence.

I took her far enough away from the other guards and the

other cells so I could explain to her the situation at hand. "We need to escape," I told her.

At first, she seemed to be without words. I hadn't heard her speak in a year, and it was all I yearned for at that moment.

"Charlie," she said through her breath. She seemed lost as she stared into my eyes.

"I'm here," I told her. "I'm here."

"When are we leaving?" Amelia finally asked me.

"As soon as we can," I told her.

Amelia covered her hands over her face, shaking her head. "I can't leave Lucie," she replied.

Lucie. "Who is Lucie?" I asked, feeling as though I had forgotten something important.

"Leah's daughter." Leah—a pregnant woman Amelia helped just before I left for Prague.

"She's alive?" I asked. I don't know why I asked that question.

"Lucie, the baby, she is alive. Leah was executed."

Shame was all I could feel. "It isn't fair." What else could I say? It wasn't. At that moment, I knew I would do whatever I could to protect baby Lucie along with Amelia. It was the very least I could do for that innocent little girl.

Amelia placed her hand on my left shoulder, allowing her fingertips to skate down the loose material of the empty sleeve.

"Your arm, Charlie."

Amelia's eyes filled with anger, but I kissed her pretty lips to remind her that I was alive. "This war could take my arm, but it could not take me." The sensation of our lips connecting after everything we had been through made me feel like, together, we had access to the key that would open the door to a future we both desired.

There was not much time for reconciliation, but I knew what I had to do.

CHAPTER 24

MAY 1943—TEREZIN, CZECHOSLOVAKIA

It was time to move. I had planned the escape out thoroughly—every moment would matter.

I had Amelia by the sleeve, the fabric gripped tightly in my hand as we entered an unused building behind the tunnel that led to the execution field. With only a weak flashlight, I lit up the stairs so we could find our way to the underground floor of the building. Many crates were lined up, filled with items stolen from the Jewish prisoners.

"What is all this?" Amelia asked.

I didn't have the strength to explain where it had all come from, but I assumed she would soon figure it out on her own since there was an entire crate dedicated to sets of false teeth taken from the dead.

Thankfully, it didn't take me long to find what I needed. I knew I needed to hide Amelia and Lucie if I had any chance of sneaking them outside of the front gates. The potato sacks I located would hopefully do the trick.

"A potato sack?" Amelia questioned, still looking in each open crate that housed horrendous items that should never have been taken from the deceased Jews. It smelled foul down there, and the fumes were making me feel nauseous, as I imagined they were making her feel, as well. Though, after living in the camp's confines for so long, one might argue the horrible aromas were somewhat typical by that point.

"Yes, and I need you to stay here while I find a way to retrieve baby Lucie." Lucie was held in a nursery cell along with other motherless babies. That would be the trickiest part of this plan.

"Hurry back please," she pleaded. Amelia must not have understood how badly I wanted to hurry back and get her out of this place.

I was nervous as I made my way through the camp, but I kept my disposition calm and walked directly into the nursery that was guarded by two night shift nurses. They saluted me upon my arrival. "I must take one of the babies for reasons I cannot disclose," I said, speaking authoritatively. The nurses knew better than to ask questions. However, the looks on their faces were no longer friendly. Underneath our uniforms, we were all people. Some had lost their minds after being brainwashed for so long, but many still had thoughts of their own.

The cell was cold and damp, and the babies were likely to get sick from that environment. It was insufferable and sickening. I hadn't had a reason to step foot into the nursery cell until that night, and I wish I never had to see how those poor babies were living. They had no hope.

"Which baby is Lucie?" I asked one of the nurses.

She walked over to a small wooden cradle and lifted the baby and then handed her over. Lucie was tiny for being nearly a year old. She didn't feel as though she weighed more than fifteen pounds. Her eyes stared up at me with wonder, but she didn't make a peep. "Here is a blanket," the nurse offered.

I wrapped Lucie in the blanket, nodded my head at the women and left in a hurry.

"I will keep you safe, baby girl," I whispered, hushing her soft coos.

It didn't take long before I made it back to the building where Amelia was waiting.

Stress was getting the best of me. Amelia wasn't moving as fast I would have liked, and sweat was beading over every inch of my body. I rushed her into the potato sack with Lucie. I didn't know if her hesitation was out of fear or trust, but I needed her cooperation so we could move quickly.

Once Amelia and Lucie were settled inside the sack, I carefully lifted them both and tossed the open part of the bag over my shoulder.

The walk to the front gate felt like it took an hour when it was just a few minutes.

"Where are you going so late at night?" the guard asked. It wasn't for the fact that I was leaving the grounds; it was because I had a full sack of something hanging off my shoulder.

"I need to get a head start for my doctor's appointment. It is first thing in the morning," I told him, lying through my teeth.

"Oh, you're the soldier who had his arm amputated," the guard continued. He was more focused on the tied off sleeve than the sack resting on my back. I was grateful for that.

"That's correct," I replied.

"And what's in the bag?" I prayed, and I prayed hard that the man was just curious. I hadn't been questioned while leaving before, and his rank was equal to mine. There was no reason to question another guard, aside from curiosity.

"I was asked to bring leftover clothing to the hospital for some of the recovering soldiers who have nothing to leave with."

The small talk continued, and I was thankful the grounds were dark, so he couldn't see the nervous expression on my face.

The gates were wide open, and I walked away casually. If I moved any quicker, I would look suspicious. Amelia and Lucie were not heavy at all, but with one arm and hoofing it a few blocks, I was becoming breathless.

In the darkest corner of an alleyway, I placed the sack down ever so gently. "Don't move," I whispered against the bag.

I was watching a group of passengers step out of a car at the corner of the block, and my plan escalated. The fastest way out of this area was an automobile. I had no choice. I was already a criminal by all German means, so stealing a car was no worse in my mind.

After a long two minutes, I lifted the bag back up and made my way to the black Mercedes, opening the back door first. I placed the potato sack down on the back seat and jumped into the driver's seat as fast as I could move.

For a few years of my life when Papa was between jobs at bakeries, he worked a side job at a gas station. He taught me the tricks he learned, one of them being how to hot-wire a car. It was a very long time ago, but I remembered how to get the job done.

There were no people in sight when I took off down the road. I got at least two miles away without a second look. "Amelia," I called out. "You can pull the bag down."

I peered into the rearview mirror, noticing the redness on Amelia's chapped cheeks. She had Lucie snuggled in her arms. "Charlie, you did it!" she exclaimed.

"It doesn't matter," I told her. We were nowhere close to being out of the woods yet.

"Where do we go now?" she asked.

"We need to get out of this country, Amelia. We're not safe."

* * *

It was only a matter of a few hours before we ran out of gas. I expected it to occur, but I was hoping to make it to the border before it happened. We were just a couple of miles away, but it was too late at night to make the hike in the dark. "We're going to have to start walking," I told Amelia.

Even still, after ditching the car in a field of tall grass, we didn't get far before we were spotted. "Hey! You there!" a man shouted toward us.

We felt cornered in the woods, and though we tried to run, exhaustion was not on our side when it came to speed.

There was silence for a golden minute, but then the voice elevated again. "Hey!"

"Dammit," I whispered. "The man is after us." I took Amelia by the arm and pulled her toward a nearby tree. All I could do was cover Amelia and Lucie with my body, pinning them to the tree with my back. I prayed Lucie wouldn't make a peep, but there were whimpers we couldn't stop.

"Where did you go now?" the man continued to shout. It was hard to tell where his exact location was with his voice bouncing off each tree.

Lucie's cries grew louder, and we were inevitably spotted. I was sure we were both about to end up dead when the man's light centered over our faces.

"You're a soldier," he said, pointing his light in my face. "And you have a prisoner. Is that a stolen car you got there, too?"

"Ja, I am a soldier," I answered.

"What are you running from?" he continued.

"We aren't running," I responded.

The man could only laugh in response. He was toying with us, or so it seemed. "It's obvious you're running from something. Most people don't dump a luxury car that looks as if it belongs to the SS, then run into the woods just two miles from the Austrian border."

"Who are you to care?" I shot back.

"Absolutely no one, but I live about two hundred yards

behind you, and I think I have a right to know who is passing through my property tonight."

"We don't mean you any trouble, sir," Amelia spoke up. I wanted to keep Amelia hidden as much as possible, but there was not much I could do to keep her from speaking.

"Now, if you tell me the truth, I'll offer you a roof to sleep under tonight. My wife and I like to keep a low profile, though, so you'll need to answer my questions first."

The man had nothing but millions of questions, and I had more than a million lies to offer in return. My lies led us to the vacant bedroom within the man's home. The man told us we could stay until morning, and we were to meet the man at his front door. I don't believe he wanted to be seen walking through the woods with us.

We waited for the man to leave us within the darkness of the hovering trees. I turned to Amelia and inconspicuously tore her Jude patch from the fabric of her sleeve. It was a telltale sign of the truth we were desperately hiding. "Take off your coat," I told her. I think she was confused for a moment, but when she understood what I was attempting, she complied much quicker. I was quick to strip her clothing of all the dirt-ridden golden stars, and then Lucie's clothing as well. I had to tell myself we would be okay, but I wasn't sure if we were walking right into a trap.

The room he let us sleep in was empty and cold, but it offered shelter from anyone else who might hunt us in the night.

The night crept by as I focused on the sounds of crickets singing outside in the woods. Amelia wasn't as quick to fall asleep as Lucie was, so I took the opportunity to hold the woman I loved. I silently promised her everything would be all right. I was afraid to speak it out loud, though. If I were to share my thoughts, I knew none of it would be a truth I could commit to without knowing what our future would hold.

Amelia was a smart woman who undoubtedly knew the facts of our situation. Even still, she looked at me as if I was her hero, and it pained me knowing it was my kind who put her in this situation.

Before long, it was almost sunrise, and I could not sleep for a second, knowing the challenges from the previous night would only lead us to an inquisition at the border. Instead, I took every free moment I had to watch Amelia sleep. I took in every part of her—her dark lashes that fluttered while she dreamed, her nose that curved slightly at the tip, and her full lips that remained parted as hushed breaths escaped. Her skin was pale, but the color of ivory. She was the picture of perfection to me, and in my heart, I knew the odds of having the opportunity to wake up beside her every morning. The war was bigger than the two of us, and maybe I helped her escape the gas chamber, but I wasn't sure I would be given the gift of life with her.

I ran my fingers through her soft, dark hair, and traced my knuckles across her cheek. I wanted to memorize every part of Amelia, knowing I would need those memories to last.

I whispered into Amelia's ear, "Are you ready?"

I'm not sure how long she had been awake, but she answered immediately. "Yes."

I wished so hard to hold on to the moment—a moment when we would wake up face to face, forgetting about the world outside of the enclosed room.

Amelia's fingers traced a few of the scars along my cheek and eyebrow, studying me as I was studying her. "My face has been torn to shreds, and my arm is missing. I'm not a full person anymore," I told her, realizing that if the situation was different, she might not want to be with a man who looked like me.

She smiled in response, as if I was making a joke that wasn't based on truth. "You could look like a monster for all I care, and I'd still only see the beautiful man you are inside. I see what my heart sees—an amazing man."

Those words drew my lips to hers, and I held my girl as tightly as I could.

"What is your dream, sweetheart?" I needed to know, because I planned to fulfill all her wishes if we could find safety.

"I want to go to the United States. Maybe New York or Massachusetts... it has always been my dream," she said.

"That sounds like heaven," I told her. "That will be our plan, Amelia. We're going to have it all." For that moment, I honestly thought we would have everything we wanted. "And I will stand by your side as you become known across the world for your magnificent talent."

Amelia looked back and forth between my eyes with a look of hunger. When she moved in closer, her intentions became clear.

Even if I had known how much more pain the next few moments would eventually cause my heart, I would still choose the heartache over never experiencing that time with Amelia. I have this night—the night I made love to the love of my life. I won't ever forget.

"Amelia, you are everything worth fighting for," I muttered against her ear.

* * *

Approaching the Austrian border was bringing my greatest fears to fruition. Amelia clung to my arm, clearly terrified as well. Neither of us knew what would come of the escape. "Charlie, do you really think this is going to work?" she asked.

"We need to be curt with them and appear calm. If we don't look like we have something to worry about, they won't doubt our story." They would most definitely question our story, but I needed Amelia to remain complacent. It was most important.

Just before we descended the hill that would lead us to the

country's border patrol, I stepped in front of Amelia and pressed my forehead to hers, sheltering Lucie between the two of us. I placed a kiss on the top of the baby's head and prayed that her innocence would always be intact. I hoped she would never remember a moment of the last year of her life. "I'll be her papa. I want to be that person for her," I told Amelia, looking her in the eyes, knowing she planned to be Lucie's mother. Could I fix these lives? My heart softened when I glanced down at Lucie and smiled.

"You are incredible, Charlie Crane," Amelia told me.

I didn't feel incredible. My people are the ones who killed Lucie's parents, leaving her orphaned and in a position where she had to escape a country just to live.

As we made our way closer to the guard's towers, I held Lucie tightly against my chest and kept my eyes set on Amelia, watching her expression change by the moment. I could so easily see forever in Amelia's eyes, but I worried that her forever simply could not be with me if we were all to survive.

I could see the thoughts bubbling in her head too.

"Charlie, how will we make it across Austria? Are we walking into another war zone?" Amelia asked.

The war was everywhere. Not one place was safe. I didn't want to scare her or lie, so I continued walking, shooing off Amelia's question.

"There's a train station just over the border. We're going to get on that train. I have some money saved up to get us to Zurich." I glanced over at Amelia as we continued to walk, noticing the apprehension written across her face. "Here," I said. "Take Lucie for a moment."

Amelia took Lucie and tightened the blanket around her small body, and I reached into my pocket, pulling out a handful of marks. "I want you to have enough, just in case," I told her.

"Just in case of what, Charlie?"

"In case you make it, and I don't," I said, trying not to choke on my words. "No more questions, okay?"

As we approached the gravel path that led to the watchtowers, a guard spotted us and walked in our direction. He was hardly in hearing range when he said, "Soldier, is everything okay?"

I had to lie, and I had to make my lie believable. "Yes, yes, we had some car trouble a couple of miles back, and my wife and I are on leave to go visit her family across the border. They plan to pick us up just inside the town." The words flowed effortlessly, almost believably so.

The guard inspected Amelia with a narrowed glance. "Your wife looks ill," he said.

I swallowed hard and looked over at the pale complexion on Amelia's face. "Oh, you know how it is in the springtime. I've had a terrible cold for a week, but it's passing now. I just hope our daughter doesn't catch it. A baby with a cold is not an enjoyable time," Amelia said, sounding believable and experienced. I was impressed with her fib.

"I see," the guard continued. "What is your name, soldier?"

I considered coming up with a false name, but the odds of that turning out better than the truth weren't high. "Charlie Crane," I said, realizing that I was supposed to be on leave for a medical appointment today, and that appointment was not in Austria. Surely, it would take a bit to find that information out, though.

"Where are you stationed?" The questions seemed endless. It was as if he was trying to trap me.

"I'm in transition," I said. "Due to my injury." I pointed to my shoulder, hoping he would see that my arm was missing and that there was nothing more than that going on.

"I suppose that's a good time for leave," the guard said. "Give me a moment to call in your name. What is your wife's name?"

I felt faint. It was over. We were about to lose it all.

"Emille Crane," I spoke on behalf of Amelia. Nothing about Amelia screamed German, especially the emaciated look she wore as a label.

The guard shook his head and went off to the watchtower to call my name in. There was no way anything positive was going to come from the situation. Or, at least that's what I assumed.

"You can go on through," the man said.

I placed my hand on the small of Amelia's back as we walked past the towers. What if we were walking into a worse battle zone? I had only hoped it was more forgiving than Czechoslovakia.

"I love you," I whispered into Amelia's ear.

She looked at me with confusion. After all, we had made it through the border.

That must have been what she was thinking.

"Never forget," I continued.

I knew Amelia could not return the words after she explained that she lost everyone she ever loved, but it did not matter to me. I needed her to know how much I loved her, especially after what happened to everyone else in her life.

The guard allowed us to believe he was going to let us pass through until his words belted out: "Jews don't belong in Austria either."

That was the end. "Don't turn around, Amelia. Keep walking and then run," I whispered into her ear, kissing her one last time on the cheek.

That was it. I didn't want it to be the end. I wanted to have the end with Amelia by my side as we grew old. It was just a dream. It was just a silly dream that could never happen.

Our eyes met one last time. Her brows furrowed and her bottom lip fell with discouragement, but she did as I told her to do and ran as hard as she could with baby Lucie.

I knew what would happen next, and I willingly stood in the path of where Amelia was running.

The gunshot sounded hollow between so many trees, but the blast went silent as I took another bullet.

I would take twenty more shots for her.

"Argh!" I shouted, falling to my knees. The momentum of the hit stole my balance.

The bastard shot me in the left shoulder. Lucky for him, I had few nerve endings left in the area. Still, I clutched the wound and grunted, "Let her go, or I'll kill you." My words were foolish. I didn't have a weapon drawn, and the guard did. We were on the same side, yet in that second, I was his enemy.

"Kill me?" the man asked through laughter.

The man shouted a slew of profanities at me for several moments until he walked toward me and yanked me toward the post he was guarding. "I am reporting you to the authorities."

"I don't care," I told him.

I prayed Amelia made it to the train with Lucie. I prayed harder than I had ever prayed in my life.

Every second that passed, more distance grew between Amelia and me, more distance than I thought I could ever erase. To love someone is to set them free.

The guard made a phone call from the post. I was reported by the guard, now waiting for what would happen next. "Why would you do something so stupid?" the guard asked.

"I don't want to be the enemy." My words were not the most intelligent to speak, but it was the truth, and I no longer cared to lie.

"I was trying to shoot her," he said, staring at the blood oozing from my shoulder.

"She did nothing to you," I explained, sneering at the man who had a mustache that looked much like the Führer's—the evil man who we were all supposed to admire so much.

"That woman is a Jew, you fool."

"That means nothing to me," I replied. "That woman was innocent and has done nothing but hard labor for the last year of her life, with nothing but hope that the work would someday set her free. She was treated worse than an animal, and this is what we think people like her deserve?"

I was not making any sense to that man, but I didn't expect my words to conjure any emotion. Most of the German soldiers had been warped to believe nothing but lies, and it was too hard to see the truth.

It wasn't long before the Gestapo arrived, detaining me as a prisoner. I was now on a different side of the war. I was officially a traitor.

It was the only side I preferred.

The Gestapo and I exchanged very few words. Instead, they took me to the hospital where I had the bullet extracted from my shoulder without so much as a numbing agent. There were no kind nurses or soothing words. I was no longer cared for as a Nazi. Instead, I was bandaged up just well enough to be transferred to a prison cell.

The Gestapo tossed me toward a dark wall, the metal gates clinked, and a key secured my confinement. My sentence was ten years in prison. I was left to rot as punishment for my act of love, for committing a war crime.

CHAPTER 25

MAY, 1945—AUSTRIA

21 YEARS OLD

It was two years later when I heard the words I didn't expect to hear for another eight years: "Crane, you are free to go." A Gestapo I had become familiar with throughout the last year released the cell door.

"Why am I free?" It might not have been the best question, but it was my only question. I was okay with a life term of imprisonment because it was the result of offering Amelia a chance at freedom.

"The Nazi regime is over." Just like that, the madness had ended, but how many lives had been sacrificed for this war? "The Führer is dead." Most of my life has revolved around the Führer's rules and laws.

The information was a lot to take in at this moment because my first realization was that everything that had happened in my life those last few years was for nothing.

Six million deaths of innocent Jewish people.

For nothing.

Hitler was gone, but the memories were not. I had done nothing for the last couple of years other than contemplate what I had been a part of since I was twelve-years-old.

I took slow steps across the cement floor toward the gated exit. Most everyone in the prison was released at the same moment. We were all there for war crimes, but most of us had gone AWOL.

The sun was overwhelming when I stepped outside, but the damp grounds smelled of rain. It was a lovely scent. It was more than lovely, in fact. I had the urge to kiss the ground. "I am heading home," one of the prisoners said to another.

"Ja, same."

Home. My last letter home was to Mama. She had been unhappy with me for good reason, but part of me wonders if she was relieved to know I couldn't get myself into further trouble while in prison.

I stopped at a payphone and dialed home, hopeful Mama would answer, but before the called connected, I hung up the receiver.

I wasn't ready to go home.

My legs ached as I made my way to the nearby train station, purchasing a one-way ticket to Zurich. I didn't have much money, only what I had on me when I arrived at the prison, but I had enough to get by for a bit.

This train ride was much different from all the other trains I had ridden. Freedom was in the near distance, but for the first time in my life, I could live as I wished. Although, I didn't quite know what that meant.

The train ride was several hours, which I embraced while peacefully staring out the window, watching the hills become snow-covered mountains. I wasn't sure what the odds were of finding Amelia in Zurich, but I would do whatever I could to locate her.

The engines from the train began to simmer, warning that we were coming to a stop. We were pulling into a railway station with a covered awning. Loved ones were waiting patiently for passengers to disembark, and I closed my eyes, imagining Amelia standing among them, waving furiously with a smile from ear to ear.

I would step down onto the platform, and she would throw her arms around my neck. Her lips would crash into mine, I would lift her into my arm, and swing her around as she drew her legs around my waist. She would tell me she loves me. She would tell me she waited here two years for me. We would run away together and live happily in a dream.

A dream.

When I stepped off the train, I heard the reunion of families and couples. "You have gotten so big!" "You look more beautiful than ever." "How could you become even more handsome while you were away." "I love you, sweetheart."

I made my way through the happy crowd, wanting to clutch my heart to make the pain go away. I wondered if she waited. I wondered if she was there, somewhere.

When I departed the area of the railway station, I felt overwhelmed by the aromas of bakeries and flower gardens. Healthy green trees were scattered, and the world felt untouched there. Locals were walking around as if life had been typical, and they knew nothing different. I was jealous of the ease most wore on their faces.

Some locals gave me a once over. I assumed it was because I was unshaven, my hair needed a cut, and I was wearing my brown trousers and pale tan collared shirt from the uniform I had been forced to wear like a second layer of skin.

I felt uneasy as if I was riding a bicycle for the first time in fifteen years. This way of life shouldn't be something forgotten, but after such a long while, it was no longer second nature.

"Flowers for a special lady, sir?" A man stepped out from beneath a small awning in front of a flower shop and reached his arm out to me, his hand filled with bunches of multi-colored flowers. The smell of lilacs and roses assaulted my senses, and I leaned in to take a closer whiff. I could inhale the delectable scent all day. I reached into my pocket and retrieved some money.

"Ja, I will take them. Danke." The man handed me the flowers with a toothy grin. "I hope your lady enjoys them."

Amelia would love these.

I held the flowers up to my nose until I reached a bed and breakfast just a couple of miles outside of town. It was the first place to stay that I came across.

I knocked gently against the hickory door, and soon after heard footsteps clamoring from within. An older woman opened the door. Her white hair was short and in curls, her skin covered with fine lines, and she wore a house dress layered beneath a stark white apron. "Hallo, may I help you?" she asked, a questionable smile outlining her lips.

"Ja, Fräulein. Do you have an open room?"

"Frau Joel," she corrected me. "Herr Joel and I run this inn together, and we do have a free room. How long will you be staying?"

"I'm not quite sure, Frau."

"Very well. Come on inside, young man." Frau Joel held open the storm door, welcoming me into the inn. The house smelled like Mama's kitchen—fresh breads and pastries, as well as vanilla and hydrangea—I had not enjoyed these scents in so very long.

"The inn is beautiful, Frau."

"What is your name, sohn?"

"Charlie Crane," I answered.

The woman narrowed her eyes at me, almost as if she was studying me. "It's a pleasure, Charlie."

"Same," I responded.

"Wait right here," she said, disappearing into what looked to be a dining area. Frau Joel soon returned with a camera and a tripod. She stood the mechanism in front of me. "One... two...

three." She took my photo, but the quickness and unusualness of it all made me snicker.

"What is that for, Frau?"

She took me by my good arm and brought me to the stairwell. Gold-plated framed photos lined the wall. "If you stay in this inn, you become family, Charlie Crane." I placed my hand on my chest, taking in the photos that looked to span at least a decade. I only had a chance to see half of them before she pulled me off toward the kitchen at the end of the oak-covered hallway. "You look starved."

"I am quite hungry, ja." I couldn't tell if Frau Joel was nervous, or always quick on her feet. She seemed a bit frazzled, but I didn't know anything about her.

Frau Joel sliced some bread and poured me a glass of milk. She whipped a placemat off the oven's railing and laid it down on a small table in the corner of the kitchen. "Sit and eat." It had been less than five minutes since I knocked on the front door. I was feeling a bit unsettled, but there was fresh bread waiting for me, and I was not one to turn down food.

I placed the bunches of flowers down on the table as I took a seat on the handmade apple-red seat cushion. After pulling my chair in, a thumping sound yanked my attention away from the food. I glanced toward the window above the sink, seeking the source of the odd thumping sound. "What is that sound?"

"Ah, Herr Joel is chopping wood in the back. There's nothing to be concerned about."

I redirected my attention back to the food, slowly feeding myself crumbs at first. "You look like you've been through a lot, Charlie."

"Ja. I have not had it easy, Frau." I should not have said that. I had it quite easy compared to most.

"You were a soldier," she said as a statement, rather than a question.

"Ja, but that's not my story."

Frau Joel's head tilted to the side. She looked intrigued to hear more and pulled another chair from the table. Frau Joel sat down and crossed her hands over the woven place setting. "I am a good listener," she said.

I took another nibble of the bread before speaking. "Well, I fell in love with a woman and helped rescue her from Theresienstadt."

Frau Joel cupped her hand over her mouth and shook her head from side to side. "Oh, Charlie," she sighed.

"Ja. However, I was caught just as the woman made it past the guard tower. They threw me in prison. I was supposed to be locked up for ten years, but now that Hitler is—anyway, I only had to remain in prison for two years." I knew I should have been more careful of who I shared my story with, but talking about the situation kept the reality of my life alive and current.

"I see," Frau Joel said. Her lips pressed together, and she patted her hand against her chest. "I—well then, I'm going to go prepare your room while you enjoy your food."

"Danke," I offered.

I should have waited a little longer before unearthing my story.

Frau Joel untied her apron and hung it on the broom closet door knob before leaving the kitchen. Before she got very far, though, she returned. "Charlie, you aren't being chased by anyone, are you?"

"Nein, Frau. I'm looking for my love. That is all."

A firm smile grew across her cheeks. "That I support, sohn. Maybe I can help."

CHAPTER 26

1945—AUSTRIA

I was counting out my francs, finding that I was quickly running out of money after just a few days of being in Zurich. It was time to find a job.

I offered Frau Joel the remainder of what I had left. "Here you are, my payment to you," I offered with an outstretched hand.

Frau Joel closed her eyes and inhaled sharply through her nose. She pressed my fingers down over the money. "Charlie, hold on to your money. I want to see you back on your feet, and I don't want to make things harder for you."

"I couldn't possibly impose," I told her, stepping closer with my hand outstretched.

Frau Joel tugged on my arm and walked me over to the sitting area near the foyer. "Have a seat, Charlie." The way she spoke to me made me think of Mama. I had not let her know that I was free from prison, and I knew it was important to do so soon.

We sat in two worn Victorian chairs with tan and pink stripes. The colors appeared worn, likely from sitting in front of the window's light. "I lost my son, Charlie. The First

World War stole him from me, and I have never been the same."

I found myself dragging my fingertips down the side of my face while noticing the monumental pain pulling at the outside corners of her eyes. "I am so sorry, Frau."

"Herr Joel and I knew we couldn't remain in Germany after Francis was taken from us. It was too painful. So, we moved here to Zurich and vowed to help displaced men and women due to the war. Francis might not be with us now, but he has brought us so much love. As I mentioned when you arrived, those who stay here with us become our family, no matter the length of their stay. We sometimes think this house finds lost people like yourself."

My heart ached for Frau Joel. To take such a loss and turn into a gain was much harder than she made it sound. She had overcome battles, some I could not imagine, and I admired her greatly. If she refused, there would have to be another form of repayment. "I will earn my keep here until it's time for me to leave."

Frau Joel allowed a smile to tug at her forlorn lips. "I will never turn down help, Charlie."

"Very well," I told her. "I will start by helping Herr Joel chop some wood, ja?"

"That would be wonderful, but I must ask how that will be possible with one arm?"

For the first time in almost three years, I had forgotten about my misfortune. I glanced down at my one lonesome hand resting on my knee. "Maybe there is something else I could be helpful with in the house?"

"I have some linens that needed to be washed and folded, and the stairwell could use a good sweeping," Frau responded with a grimace. Maybe she thought I was feeling emasculated, but I wanted to do whatever she would find helpful.

"I will do a great job at that," I assured her.

"Wonderful," she said, slapping her palms down gently on the armrests of her chair. "Charlie, I do have a question for you before you go."

"Ja, Frau?"

"Are your parents well?"

I drummed my fingers on my lap, staring at a scar on the knuckle of my thumb, losing myself in thought as I recalled how I earned that stripe. I was helping Papa slice bread one day, and the knife slipped from my hand. Blood was everywhere, but I didn't care because Mama hushed away my concerns, while Papa quickly cleaned the wound and wrapped my hand up. They never let me know of fear and pain.

"My papa was infected with influenza a few years ago and passed. My mama is still living in Bavaria," I informed Frau.

"Does she know your whereabouts?"

"Nein. Not yet, Frau."

"We have a telephone, Charlie. Please ring her and let her know you are okay, ja?"

"Of course," I replied, relieved she offered to let me use her phone. I didn't want to be intrusive by asking to make a long-distance phone call.

Frau Joel stood from her chair and retrieved her shiny black rotary phone from the corner of the room and pulled the cord taut so it would reach the tea-table beside my chair. "I will give you some privacy."

Another guest was descending the stairs just as Frau Joel left the sitting room. "Ah, Herr Pierce. I have your breakfast. Are you hungry?"

"Ja. Very much, Frau. Danke," the man asserted.

Frau Joel pulled the sliding door closed, leaving me in the room alone with the phone. I knew the conversation was not going to go well, explaining to Mama that I would not be coming home.

With trembling fingers, I pulled against the digits, allowing an extra lingering second to occur before each spin. Mama didn't tend to sit in the house all day. She would often be delivering clothes and linens to neighbors. Therefore, I was surprised when the phone connected right away.

"Hallo," she answered with a sound of hope as if she was wishing it was me calling.

"Mama," I spoke into the receiver.

"Charlie, sohn." Mama's voice croaked with a raucous sound. "Charlie, are you well?"

"I am well, Mama. I am now free from prison."

A sigh with a hint of a cry stung my ear. "Thank you, God," she uttered. "Where are you, Charlie? When will you be coming home?"

I closed my eyes, wishing away the next moment. "Mama, I'm not ready to come home."

There was a pause, a much longer pause than I hoped. "Well why not, Charlie?"

It was clear at that moment that I was a selfish man after what I had put Mama through, but the thought of returning to Germany made my stomach ache. "I don't want to go back to Germany, Mama. I was going to ask you if you might want to come to me and stay in Switzerland for a while?" The thought hadn't crossed my mind before that moment, but Mama and I could find a place to live here until we could move to America.

"Switzerland?" Mama questioned.

"Ja, Mama. I took a train to Zurich after being released from prison." I'm sure she was wondering why I didn't take a train directly home, but she must understand how much I despise Germany at the moment.

"Charlie, my roots are here. I cannot simply get up and move to another country on a whim."

I understood, but I didn't want her to think I was running away from her. "Maybe just for a holiday?"

"Charlie, listen to me, sohn—this is hard for me to say, but if you don't feel like your home is in Germany, then I want you to find a place that you can call home. I will support your dreams because I feel responsible for stealing every dream you have had up until this point."

"Mama," I lamented. "The war was not your fault."

"No, but I believed in things I shouldn't have, Charlie, and it deeply affected your life."

"I don't hold you responsible, Mama."

"I love you for that, Charlie, but now I want you to go on and live your life. But please, don't forget about me, ja?" I didn't know how she could think I might forget about her.

"Mama, I want to move to the United States someday when I have enough money saved. Will you come with me?"

Mama exhaled heavily into the phone. "America? Oh, Charlie, I don't know. Maybe someday, but remember that everything in life takes time."

"I plan to do whatever it takes, Mama. I want the life of freedom. America is the dream, ja?"

"Charlie, you are a smart boy, and I know good things come to those who work for them. Therefore, if that is your dream, then I believe it will happen."

"I will work hard, Mama. I will make you proud."

"You have already made me so very proud, Charlie. I can hear your papa now. He would be saying: *That is my sohn*," Mama sighs into the phone. "Charlie, nothing got in your Papa's way and I would expect nothing less from you."

"You aren't angry at me for not coming home, Mama?"

"I miss you, Charlie, I do, but I will not hold you back. A mother's job is to raise her sohn and watch him fly on his own." There was silence following her statement. I wish I could have pretended she was truthful with her words, but I could hear the pain. We were both in pain for different reasons.

"Thank you for understanding," I offered.

"Please try to phone me as often as you can because I will always miss my boy."

"I miss you too, Mama."

"Anja," I hear Mama's name shouted from the background. The voice sounded like it belonged to Frau Taylor. "We're going to be late for tea."

"Charlie, Frau Taylor is calling for me so I must be going. Oh, and Claude has some exciting news to share with you. Write to him when you can, sohn. Take care of yourself, please. I love you, and I am thinking of you always."

"Ich liebe dich, Mama." *I love you too.*

Mama took the news better than I expected she might. I also suspected after she gave the information some time to settle in, she might think differently of me not coming home. Part of me wondered if Mama had convinced herself that I was never coming back. If that were true, knowing I was alive and out of prison might have been the relief she needed.

Upon ending the call with Mama, I made my way into the hallway near the kitchen where I retrieved a broom from the small closet. Sweeping the stairs was the first task on my list.

I started at the top step and worked my way down, trying my best to keep the broom steady with my one hand. I hadn't done much in the last couple of years to notice how many tasks would give me trouble without two hands. Sitting in a cell hardly required one good hand, never mind two.

The framed photos on the wall caught my attention as I swept. It seemed the years of guests were blended as some photos appeared more recent than others. Most were pictures of lone people, and it made me wonder if they were missing someone too. Were they on the run or searching?

One photo stood out because it was the only photo that had two people posing. The woman was smiling, when most of the other images showed people with straight-lined mouths. The portrait was of a mother and a child.

When I took a closer look, tilted my head to the side and narrowed my eyes, I dropped the broomstick against the wall.

The thud seemed muted next to the sound of my drumming heart. *It couldn't be.* I removed the framed portrait from the wall and inspected it for a moment longer. I shook my head in disbelief as I hiked down the stairs, holding the broom under my arm. "Frau Joel?" I called out.

"In here," she hollered from the kitchen. I knew where she was, but I was hardly thinking straight while staring at the woman in the picture. *Could it be possible?*

I nearly tripped on the black and red oriental runner as I entered the kitchen, finding Frau Joel stirring a wooden spoon around an open pot on the stove.

"Who is this?" I asked her, holding the picture out. "Did she stay here too?" I already assumed the answer since she mentioned taking photographs of all her guests.

"Guten tag, Herr Crane," Herr Pierce spoke from the small table, shoveling oatmeal into his mouth.

"Guten tag," I responded with haste, refocusing my attention on Frau Joel.

She took the portrait from my hand and peered down at the image, smiling faintly. "Do you know this woman? It's been a few months since she left here—Amelia—the girl with her arms full."

"Amelia?" My voice broke, my chest heaved, and my knees gave out as I fell to the wooden floor.

"Charlie! Are you all right?" Frau Joel exclaimed, lunging for me with her hand outstretched.

"She was here?" I questioned. "Amelia Baylin?"

"Ja, ja, she was here for almost a year, in fact. Amelia—oh, that girl—the poor thing. She was starving and weak, and yet it was as if her heart hurt more than her belly. She was more concerned about waiting here for the love of her life to find her than she was for her health. Come to think of it, she was much like you, ja?"

"Ja," I muttered.

"Wait a moment," Frau Joel said, standing up and brushing her apron off to straighten the fabric. "You mentioned the name Amelia. Is—this couldn't possibly be your Amelia? Are you the one who saved her life?"

My head was spinning. I had so many questions, and yet, all I wanted to do was run out the front door like a mad man to chase after my girl. She made it here. She was alive. The thoughts were endless.

"Ja. That's my Amelia," I said, pointing to the portrait she held.

"Oh Charlie," she sighed. "We helped Amelia find a sponsor in America. She emigrated not long before you arrived here. She was sure you were—"

"Dead. I know. We were separated after I was shot down by another guard. I was trying to save her."

"You did save her, Charlie. You gave her a life."

"I have to go to America," I said as if it were my only option —as if I could jump on a boat and go that very same day.

"Ja, but it is costly, and we will have to find you a sponsor too. It takes time, Charlie."

"Do you know where she went when she got to America?"

"I only know she was looking for a place to stay in New York City," Frau Joel answered.

Amelia's dream. It was coming true, but I wanted to live that dream with her. "I need to find a way—"

"Don't we all," Herr Pierce added in. "You are a smart man, Charlie." Herr Pierce was a new visitor, a quiet man who didn't often speak. Therefore, I didn't know much of his story, but he seemed as though he didn't have much direction, or maybe he was trying to figure out what was next for him. He was a soldier too, but had been stationed in Zurich. He had more or less served his time but didn't have to see a whole lot, or so he had led us to believe. I envied whatever innocence he still had intact. However, no one truly knows anyone else's story. I suppose he could have been hiding his life better than I hid my own.

Frau Joel helped me back up to my feet, swept some dust off my shoulder and then grabbed my chin between her fingers. "Look at me, Charlie." I peered down at her five-foot-three stance, wondering what she was about to say. "Go on into town, find yourself a job, and start saving every nickel you can. We will get you to America. Ja?"

I pressed my lips together and silently thanked God and Frau Joel before the words found a way off my tongue. "Danke, Frau. Danke."

"This is why I keep this house running, Charlie; for moments like these." Frau Joel handed me the portrait. "Keep this. Keep it as motivation for what is next in your life, sohn."

"Danke," I offered before ambling up the stairwell to my room where I placed the picture down on the nightstand. She may not have been with me in person, but she could still be the first thing I saw in the morning and the last thing I saw before I went to bed. Amelia was my encouragement to work harder and faster.

I swept, I washed the linens and hung them to dry, and I grabbed my coat and ran for the village. It was suddenly like I had a precise direction, and I walked directly into the bäckerei, feeling as though the pieces were falling into place.

The signs were everywhere. I just hadn't been paying enough attention. "Hallo," I greeted the baker who looked to be helping patrons and preparing goods from behind the counter. "My papa worked in a bread shop most of his life. He taught me everything he knew, and I would love nothing more than to help you in your bäckerei. I won't ask for much," I assured the man.

'You want a job, sohn?" he asked in response.

"Very much so."

"You only have one arm," he said, inspecting me from head to toe.

"I can make do quite well without my arm."

"Can you sweep?"

"Ja. In fact, I can make the floors shine."

The man's lips curled into a smile, just on one side of his face. I guessed he might have been impressed with my answer. Papa always said the cleanliness of a floor could make a big difference to a patron walking into a bake shop. I didn't quite understand what he meant by that as a child, but I understood as a man. "I can pay you five francs a week."

"I will take the offer," I told him. With that kind of pay, I hoped that I could save enough for my trek to America within a year. "I won't let you down, Herr. I am a hard worker."

The next year would not be easy. I would need to work hard at both the bäckerei and at the house with Frau Joel to earn my keep. I didn't feel like I deserved the gifts of a job and housing after the life I had lived, but I was counting my blessings and doing my best to keep my sights on the future. If I could make it to New York City, surely, I could track Amelia down, and life would be perfect.

CHAPTER 27

PRESENT DAY

I don't know how many hours the surgery took, because I couldn't bear the thought of staring at a clock. The wall in front of me, white and empty, was a blank canvas for my mind to paint beautiful portraits of a life I have dreamt of many times. My heart hurts to think of the years we lost; raising children together, curling up on a sofa while watching late-night television, and our knuckles sweeping against each other's, while reaching for more popcorn. The imagery is simple, but so far out of reach and so far in the past that the thoughts are becoming unfathomable.

My mindset might not be status quo after spending so many years waiting for something I did not deserve. Yet here I am, digesting the truths Amelia has shared with me these past two days, including my connection to the two women sitting to my right.

"We have a daughter, Charlie," Amelia said. I keep replaying those words. "We also have Annie," whose name was changed from Lucie. I promised to be her papa, and I was not able to keep that promise.

The understanding of what I have... have had all along...

should have made my heart stop beating. All this time, my dream was unraveling into a reality, just without me playing a part. My daughters, one biological, and one inherited by being a savior. Clara and Annie—they both sat beside me, unknowing of our relationship. Amelia did not tell them about me, fearing how much turmoil it would cause the girls. I knew she was right, but as I tried not to stare directly at them, I yearned to tell them the truth—that I was their papa and would have done anything to be that man in their lives.

I had to understand the repercussions of being selfish. They were far too advanced in life to find out something as such. Maybe Amelia would change her mind someday.

"Mom never mentioned having a friend named Charlie," Clara finally speaks after hours of silence. Clara, Annie, Emma, and I have been sitting in this waiting room for hours, waiting to hear news about Amelia's fate. Many times throughout the hours, I felt that I should excuse myself. Who was I to be seated in that room after these three women have spent their lives with Amelia?

However, I could not leave, not after being reunited with my girl.

"We haven't seen each other in many, many years," I say to Clara.

"So I've heard," she says. I'm sure she doesn't appreciate the fact that a stranger—as far as she's aware—is seated beside her in this room. Emma, however, hasn't taken her eyes off me. Emma is the only one who knows the truth, because Emma is the only one who has read Amelia's journal. Amelia asked Emma to keep her secret safe to prevent pain on her mother and aunt.

The waiting room door opens slowly, and my heart nearly stops beating. My face becomes cold, and my hand is clammy. We all stand at the doctor's presence, and I notice the tired look in his eyes. "That woman," he begins. "She is a fighter. It was a close call a couple of times, but she pulled through like a champ. Amelia—she is going to be just fine."

Amelia is going to be just fine.

Today is the first day of my life.

Clara and Annie are both in a mess of tears, moving toward the doctor to hug him. And Emma, she's standing back waiting her turn, but she's staring at the doctor with a different kind of look than her mother and aunt. Emma has taken a liking to the doctor, I have noticed. I can understand why, after saving her grandmother's life.

I want to hug the man too. He saved my Amelia—something I couldn't do this time.

It is best for me to keep quiet as Clara and Annie ask many questions about Amelia's future. Maybe I should be concerned with the same, but in our nineties, every new day we wake up is a gift, and rather than worry about the future, I plan to live each day fully, thanking God for the time I am lucky to have with Amelia.

I take my seat, knowing it is the right thing to do. The girls all need to see Amelia, spending their time being grateful to have her still. I can wait for my turn.

"What's in the bag, Charlie?" Emma asks as Annie and Clara rush out of the room to go on and see Amelia in recovery. I have a leather briefcase that contains the letters for Amelia. I need to keep them hidden, as they are for Amelia's eyes only.

"Just some things I wanted to give to your grandmother," I tell her.

"Like what?" Emma smirks, and this time as I stare at my granddaughter, I notice my smirk etched on her face.

She is mine. *She is mine.*

My eyes soften and fill with tears. I can't stop the emotions from taking control of me these past few days. "You are very strong-willed, aren't you?"

Emma smiles gently. "Am I?"

"I'm proud of you, Emma."

Emma bites down on her bottom lip. "Charlie, I'm really upset that I didn't know about you all this time. You're my grandfather, and I deserved to know you."

I stand up from my seat and move down two chairs to be next to Emma. "Titles do not matter. What matters is today, how we feel in this moment, and what we take forward with us." I wrap my arm around Emma's shoulders, and she leans her head into my arm. I close my eyes, feeling a tear fall.

"Well, I won't take any day for granted now," she says quietly. "I want to know everything there is to know about you —my grandfather."

This is what I have always wanted.

"Thank you, Emma," I utter.

"What's in the bag?" Emma asks again.

I glance down at the worn leather handle I'm gripping. The stitching has come loose after years of wear and tear. "Letters."

"Letters?" Emma asks.

"I had nowhere to send the letters, but that doesn't mean I didn't want to write them."

"You wrote Grams letters, all these years?"

"All of the years," I answer simply.

"Isn't it sad that you both went so long, obviously loving each other, but not being able to be together?"

I chew on the inside of my cheek, trying to find pleasing words to offer as a response. Being positive is something I strive for, but her question—I can't spin it in the right way. "Yes, darling. It is quite sad, indeed."

The door to the waiting room opens again. This time it's a nurse. "Emma, your grandmother is asking for you. We'll allow one more in right now."

Emma glances over at me. "I'm sorry. I know you've been waiting a lifetime to see her."

"Another couple of hours won't feel like much in comparison," I tell Emma.

* * *

Less than an hour has passed when I see Annie and Clara walk past the waiting room. When the door opens, Emma pokes her head inside. "She's asking for you," she says with a twinkle in her eye.

It's my turn.

I collect my briefcase—my letter carrying bag—in my right hand and walk as properly and yet, as quickly as humanly possible down to Amelia's recovery room.

A deep breath calms me before stepping inside the room. The scent of hand sanitizer is stronger inside than it was in the hall, and the beeps are much more alarming. Amelia is alert, her cheeks are rosy, and her hair has been pulled up in a neat twist. I'm assuming Emma has helped her.

"Charlie," she croaks, lifting her hand as if she's reaching for me.

"Amelia, sweetheart." My legs move on their own, and I nearly fall to the seat beside her bed. "You are a fighter."

"I wasn't ready," she says. "I need at least ten more years so I can live my life with you." I don't know if the odds are in our favor to make it to a hundred and two, but if it is possible, I will do what it takes to make it that far if Amelia is by my side.

"Good. Because we have a life to tend to."

"We certainly do, Charlie Crane."

"Are you in much pain?"

Amelia moves her head from side to side with subtle movements. "Not much. How could I feel pain when my heart—this trusty heart of mine—is filled with so much joy and contentment?"

The weakened muscles alongside my lips stretch as I smile at my girl. "You haven't changed a bit."

"Do you have those letters?" She doesn't want to hear my flattery. "I need to read my letters."

"I do have every single one of them," I tell her.

"Is that what is in your briefcase?" she asks.

I unclip the buckle holding the case shut and reach inside for the first stack. The paper from the envelope is yellowed and soft like pressed cotton. "It all begins here."

"Read me the first letter, Charlie. Please." Amelia pulls her hands together in plea.

"Of course, sweetheart."

With a shaky hand, I slip the first letter out of the rubber band's tight hold. I open the flap and slide the notepaper out, unfolding the pages with care. "Amelia, some of these letters are a little dark. I want to let you know that my mind is no longer in that place, and I am well—I have been well for some time, but writing to you, it always made me feel a little better in my worst moments."

"I have been there too, Charlie. I understand," she says.

"Okay then," I begin to read.

My dear Amelia,

I should have known today would be glorious. The sun is high in the sky and warm today—the kind of warmth you feel after a cool breeze forces the hairs on your arm to stand.

I thought the day couldn't get any better, but it has, Amelia. My day has become tremendously better because I found hope. It has been years since I last saw your beautiful smile, but when I close my eyes, I can still feel your presence. You changed my life, Amelia.

These past years, I was locked away in a prison cell where I deserved to rot and die. However, because Hitler has died, I have been released and given a second chance at life, which means I have the opportunity to find you. I wasn't sure if you were still in Switzerland. I wasn't sure if you had even made it this far. I prayed—it's all I could do, Amelia.

I found myself stopped in front of a quaint bed and breakfast a couple of miles outside of a village in Zurich. Frau Joel has taken me in, and I couldn't be more grateful. I am working hard to earn my keep here and just secured a job at a bakery down the street. I am going to save every dime I can so I can make it to the United States. I know now that's where you are because I found your photo hanging on the wall in Frau Joel's house.

My heart stopped when I saw your face, Amelia. I hope you have not forgotten me, and in the case that you are missing me as much as I am missing you, please know that I am doing everything in my power to find my way to you—wherever you might be in the United States.

I hope Lucie is doing well and you two are keeping each other happy. I am sorry you had to travel alone. I am so sorry, Amelia.

I love you more than I had time to express. Be well, darling.

Forever yours,

Charlie

As I fold the letter up and replace it within the envelope, Amelia's hand rests on my wrist. "I wanted to wait longer, but I had an opportunity to emigrate, and I thought I would be foolish to pass it up, especially after finding out I was pregnant with Clara."

"It was my punishment to bear," I tell Amelia.

"What am I supposed to say, Charlie? Hadn't I already been punished enough?" She's right. My statement is selfish.

"More than enough," I tell her.

"It isn't fair, Charlie."

"You're right."

Amelia stares up to the ceiling, the fiberglass panels of white reflect our shadows below. "Frau Joel was wonderful to me," Amelia says. "She asked for nothing. I told her all about you, how you had saved me—us, and she didn't judge our situation. She was one of the first impartial people I had met in a long time, especially since she was still hiding a Jewish woman, too. She could have been killed if anyone knew I was living with her."

I didn't quite consider how dangerous it was for Frau Joel to have taken Amelia into her home. In my mind, Switzerland was a safe place, but nowhere was safe when I helped Amelia escape Germany.

"How was your pregnancy? Were you all right? I—I had no idea—"

"Well, Charlie, sometimes when a man and woman—things can happen, can't it?"

"I suppose it did," I tell her.

"It was that night—the night before, at that couple's house." Amelia smiled weakly and stared at me for a long moment. "It was a beautiful moment, Charlie; one I would never take back."

"I remember it as if it was yesterday," I tell her, feeling my cheeks become warm.

"You gave me a gift—a part of you to hold on to all these years. Clara—she is just like you, Charlie. And Emma, my goodness, Emma—she is almost all of you, but a little of me too."

Amelia struggles to peek over the side of the bed at my briefcase. "What else do you have in there, Charlie?"

I smile at Amelia, watching her hand try and snag my briefcase. "Darling, you just had surgery on your heart. Let's be careful."

"Well then, tell me what else is in your bag."

"More letters mostly."

"Mostly?" she questions. Amelia does not skip a beat.

"All in due time, my dear."

"All time is overdue, Charlie Crane."

CHAPTER 28

1945—ZURICH, SWITZERLAND

Life had fallen into place with a sense of normalcy. It was the most normal I had felt since childhood, and while there were things I would still change, I knew I was on a path that would lead me to the future I desired.

I had been working many hours a day at the bakeshop. Herr John, the owner, had offered me more responsibilities along with sweeping, and I was now preparing loaves of bread before sunrise.

The quiet hours were a time of contemplation as well as daydreaming. I imagined Amelia in the bäckerei: her auburn hair in tight curls, red painted lips, and matching nails. She would be leaning her elbows on top of the front counter, staring at me as I rolled the fresh dough. She would call me charming, and I would tell her she looked radiant in her new dress that I saved three weeks' worth of pay to buy. Amelia would kiss me on the cheek, hand me a bagged lunch, tell me to have a wonderful day, and then she'd be off to the art gallery down the street where she would spend her time drawing and painting commissioned pieces of work.

The quiet hours were also a time of darkness. As the

daydreams would end, the silence would creep in, and I would think of all the things I should have done differently throughout my life.

When I had made at least fifty loaves of bread, I could leave for the day. The early shift would usually end just after lunchtime, and I would head back to the bed and breakfast to offer Frau Joel a hand.

The summer's heat was extraordinary that year. Children were not even playing in the streets as they usually would be. It was simply too hot. My shirt was practically drenched by the time I arrived at the house, yet, Herr Joel was still outside pruning the gardenia bush. He must have been used to that type of heat because he was hardly breaking a sweat.

"How can you stand the heat?" I asked him, approaching the front step.

"Lots of water and lots of breaks," he answered. Herr Joel was a man of few words, but he was a pleasant person with a heart of gold just like Frau Joel.

"I brought home a few loaves of bread," I told him, lifting the paper bag a little higher.

"You're a good man, Charlie Crane," he said.

I started up the stairs, but Herr Joel stopped me in my tracks. "Oh, Charlie, could you check the post box? I think there is a delivery."

"Ja, of course," I told him. Maybe Claude had written. We had been writing back and forth for some time, but his letters had stopped as of late. Mama assured me he was fine. She had seen him around town a few times, but he always seemed busy. Sometimes he seemed so busy he didn't notice when Mama passed him on the street. It wasn't like Claude to have his head in the clouds, so I had written a few more times in the previous few weeks to make sure he was all right. I was worried, as I knew the nightmares kept him awake a lot too.

I opened the mailbox, finding it empty. "Nein. There isn't any post, Herr Joel," I called over.

As I closed the mailbox and turned back for the house, a sight knocked me off my feet.

"Brother!" he shouted, a smile stretching from ear to ear.

"Claude!" I jumped on him, nearly knocking him flat to the ground. "What are you doing here?"

"You said you wanted me to come and visit. So, here I am."

My hand was around his shoulder, gripping it so tightly. I couldn't believe he was there, in front of me. I hadn't seen him in so long. "It is so good to see you."

"Same, brother. It's quite nice here."

Herr Joel clomped over to us in his work boots. "Sorry to startle you, sohn. When your friend arrived, he said he wanted to surprise you. He told us how the two of you had grown up together. It's nice to see you have a friend, Charlie," he said. I had wondered if they talked about my habit of loneliness, and I figured after that comment, they must have. "Claude, I hope you and your lady—"

"Uh, Charlie, I have someone I want you to meet," Claude interrupted Herr Joel. I was caught looking between Herr Joel and Claude, trying to understand what was happening. I didn't see anyone else around.

Claude craned his head to the side, looking toward the back of the house. "Juliette, darling."

Juliette. Darling?

A petite young woman with long blonde curls, rosy cheeks, dark eyelashes, and big doe-like eyes came bouncing around the corner, running right into Claude's side where he wrapped his arm around her shoulders. "Charlie, this is Juliette. Juliette, this is my brother, Charlie."

Juliette held out her hand as a smile grew across her perky cheeks. "Charlie, it is so nice to finally meet you. Claude talks about you all the time."

She seemed sweet and very fond of Claude as she batted her lashes at him, waiting to hear what he had to say next. I took Juliette's hand and placed a small kiss on her knuckles. "The pleasure is all mine, Fräulein."

"As I was saying," Herr Joel chimed in again. "I hope you and Fräulein Juliette will stay with us. We do have empty rooms if you're interested."

Claude and his red cheeks turned to face Herr Joel and shook his hand wildly. "Yes, Herr Joel. We would be most grateful."

"Wonderful. I will tell my wife to make a couple of beds up for you."

I was running my fingers through my hair, taking in the sights of Claude being so smitten over a woman. He had never shown much interest in settling down. I knew Juliette must be a special woman.

"Fräulein Juliette, come inside, dear. It's too hot to be standing outside for so long," Frau Joel shouted at us, making it known she had already met Juliette before I came home.

Juliette glanced over at Claude for approval before leaving his side.

"Go on, I'll be right inside," he told her before leaning in and placing a kiss on her cheek.

"I am so happy for you," I told him.

Claude cleared his throat, pulled a handkerchief from his pocket, and dabbed his forehead. "Brother, I was worried to mention Juliette, never mind bringing her here to meet you, unannounced at that."

"That's foolish. Why would you be worried about mentioning a beautiful woman like Juliette?"

Claude placed his hand on my shoulder. "Charlie, your mother has spoken to me. She's worried about you, as am I. You're out here alone, chasing after a woman who is in America."

No one understood.

"Well, to be fair, the last time I was being scrutinized it was for following a Jewish woman. Now, it's because she is in America?"

"Mama says you talk about her a lot when you write and call."

"I love Amelia, Claude. That will never change. Plus, I plan to move to the United States within the year. I have been saving money since I arrived here in Zurich."

Claude forced a grin. "That's good to hear, Charlie. I want to see you happy; that's all."

"Me too," I told him.

"Well then, America sounds like a fantastic idea. In fact, Juliette and I have been speaking about it a lot lately, too. She wants to be a singer, so it might be in our future. Who knows, ja?"

"A singer? That's wonderful." Everything sounded so great for Claude. I was happy for him, but internally sad for myself.

Claude slapped his palm against my back. "Come, Charlie. Let's go inside."

I followed Claude up to the front door and inside where we heard Frau Joel and Juliette having a friendly conversation. We stepped into the kitchen, finding Frau pouring a pitcher of water into three glasses. "You all must be parched," she said.

Juliette was the first to take a helping of water. When her dainty fingers wrapped around the yellowed crystal goblet, I noticed a sparkle on her left ring finger. I almost choked. The love between them was noticeable, but I didn't realize they were that serious. I had to digest the information before responding, or my reaction might have come off as crass. Claude deserved every moment of happiness. Didn't he?

We had both been in the trenches; both almost lost our lives. However, we both watched thousands of Jewish people perish, or worse, had sent them to their death. Did either of us deserve happiness in life?

I couldn't understand why I was suffering so much.

"Let us hear a song, Juliette," Frau pleaded.

Juliette's cheeks turned a shade of red as she brushed a fallen strand of hair from her cheek. "Oh, I couldn't."

"Oh, darling. Let them hear your voice. It's simply beautiful. You know, that is how Juliette and I met. I was out at a pub one night, and they were featuring a pianist and a singer. The spotlight lit up Juliette's face, and then I heard the sweetest sound I have ever heard in my life. I thought my heart was going to explode out of my chest." Claude told his story with theatrics. He was most definitely in love.

"When did you turn into such a romantic?" I jest with Claude, though I realized soon after it might not have been the right time for a joke. Claude's eyes studied me with a sense of anger. I had insulted him.

"When I found the right woman, of course," he responded. "Anyway, I rushed up to the little wooden stage after the show and begged to take her out for dinner." Claude turned to Juliette and swept his thumb across her cheek. "These rosy cheeks of hers were a telltale sign, but it wasn't until the tip of her nose turned red that I knew she might comply." Claude tapped Juliette on the nose and placed a kiss on her cheek.

"You two are to be married, I see?" I felt hurt that Claude hadn't told me. He hadn't mentioned Juliette in a letter, but I assumed now that was why he had stopped writing.

"Yes, Charlie. I was easing into the news to make the introduction less jarring," Claude said, his laughter sounding as if he was full of nerves.

Juliette set her glass down on the table and held out her hand, the hand I did not kiss earlier. I stepped in closer to take a better look. "What a beautiful ring," I tell them both. "I'm very happy for you."

I don't know if I sounded honest. "Charlie, come help me make their bed up in the spare room," Frau Joel said, taking me by the arm and leading me out of the kitchen.

We were upstairs and closed into one of the empty guest rooms when Frau Joel slapped her hands against her hips. "What is the matter with you, Charlie Crane?"

I was taken aback by her question. "What do you mean?"

"Claude is your closest friend, ja?" she asked.

"Ja," I confirmed.

"Why are you acting so doleful toward him? He's happy, Charlie. Shouldn't you be happy for him too?"

I didn't realize my reactions were so obvious. I had never been a jealous man, especially not of Claude. *A jealous person is weak and unlikeable*, Mama would always say. "Of course I'm happy for my friend," I told her.

"Nonsense. The look on your face spoke before you had a chance, Charlie. He clearly wants your approval. Why not give it to him? Fräulein Juliette is lovely."

"She is," I agreed.

"So, what is the problem?"

"There is no problem," I replied.

Frau Joel's eyes rolled around with frustration, and she huffed a loose hair away from her eye. "You are stubborn like my sohn was," she said. "Listen to an old lady, Charlie. Be happy for your friend and then happiness will soon find you. That's the only way life works, ja?"

"I understand," I responded. She was right. It wasn't fair to take my sour feelings out on Claude. Just because I could not be with Amelia, did not mean he shouldn't be with someone he loves.

I helped Frau Joel secure the bed linens and then followed her back down to the kitchen where we found Claude and Juliette having a quiet conversation, both smiling, both fawning over one another.

"We must celebrate," I said, making them aware I had stepped back into the room.

"I will make a feast tonight," Frau Joel said, following up my statement. "We will all celebrate your prenuptial plans."

"I am so happy for you both. Juliette, Claude is a wonderful man, and I know he will make you quite happy," I told her. He would. That much I knew for sure.

"He already has," she crooned.

"Charlie, I will need a few items at the store. Could you be a dear?"

"Ja, anything you need, Frau."

"I will stay here and help Frau Joel. Claude, why don't you go along with Charlie and keep him company. You two need to catch up. I'm sure you have war stories to exchange," Juliette said with raised brows.

Juliette must not know what our war stories consisted of, or she wouldn't have made such a comment. It's best not to know, so if Claude chose not to share, I could understand and agree.

Frau Joel took a moment to write up a small list, and then handed it to me with a pocket full of francs. "Thank you, boys."

Claude and I made our way out of the house. Several minutes passed before one of us spoke. "I apologize for not telling you sooner, Charlie. I didn't know how to say something so important in a letter."

"There is nothing to apologize for," I told him. "I am happy for you."

"But, I am sad for you, brother. I know you are hurting."

"This should not be about me, Claude. I am a grown man. I can handle my issues."

"I do love her, Charlie. She's an incredible woman. I want you to be at our wedding. I want you to stand by my side, as my brother. It would mean the world to me."

"I will be by your side; I promise."

Claude's lips pressed together and curled into a slight smile as he slapped his hand against my back. "Great. Now, tell me. How is that arm doing?"

I glance down at my tied off sleeve. "Well, it's gone."

Claude and I erupted into a fit of laughter. What else was there to do but laugh at our woes.

"At my last doctor's visit, I mentioned a pain I was having in my chest. It turns out I still have some shrapnel stuck, but they can't do much to help," Claude said. "They said it shouldn't cause me too many issues, but I might feel the pain here and there."

"We are alive," I told him. "We should be thankful for that."

"That we are, my friend," Claude said.

The streets were quiet, which gave Claude a good view of the area. I had grown to love living in Zurich. The peacefulness was the best part. "How is my mama?" I asked.

"She is well," Claude said, without missing a beat. "She told me to slap you if you appeared to be out of line in any way. Do I have to slap you?"

"No, brother. I think I'm in line," I told him, pointing across the street to the bäckerei. "I work there now. Just like Papa."

"That's fantastic, Charlie. I am proud of you."

"My mama told me not to fall in love with Zurich. She's afraid of losing me like your mama lost you." Yet, Claude was looking around with wide eyes as if he was falling in love with the small village.

"I simply cannot go home to Germany. I can't shoo away the feeling of being neglected by our country. It's a terrible thought and feeling to have, but I can't move on from it," I explain.

"I do understand," Claude agreed. "Other than meeting Juliette this past year, home does not feel like home—it feels like the dust has settled all over Germany. I have been telling Mama for a while now that I was planning to leave. She isn't happy, but like your mama, she doesn't want to hold me back from what will make me happy either."

I didn't want to influence Claude into a decision that might not be right for him, but Zurich was a good transition for me. "I understand completely."

"Honestly, Charlie, while I came here to see you, I was hoping I would like the area. I assumed since you had been here for a while now, you must like it enough to stay."

"It is my last stop before America, so ja, it is a good place."

"I think Juliette and I might move here until we can make our way to America, as well. Would that be all right with you?"

I stopped walking and turned to face Claude. My heart felt full for the first time in a while, and I threw my arm around his neck, hugging my friend tightly. "I would be quite happy to have you nearby. We're brothers, Claude. I always want you around. We can travel together, make peace in our lives, and do good things."

"Ja, that is what I want, Charlie. Annika had already told Mama that she planned to leave for America as soon as possible too. I don't see it happening, but the conversation has been alive and running for almost a year in our house. Annika and I both agreed that whoever makes it to America first, will make sure Mama comes along. She keeps hesitating, but your mama and my mama and papa are not getting any younger, ja? Mama has declined the offer every time we brought up the topic."

"I told my mama the same. I will be sending for her as soon as I am settled in America. It will be good for them."

"We deserve our freedom, don't we, Charlie?" Claude's question was the same one I asked myself too many times a day.

"I don't have a good answer to your question," I answered truthfully. "However, I don't think any answer I have would be a positive one."

"I would have to agree," Claude said.

The guilt of the war we were a part of would always feel like a scar on our foreheads. It was not something that could be forgotten or covered.

"You know, just before the soldiers were released, when the Führer ended his life, there were riots. The Russians were fast, Charlie. They came in and were ready to eradicate us all. Part of me thought I should surrender, but I was a coward and ran with the freed civilian Jews. The guilt—it's unreal, brother."

"I suppose rotting in prison was better after all," I said, trying to lighten the conversation. But there was no way to make this better. We would forever live with the guilt imposed on us.

"You remember Sven?" Claude asked as I opened the door to the grocery store.

"I wish I didn't," I said.

The scent of fresh produce filled the air around us, but the humidity level made it almost hard to breathe in at the same time.

"He caused a final scene for all to witness and hung himself at the front arches."

I wasn't expecting Claude's comment, and my initial thought was that Sven took the easy way out. I can only hope he suffered long enough. One might think, living a life with the memories of what he did would be a more suitable punishment.

Maybe I shouldn't be one to talk about such a thing. However, the difference between us and Sven was that we didn't get any joy in hurting others as he did.

"I guess we all have our breaking points," I told Claude.

"Many of our comrades—the other soldiers have already ended their lives. It's almost common," Claude said.

I honestly feared my own breaking point.

CHAPTER 29

1946—NEW YORK CITY, NY

EIGHTEEN MONTHS LATER

The ocean liner was preparing to dock. The sun was casting a golden glow across the sky and scattered clouds, the ocean was a piercing blue—a perfect reflection from up above. The day had finally come—I was in New York City. The Statue of Liberty was staring down upon me, welcoming me to a new type of freedom. I removed my hat and tipped my head toward the green icon and departed the ship, following hundreds of others who were also arriving at their dream come true.

The arrival process was long and came with paperwork approval, questions, a medical checkup, and endless lines. It was all worth it.

She was nearby; I could feel it.

My vision was so clear, I couldn't see how it wouldn't turn out the way I hoped:

I will be walking along a curb, heading for a coffee shop on an early Sunday morning. I will spot her—she will be dressed in a long black overcoat. Her hair will be up, held together with sparkling pins. One white-gloved hand will be holding Lucie, and the other will be carrying a leather pocketbook. She will have her chin up and her shoulders back, walking with pride.

Amelia will approach the corner from where I spotted her, and she will walk past my presence, not expecting to see me in New York City of all places. I will speak out: "It has been two long years, but your beauty is timeless."

Amelia will turn at the sound of my voice, and she will spot me. Her beautiful mouth will fall ajar, and she will press her white-gloved fingertips to her lips. I will hear my name spoken from the sweetest voice. She will pause, and then she will run into my arms as if no time had passed.

"I secured us an apartment," Juliette said as we boarded a ferry to take us to the main island. This part of the trip was to be quicker than the last.

"Yes, it's near Broadway," Claude gushed, wrapping his arms around his bride. "My girl is going to be a famous Broadway singer. You just watch."

The three of us stood by the stern of the ferry, watching the Statue of Liberty wave us off with her undying flame.

"I'll bet on it," I added to Claude's statement about Juliette making it to Broadway. She does have the voice of an angel, and I have fallen asleep many nights listening to her practice.

I might have said more, but I was starting to feel like a third-wheel to my best friend. He just married the love of his life, and they should be living in their own home sharing their marital bliss privately, but the cost of living in New York was unfath-omable, and it would only work if the three of us could live together under one roof, at least for the time being. The three of us planned to secure jobs as quickly as possible, but only time would tell how long that might take.

"There are two bedrooms, Charlie. We will all have our privacy..."

"I wasn't worried," I responded, trying to prove my state-ment without a look she could decipher.

"Well, I can see the concern written in the way your eyebrows are arched," Juliette said.

"I will do my best to give you space," I offered.

Juliette dropped her small bag and took ahold of my arm, pulling me to turn toward her. Claude followed in suit, turning around to face Juliette, but at the same time, keeping his focus on the paper map he held in his hand. He was determined to find his way around the city without guidance.

Juliette stepped in front of me and placed her hands on my shoulders. She had kind blue eyes; the color was so light they sometimes appeared transparent in the sun. "Charlie," she spoke. "The three of us agreed to move to America. We knew we couldn't do it alone. The apartment is just as much yours as it is ours, and I don't want you to think of it any differently."

"Yeah, brother. Stop worrying," Claude said with monotony as he traced his finger down the center of the map.

"I can cook," I offered. "I'm good at laundry and dishes, too."

"We are all good at those things, Charlie," she said, placing her palm on my cheek. "Please, do not worry. We're in America. We're here, and we're going to help you find Amelia, ja?"

That statement helped me perk up and forget about the awkward living situation.

"Our apartment is just about six miles away from Battery Park, where the ferry will bring us. We will need to find a cab," Claude said, lifting his suitcase and marching toward the port side of the ferry.

It wasn't long before the three of us were crammed in a yellow cab with a stripe of red painted down the center. It was New York fashion all the way. My heart was thudding, just trying to come to convince myself that I was actually in America. The air even smelled free.

We drove through the theater district where billboards appeared as large as the buildings, all covered with red and black showcase letters. Juliette was bouncing in her seat with excitement. She was much like a little girl on Christmas morning. "I simply cannot wait to start searching for auditions. Claude, can you imagine?" she gushed.

Claude wrapped his arm around Juliette, tugging her in close to his shoulder. "They will be looking for you before you know it, darling."

Juliette presses her hands together in prayer. "I can only hope," she said.

The cab dropped us at our new address in between several overshadowing buildings that seemed taller than the sky. People were bustling along the streets just as they did in Zurich and Bavaria, but New Yorkers walked around as if they had a bigger purpose—as if they had reason. How could they not?

"That's it. Right over there," Claude said, pointing across the way at a large building with a red brick facade and wrought iron decorative framed windows at the corner of each level. The building must have at least a dozen floors of apartments.

There was a black awning and an oversized door at the top of a steep cement stairwell. We collected our belongings from the cab driver and pulled our trunks and bags up the steps, one by one.

We piled into the building—the interior smelled of pie—someone on a lower level must have been baking. "The building manager said he would be in his office until later today," Juliette explained. "He said his office was here on the first floor. Wait with our things, and I'll find him."

Claude and I watched as Juliette strode down the hallway, stopping in front of the last door on the right. She knocked loudly, and the door opened almost immediately. Juliette held up her forefinger as she disappeared into the office.

It wasn't five minutes before she reappeared in the hallway, gleaming from ear to ear as a key dangled from her fingers. "Boys, we're on the twelfth floor. I hope those muscles of yours are up to the task."

By the time we lugged all of our belongings up the stairs, I had vowed never to move out of the apartment. Claude and I both dropped to the ground once we could close our front door.

Our apartment was pleasant, with two bedrooms, as Juliette had mentioned. The appliances were quite outdated, but everything seemed to be in working condition. Our view was of a theater, and I imagined what it would look like at night with the marquee of lightbulbs lit up.

* * *

It took us a week to settle into our new apartment, and we had all been assiduously searching for jobs. We had given ourselves two months to fall back on with our finances if need be, but we all wanted to secure jobs sooner rather than later.

"I have an audition later this morning," Juliette told me as she scrambled some eggs in a frying pan. "I am quite nervous."

"You are going to do wonderful," I told her, sipping on a cup of steaming coffee.

"How about you, any closer to finding a job?" she asked.

"Actually, yes. There's a large bakery a few blocks away, and they told me to come back at the end of the week because they might have a position available then."

"Fantastic," she chirped.

Claude had been out since the wee hours searching for hiring signs in shop windows. He was determined to find something by the end of this week. "Charlie," Juliette spoke up, sounding unsure in the way she said my name.

"Yes?"

"We overheard you talking to someone last night, in your bedroom."

I felt confused by her statement. I was certainly not talking to anyone in my bedroom. In fact, I fell asleep early. "I'm afraid you must have heard something else. Perhaps you were listening to a conversation next door. I had heard them speaking now and then."

Juliette removed the frying pan from the stovetop and placed it down on an oven mitt next to the sink. She wiped her hands on her short blue apron, and her blonde barrel curls flipped over her shoulder as she faced me. "Charlie, you were talking to Amelia. We heard your voice, and you said her name more than a few times. Of course, I'm not trying to embarrass you. We are just concerned, is all."

We. It was always *we.*

"I must have been having a dream," I told her, simply.

"You were crying, Charlie," she added. "You were crying out, 'Please don't go, Amelia.'" That comment made my cheeks hot. I was embarrassed to find out I was crying in my sleep.

"It won't be an issue soon, Juliette because I am going to find her. We can't be more than a few miles apart at this very moment, ja?"

Juliette did what she always had when I made a comment she didn't agree with—she pressed her pink lips together until a straight line formed across her cheeks, and then she would smile ever so slightly and nod her head.

I had spent more time roaming the streets for a familiar face throughout the past few days than I had seeking out a job. I had got lucky with the first bakery I visited. However, that information was for me only.

"Well, if you ever want to talk, I am a good listener," she offered, taking two plates down from the cupboard.

"Thank you, Juliette."

Again with that smile.

We were almost done eating our eggs when the front door flew open. "I got myself a job!" Claude shouted, clicking his heels in the air as he ran toward us. He had been putting in more effort than usual with his appearance. He looked good with his fashionable attire, a nice green-blue button-down, a chocolate brown tie, and a matching pair of trousers. Even his hair was slicked back, not a strand out of place. Someone might have thought he was off to some Ivy League school in the city.

A squeal came from Juliette's throat, followed by a shrill scrape from the bottom of her kitchen chair against the linoleum tiles. In a matter of two seconds, Juliette wrapped herself around Claude's body, her legs tangled around his waist, and her arms squeezing the life out of his neck. She peppered his face with kisses amidst a fit of giggles.

My stomach hurt.

I was jealous.

"That's really great, brother," I offered, lifting my coffee mug in the air in the form of a cheers. "Where's the job?"

Claude lowered Juliette, helping her feet find the floor. "Come on, I'll make you some breakfast, while you tell us everything," she said, rushing into the open L-shape kitchen.

"It's just three blocks away at a pub. They hired me to slay drinks. I know my way around a bar, so I knew all the questions they asked. Apparently, my knowledge impressed them enough to hire me on the spot. In fact, I start tonight."

Knowledge of liquor—it was a side effect of being a former Nazi. There were not many options to numb the haunting memories.

Claude had filled me in on his life during the year I was in prison. As I rotted externally, he rotted internally. Claude found himself at pubs nightly, drinking until someone would help escort him home. It wasn't until he ended up in a hospital bed under the care of his sister, Annika, that he slowed his habit. She followed her brother around like a lost puppy for months, making sure he didn't find more trouble at the bottom of a bottle.

I wasn't sure tending bar at a pub was the best job for Claude, and I could see by the look on Juliette's face that she might agree.

She was cracking an egg as he said the word "pub." The yoke was now covering her hand. She rushed to the sink, cleaning the remnants, and we stood still watching her digest Claude's news, wondering what she might say. Now that they were married, it was her place to make the first comment, not mine.

"Juliette," he said, walking toward her. "You all right, darling?"

"Oh yes, yes, of course, sweetheart. I just spilled some egg. Give me a moment."

She dried her hands on a dishrag for longer than necessary, and when she turned around, the response was shown in the form of tears. "I don't think a pub is the best place for you to work," she said. "Don't you remember—"

Claude pressed a smile on to his lips. "Oh, darling, I remember as if it was yesterday, but I'm well now. You know this, ja?"

Juliette pressed the dishrag to her cheeks, blotting a fallen tear. "I know you are better," she said.

"Then what's the problem?" Claude looked confused as if he couldn't understand the concern.

Juliette forced a phony smile and sniffled through a soft laugh. "There is no problem, sweetheart. I am so proud of you." Apparently, arguing beliefs was not part of a first year in marital bliss.

"Good for you, brother," I offered, supporting Juliette, but still knowing we felt the same way.

"This day is going so well already, and it's hardly nine o'clock. I bet something is in the air for us, and you will snag that role with your audition today," Claude said to Juliette. "And you, Charlie, you're going to get that position at the bakery. I can feel it in my bones."

"Yes, yes," I agreed.

"In fact, I found a tasty looking sandwich shop on my way home. I'm buying lunch today," Claude offered.

"I have my audition at noon," Juliette added.

"After your audition, we will meet you and go, ja?"

"Ja," she said quietly.

Claude poured himself a mug of coffee and sat down at the breakfast table with me as Juliette cooked him up some eggs and bacon. We were both quiet, awkwardly quiet, so Claude took the newspaper from a side table. He wasn't looking me in the eye, which told me he was aware of his bad idea as well as we were.

As soon as Juliette placed Claude's breakfast down in front of him, she untied her apron and hung it on the hook next to the row of cabinets. "I need to go freshen up and prepare for my audition," she said.

When Juliette was closed up in the bathroom, Claude laid his paper down and began shoveling eggs into his mouth. I did my best to stare out the window behind him, avoiding the thoughts that might slip out in the form of a lecture.

"I know you think this is a foolish idea, brother, but I don't have any skills other than assisting in the murder of innocent people."

I understood that part. I also understood what that part caused us to do—drink. "This will never get easier on us for as long as we have our memories," I told him. "However, it is easy to fall into a dark hole we will never escape, and that is what I fear the most."

"With all due respect, you are not one to talk, brother."

I should have figured he would point out my flaws during the conversation, but if it helped him realize his weakness, I would allow him to elaborate as much as he needed. "I am aware," I conceded.

"Maybe we should both find a doctor to talk to," Claude suggested.

"We mustn't. We need to keep our past quiet, especially here. I don't believe New Yorkers will take kindly to the thought of Nazis living among them. Let's agree not to tell a soul that we were Nazis, ja?" It was a thought that was too often crossing my mind. We were not of the general population who emigrated to America. We were not the ones who deserved that type of freedom.

"You're right," Claude responded. "Therefore, we need to be responsible for ourselves, learn from our mistakes and wrong-doings. It's the only way to move forward. I promise I will be okay working in the pub."

I leaned forward and cupped my hand on Claude's shoulder. "I believe you, brother. You are strong enough."

"As for you," Claude continued. "We should talk about finding you a nice lady to fill up your time, ja?"

Rage. It's the only way to explain the feelings I had. I was trying my best to believe in him, and he was giving up on my hopes. "Nein," I argued. "Nein. I will find Amelia. This city is not that big."

"Her name was not in the phone book," Claude added.

"I am aware."

CHAPTER 30

1946—NEW YORK CITY, NY

Claude and I stood patiently beneath a marquee encased with Edison light bulbs. Juliette needed this job. She wanted it more than anything in the world, and after this morning—the look of despair with worry for Claude's well-being—I wanted this good news for her. Juliette had become much like a sister to me throughout the last couple of years, and while the two of them often made my stomach turn due to their public displays of affection, I loved them both dearly.

Claude had checked his watch no less than ten times in the past five minutes. "The later she is, the more chance of good news," I told him.

"Ja," he said quietly, looking behind him toward the over-sized golden arched door that was to open when she was through.

We leaned our backs up against the white brick facade and watched people pass. Some were on bicycles, some on foot, cabs and cars, and even an airplane flew overhead. The city was alive, and we were taking in all of our surroundings.

A pigeon swooped down for a fallen bread crumb, pulling my attention from the center of the road. When the pigeon was startled by a passerby, my gaze was drawn to the person disrupting the bird's feast.

She had a long black overcoat. Her hair was tied up with glittering pins, and she wore white gloves—one that held the hand of a little girl. I hardly had a second to see more than the profile of her face, but she had rosy cheeks and a slightly upturned nose. She was relatively young, maybe my age, and I was sure...

I stepped away from the wall, jolting toward her. My hand made contact with her shoulder. "It has been two years, but your beauty is timeless," I shouted, sounding breathless, and not at all how I planned to sound when I would finally see her again. "Amelia, it is me. It is Charlie."

The woman stopped but didn't turn around that quickly. My heart pounded so hard, I thought I might faint, or at the very least, fall to my knees.

It had been a minute, I was sure. "Please, look at me. I have missed you so much."

A faint cry cooed from the woman, and a sniffle followed, "Please, sir, don't hurt me. You can have my money, just don't hurt me."

With caution, I stepped around the woman to admire her face, but my world came crashing down in that instant. It was not Amelia. "I apologize, Fräulein—madam, I was sure you were someone else."

The woman took her child into her side. She was shaking, and her eyes were watering as she ran off. I could only stand and watch them from behind.

My heart shattered all over again. I was sure it was Amelia.

A hand clutched my elbow. "Brother, let's get out of the street."

I didn't move. I couldn't move. My knees buckled, and I fell to the cobblestone. "I thought it was Amelia," I cried out.

Claude continued to try and help me off the ground, but nothing within my body wanted to comply.

"Just leave me here," I snapped.

"You're out of your mind, Charlie. Get up right now."

"I need to find her. You don't understand. What if you were separated from Juliette? What would you go through to find her? Would you give up?" My words sounded like sobs, though there were no tears left to cry. I had already cried them all.

"Of course not," Claude said, sounding less confident than he had while giving me his advice throughout the past year. It was as if I had finally gotten through to him, explaining my devotion to finding Amelia.

"God saved me from that battle in Prague so I could save Amelia, and all along I thought it was so I could take care of her and love her after all had been taken, but I am coming to realize now that I was only meant to save her from the war because I do not deserve the rest of the story."

Again, Claude tried to lift me to my feet, and I pushed through my weakness to stand. He buried his shoulder under my good arm and helped me back to the curb where we spotted Juliette standing complacently with her black-gloved hands gracefully holding a silver clutch. "Are you all right, Charlie?" She had concern and pain written across her face. Her brows furrowed, and her nose scrunched slightly. She ran to me, wrapping her arms around my neck. "I saw everything. Charlie," she choked. "I am so sorry."

I needed that embrace, but I shook away my selfish pain and pulled away, grabbing her hand and squeezing. "How did it go?"

"Yes, darling, tell me it went well?" Claude questioned, taking her other hand.

Juliette's pearly teeth appeared from within her wide smile and she began to bounce on her toes as a small shriek grew in her throat. "I got the job!" I knew it was a moment where I needed to take a step back and allow Claude to share that good news with her.

Her shouts and excitement with details sounded hazy as I watched from a few feet away. Claude was swinging her in a circle. His happiness for her was palpable.

I lost my focus, imagining myself in Claude's shoes—imagining Amelia in Juliette's.

We would be standing outside of an art gallery. Amelia's painting would have been chosen as a featured piece of work for all of New York City to see.

Amelia would be beaming with pride, and I would be swinging her around, kissing her cheeks and her lips. I would be whispering into her ear how proud I was; how I knew she was meant for this life. I would tell her I was taking her out for a fancy dinner with candlelight and jazz music so that we could celebrate. Then, she would kiss me back while giving me those eyes that told me how happy she was.

"Let's go celebrate, ja?" Claude shouted out, pulling me from my daydream. Juliette ran toward me, grabbing my arm.

"Let's go, Charlie. Did you hear, I'm allowed to give you and Claude front row tickets to my shows. I hope you like the theater," she gushed.

"Of course. I wouldn't dream of being anywhere else." That was a lie.

During the short walk to the sandwich shop, I came to realize how many women passed by who were all wearing long overcoats with their hair pinned. At least half of them had a young child, as well. I was beginning to realize the lack of serendipitous odds there would be of running into Amelia, or just spotting her in the city. She would look different after not being starved. What if I didn't recognize her when she passed? Would she recognize me? Would she stop if she did?

My questions could have gone on forever, never to be answered.

The sandwich shop was bustling with people waiting for their turn in line. The line was out the door, and wrapped around the corner. "I heard the food is worth the wait," Claude said, taking his place at the back of the line. "Tell us about the show, darling."

"Oh, it's just wonderful. The show is called 'La Bohème' and it's an opera. Claude, they want me featured in an opera!" she squealed, covering her mouth to hide the emotions. "It's about some starving artists in Paris. The story is phenomenal. I'm just beside myself."

A starving artist. Bohemia. It must have been a sign. Everything seemed to be a sign.

Just as I was thinking of coincidences, I spotted another woman in line with a long overcoat. She had a daughter, too. I could only see her from behind, but there was just as much of a chance that it was her as any of the other women I had seen. She turned to talk to her child, and I pressed up on my toes to see over several heads, hoping to get a glance at the side of her face, but she quickly repositioned her stance, leaving me without a view of much more than her back.

"Brother, that's not Amelia," Claude whispered.

"Well, how do you know?" I asked.

"I saw her a turn around a few minutes ago. I assure you it isn't her."

I knew I should stop looking after hearing it wasn't her, but my only thought was... Claude could be wrong.

"Some of the other girls I'll be working with on set are so lovely," Juliette spoke up. "In fact, one of them asked us to meet her out tonight at a jazz club near Times Square."

"Well, that sounds wonderful," Claude replied. "I think it's a fine idea to get to know some of the other actresses."

"Her name is June. She's around our age and soft-spoken, but with a beautiful voice. I was in awe listening to her practice."

Claude appeared enamored just listening to Juliette. I could see the pride and happiness he felt for her—it was as if his gaze was slipping through her as he tried to see whatever she was imagining. I suppose that was what true love looked like from the outside. It must have been the way I looked at Amelia when I had the chance.

"I can't wait to meet her, darling. Anyone who makes you happy will surely make me happy, as well."

Juliette swallowed hard, raised her eyebrows, and glanced over in my direction. "Charlie, you must join us tonight too."

"That's nonsense. You should get to know this girl without me crowding the space."

"But, I want you to come," Juliette insisted. "Please, Charlie. We have only been in the city a week. You should get out of the apartment and live your life here. Plus, you never know who you might run into, right?"

I did not miss the fact that Claude nudged his elbow into Juliette's side. I knew what she was doing, and I knew what he was telling her to stop suggesting—both for different reasons. Juliette's reason won my attention. She was right. If I had any chance of seeing Amelia, I would need to be outside of my apartment. "Okay, I will join you," I said.

"That is fantastic. We will have a great time, you'll see."

* * *

Unlike Claude, I had not put much effort into changing my style, adhering to the New York fashion. Therefore, Juliette insisted on dressing me for the outing. She had made a couple of shopping trips to find new clothes for herself and Claude over the past week, and it was apparent she was falling in love with fashion more and more each day. I had been watching the attention she was giving each accessory and matching her clutch or pocketbook. Juliette wanted nothing more than to fit in with the lifestyle. She had said this on more than one occasion: "If it weren't for my thick German accent, I would fit in perfectly here. No one would know I just emigrated." I suppose she could have been right. I, for one, thought the three of us stood out quite blatantly.

"This is the trend, Charlie," she argued as I loosened the tie she had set in place.

"I was hoping never to wear one of these choking devices again," I muttered.

Juliette slapped my hand away from the tie. "Stop, Charlie. You look dapper." When she spoke those words, I remembered it was the only way I would want to look if I was to see Amelia.

"Fine, it will do," I told her.

"You look very charming," she said, standing back to admire her work.

"You look lovely, yourself," I told her. Juliette always looked nice, though. It didn't seem she had to try very hard.

"Darling, we're ready to go," Juliette shouted into her bedroom, seeking Claude.

Claude dressed to the aces. He looked as if he stepped right out of a storefront window of Brooks Brothers. "If you keep dressing like that, I won't recognize you soon," I joked with him.

"Got to look the part, my brother. We're New Yorkers now, ja?"

I stepped into the bathroom to take a glance in the mirror. Juliette styled my hair, and I liked the way I looked.

The three of us made our way toward Times Square, where we located the jazz club. An orange glow dimly lit the interior, tea lights decorated each white linen-covered table, and the saxophone's tunes echoed between the walls. The smell of cigarettes and cigars had stolen most of the fresh air, but the mild scent of garlic and fresh bread offered the area a pleasingly rich aroma.

Juliette nearly startled me when she began waving furiously toward the back of the restaurant. "June is already here. She has a table for us in the corner," she squawked as she continued to wave above our heads at a brunette with vibrant burgundy lips and smoldering dark lashes. She was indeed a sight for sore eyes.

I followed Juliette and Claude through the crowd, taking the vacant seat beside June. "June, this my husband, Claude, and this is our closest friend, Charlie Crane," she said, opening her hand toward me.

June offered Claude her hand first, and he placed a kiss on the top of her black satin glove. "It's a pleasure. Juliette was going on and on about you earlier." Next, June twisted in her seat to face me. "Juliette told me a great deal about you, as well. She wasn't lying when she said you were quite a looker."

Juliette and Claude both snickered, and I likely blushed. It was a good thing it was too dark to see the redness on my cheeks. Before long, Juliette and Claude had gotten up from the table to secure a few beverages, leaving June and me alone. I might not have been one for many words, but June took care of that situation nicely. She began to chatter about Broadway and the lifestyle of an actress, and I pretended to listen by nodding my head and offering a snicker here and there. Truly, I was peering over her shoulder, taking in the sights, and looking for a resemblance of Amelia.

That's when I saw her.

This time I was sure it was Amelia. It was kismet. "Will you pardon me for a moment?" I asked June, standing from my seat and rushing toward the beautiful woman.

"Amelia?" I called out.

She turned toward me, and my hand fell to my chest, checking to see if my heart was still beating, or if maybe I had died and gone to heaven.

CHAPTER 31

PRESENT DAY

Amelia is wide awake and staring at me. I would have thought my stories would have put her to sleep, but here she is after all this time, apparently fascinated by what I have to say.

"I had no idea you were searching for me. I truly thought you were dead, Charlie. I knew what they did to insubordinate Jews, never mind a traitor of their own kind. I didn't know how to digest the fact that I might never know if you survived, but I recall telling you about a dream I had—a dream of moving to New York City. You told me I would get there someday, and I figured that if fate wanted us to be together, we would find each other again."

I chuckle and take Amelia's hand. "It seems fate took a bit of a detour."

"Fate just works on its own time, Charlie." Amelia tries to press herself up along the elevated portion of the bed, but by the winces pinching along her face, I can see she's trying her best to hide the pain.

"I—I had some weak moments, some I'm not proud of, you know? Someone once told me that when time passes, the pain lessens, but that was not the case for me, Amelia."

"You don't think I was foolish for thinking I saw you all over Manhattan?" I ask her. Everyone thought I had lost my mind back then. In fact, I was sure I lost my mind too.

"I did the same thing, Charlie, and I didn't have any reason to believe you were in New York City."

I had no idea she was looking for me. How could I have known? The same reason she didn't know I was looking for her. "Were you happy in New York?" I ask. "It must have been quite a dream come true after living in such horror."

Amelia smiles at first, and her cheeks brighten to a light shade of pink. Her gaze floats to the ceiling as she closes her eyes. "I was more than just happy, Charlie. I was alive. One thing I have never done since the day I last saw you was to take any day for granted. It was the least I could do for you."

A knock on the door interrupts our conversation. "Grams, you're still awake? Dr. Beck said you would be exhausted after your surgery," Emma says, walking in. She takes a seat on the other side of Amelia.

"How can I sleep when my life is just getting exciting, Emma?" she responds.

"Grams, he will still be here in the morning," she says. I can see Emma has taken on the role of parenting the grandparent. I have come to terms with the fact that at some point in life, the young have to be the responsible ones. Emma leans over Amelia and pulls the blankets up to her chest, and then gently places them down.

"I suppose," Amelia says, rolling her eyes around as if Emma is ruining her fun. "Charlie, how about a bedtime story? Do you have another letter to read?"

I stare down at my briefcase full of letters, knowing that if I read them in order, the next few letters are more dreary than I wish to remember. "They aren't exactly bedtime reading material," I tell her.

"Then tell me what happened next, Charlie. Surely, it wasn't me who you saw in the jazz lounge that night, right?"

Emma looks intrigued, and while I'm not sure I want her to hear this side of the story, maybe it's best she knows the truth, rather than just the part where I went missing for seventy-four years. "Do you mind if I listen too?" she asks.

"Only if you promise not to judge me based on the behavior of my twenty-something-year-old-self."

"We have all lived and learned, Charlie," Emma says.

"Oh, not my darling granddaughter," Amelia croons. "You're supposed to be perfect." Amelia grabs Emma's chin and shakes her head. I can imagine Amelia has been doing that very same thing to Emma since she was a little girl. The thought makes me smile for a moment. Then I remember what part of the story Amelia is waiting to hear.

I pull a brown envelope out of my briefcase—it's different from all the other yellowed-envelopes. When I remove the letter and unfold the paper, the memories come rushing back.

My dear Amelia,

The woman wasn't you. Her name was Amelia, but it wasn't you.

I am being punished, deservingly so.

Tonight, marked the end of one chapter and the beginning of the next. I don't know of many ways to make my heart feel better, and I'm suffering greatly. The pain is immeasurable, Amelia. I searched for your name in the phone directory, but there was no one by your name. I have spotted every young woman with dark hair, praying it was you. None of those women have been you. I fear the worst. Did you become ill on your way to America? I know it was common. Were you not allowed through customs? I know that was also common.

Whatever the case may be, Amelia, I don't feel like you are nearby anymore. I don't feel like you are anywhere here.

You were my purpose to survive.

Now, I feel as though I have no purpose.

This is my goodbye letter, Amelia.

I was once called a coward. It was the day I refused to murder your mama.

I may not be a coward, Amelia, but I feel broken.

In the case you are ever to find this letter, I do not want to leave you wondering. I am about to ingest an overdose of aspirin. It will be painless and quick, much like what I don't deserve. It's the only way out. I am so sorry we didn't get the chance to be together, but if life chooses our paths, it is clear you were not meant to be with a monster. You were meant for much more than me.

I love you, Amelia. Always and forever.

Charlie

I refold the letter and place it neatly back inside the envelope. Two pairs of eyes are staring at me as if I am a ghost. My hand is shaking as I place the envelope back inside my briefcase. My gaze is set on Amelia's face, wondering what thoughts are running through her mind. "You were supposed to kill my mother?"

"Yes."

Amelia glances down at her hands as she intertwines her fingers. "I had my moments too, Charlie. I'm not proud of those moments, but there were times where I thought I couldn't live with my nightmares." I should have prepared myself for that kind of truth, but I'm not sure anyone is ever ready to hear those words. "Life is full of challenges, and it is those moments that shape us for the future. We learn from our mistakes."

She is correct, though, I was not quick to learn. "It wasn't a mistake, Amelia. I had full intentions of falling asleep and never waking up again."

CHAPTER 32

1947—NEW YORK CITY, NY

It was a year after we had moved to New York City. I was holding down a stable job at a bakery. Claude was slinging drinks at a pub, and Juliette was becoming more popular and famous by the day—she worked the hardest of us all with nightly performances five nights a week. From an outside perspective, we were three lucky emigrants, living what should be a dream.

A dream would have included Amelia.

Three days after swallowing half a bottle of aspirin, I was waiting for my release papers from Bellevue Hospital where I was treated for an overdose. Claude and Juliette found me while my heart was still beating. They rushed me to the hospital where I was saved from what I didn't want to be saved from.

Both Claude and Juliette sat by my bedside for three days, angry at me—disappointed.

"I still don't understand what in the world was going through your mind, Charlie. We have spent so long trying to get here, to America. It was our dream. Then, you get here, and you lose the will to live. How does that just happen?" Juliette scolded me.

"I wish you hadn't saved me," I told them.

Claude was more than just frustrated, as was Juliette. She threw down her magazine, and the pages slapped against the tiled floors, and then she stormed out of the hospital room with her hand cupped over her nose and mouth. "She loves you like I do, you know. You are being selfish," Claude said.

"So be it," I said. I was not backing down from the way I felt. "You should not be one to talk. Have you already forgotten what you did to yourself just before you met Juliette?"

"I wish I never told you any of that. I didn't think for one minute you would hold it against me," Claude snapped. He pushed his chair out from beneath him. The wooden legs scraped sharply against the floor.

"You're just angry because you understand how I feel. You agree with the way I feel, and you have considered the same solutions like the one I had."

Claude pressed his fingers into his temples. "I need a break. I need air." Claude left, following in Juliette's footsteps.

A doctor visited while Claude and Juliette were away. I was asked a few dozen standard questions and gave untruthful answers to most. It wasn't a mystery on what I had to do to receive my ticket out of the hospital. I needed the doctors to believe that my lapse in judgment was just that—I had learned my lesson.

Truthfully, I had not learned a lesson.

The three of us were taken back to our apartment by a cab. The ride was quiet, and the interior of the vehicle smelled like menthol and body sweat. The seat was sticky and the air was thick. I felt as though the space was becoming smaller by the second. I didn't want Claude's arm leaning against my shoulder. Space was all I desired, but it was a challenge since I shared a home with them.

My air was polluted.

Nothing would change between us three until I convinced

them that I made a mistake. If not, they would hover and watch over me like I was a child. It was the very last thing I wanted.

"I am sorry," I offered as we walked into our apartment.

Claude hung up his coffee-brown trench coat, and Juliette hung up her lavish fox fur coat that she proudly purchased with her extravagant income. I watched and waited for a response to my apology.

"We love you, Charlie, but what you did is unforgivable," Juliette said, walking past me toward the bedroom she shared with Claude.

Claude dropped his hands into the pockets of his trousers and leaned back against the wall. "We thought you were dead, brother. You have to understand that an apology is not going to fix that right away. She loves you like I do. You already knew that, though."

I couldn't look Claude in the eyes anymore. I knew they both cared about me, as I did them, but something was standing in the way of my emotions. I was drowning in my sorrow.

"I love you both too," I muttered.

"Lean on me, brother. I am here to help you. And, you're right; I went through something similar, and it was terrible, but I survived, so let me help you now."

I didn't want help.

"I will be all right, Claude. I will not take any more pills."

"Good," he said. I could tell he didn't believe me, but I had nothing else to offer as a statement. "I need to get to work, and Juliette has a show in a few hours. I hate the thought of leaving you alone."

I glanced down at my watch, trying to appear like I cared about the time. "I should run by the bakery and apologize for missing the last few days of work."

"Ja. That's probably a good idea. If you don't want to be alone tonight, come by the pub."

"Will do," I told him.

* * *

"I was ill, sir. I apologize for not letting you know sooner. In fact, I was so ill, I had to be hospitalized," I lied to the owner of the bakery.

I was not sure if he believed the words I was feeding him, but he nodded his shiny bald head, pressed his lips together firmly allowing his mustache to fold over his bottom lip, and said, "I'm glad you're well now. Will you be returning to work tomorrow?" Mr. Rao was not the type of man to show his anger. He was quite laid back and had very few rules to abide by. However, after not showing up at work, I might have deserved more than just a cold response. I figured he was taking his silent anger for me out on the dough he was beating. I was lucky he didn't fire me on the spot.

"Yes, sir, I will be here tomorrow."

"Very well. I suggest you take care of yourself tonight and get a good night's sleep. I'll see you bright and early in the morning, Charlie."

I exited the bakery almost as quickly as I arrived. I was not supposed to have to reclaim my job because I was supposed to be dead.

The air outside was frigid, and I pulled my overcoat tightly over my chest, wishing I had worn a scarf. The temperatures were due to drop below freezing, and my mood was beginning to match the weather pattern. I stood still on the curb outside of the bakery as people brushed by in a hurry to wherever they were going. It was as if I was lost and unseen. No one noticed me. No one wanted to know me. I was nothing.

Claude's idea of sitting in a pub for the evening didn't seem all that bad, but I didn't have the desire to be at the receiving end of his sympathetic glances, so I planted myself on a barstool of another nearby pub.

It was best no one knew me at that moment as I slugged

several glasses of cognac. With each drink, the weight of the world slowly lifted its hands from my shoulders. Relief set in.

When I had enough to make me wish for sleep, I paid the tab and stumbled through the streets, circling a few blocks until I found my building.

Two men were outside on the front steps. I recognized them. They lived somewhere in the building and spent a lot of time out front smoking cigars. "It looks like you had a fine time tonight," one of them said as I tripped up the first step.

"It is a necessary part of life sometimes, ja?"

"You're not from around here, are you?" the man asked.

"Nein. I have been living here just a year now. It's a lovely city." The two men laughed, and I knew they were not laughing with me since I was not finding humor in anything at the moment. It was immediately apparent that I was purely the center of their entertainment.

"Nein?" the man questioned. "That's German, right?"

"Ja," I responded. I wanted to respond in the English way, but my lips and tongue were moving on their own accord, it seemed.

"What was it like over there?"

"It was awful," I said honestly.

"I'm sure it was. Did you ever meet Hitler?" I couldn't understand why that was a question anyone would ask. Of course, the people of Germany bowed down to Hitler for a long time, but that was before many of us knew the truth behind his plans.

"Nein. I saw him in passing once, but thankfully never met him," I continued.

"Thankfully?" the man followed. "I thought the Germans admired Hitler." The man pinched his cigar, focusing on the unlit end. He paused his statement and reached into his pocket for a match, working diligently to reignite the smoke. I should have taken the opportunity to say goodnight, but I stood there watching him, feeling lazy in my inebriated condition.

I shook my head. "He was a terrible man. He ruined my life, made me see and do things I will never forget—not for as long as I live."

The man snickered as if what I was saying was foolish. "If you never met the man, what could he have made you do?"

My gaze dropped to my shiny leather brown shoes. "I was one of his soldiers, but not by choice."

The man looped his forefinger around the center of his cigar and pulled it out from between his lips. His eyes narrowed, and he stared at me for a long moment. "You were a Nazi?"

"Whatever you want to call it," I told him, deciding the conversation was over. I immediately regretted sharing any information. "Have a good night, fellas."

"Wait, come back," he shouted after me. "I have more questions."

"Take care," I said, opening the front door to the apartment, waiting for the swoosh and clapping sound to tell me the door had closed behind me. I ran up the stairs as fast as my heavy legs could carry me and nearly fell into the apartment, closing myself inside. Neither Claude nor Juliette had come home yet, and I was thankful for the solitude—something I thought I would never want again after being imprisoned for a year.

As I sat with my back against the wall, the room spun in circles. I squeezed my eyes closed, wishing the world would stop encircling me, but it was no use. I felt the same with my eyes open and closed. There was no choice but to crawl to my room, where I peacefully fell asleep on the cold ground beside my bed.

What I learned was that if liquor could allow me to fall asleep on a cold hard ground, it could make me forget about my problems, too.

The sun was quick to rise the next morning, blinding me

with its sharp rays. The pain swelled in my head and worked its way through my body.

I hadn't lifted my body from the ground when a knock on my door sounded as great as a blasting cannon. It was my motivation to stand, feeling the heavy weight of my body keeping me in place.

"Charlie?" Claude called out. "You in there, brother?"

"Yeah—" I cleared my throat, "I'm putting some clothes on. Just a minute."

In truth, I was still wearing the same clothes from the night before. I did my best to change in the minute I had, but by the time I told Claude he could open the door, there was a frazzled look upon his face. "Charlie, we have a bit of an issue. Come here."

I followed Claude out of my bedroom and down to the main living area where our large main window took up half of a wall. Claude placed his hand on my back and pointed down toward the street. "Do you see that?"

I could see clearly what Claude was looking at and why he had a disturbed look written across his face. There were at least twenty people with signs that read, "We don't want Nazis. Go home." Beneath the writing was a circled swastika with a slash line.

"How do you think they know about us, Charlie?" Claude asked just before he pulled our taupe curtains closed.

"I have no idea—" The memories from the night before came rushing back, and I remembered how someone might have found out about Claude and me—mostly just me. "When I was coming home last night, there were two men on the front steps. They started talking to me and called out my accent. Question after question led to their assumption that I was a Nazi."

"You didn't tell them though, right?"

I ran my fingers through my hair, tugging at the roots. "I told them to think what they want."

"Christ, Charlie. They're going to run us out of our home. I have to go to work in a few hours. How am I supposed to walk through this? We talked about this. We knew we couldn't tell a soul what we had done because this would happen. You just put us all in danger," he shouted.

"If you had just left me to die—"

"No, don't use that every time you screw up, Charlie. Just, don't."

"I'm sorry," I offer. Again, another apology, another day. It seems to be all I had been doing as of late.

"This isn't like you, brother. What made you say what you said to those men?" Claude swung away from the closed window and dropped his hands onto my shoulders. "Look at me, Charlie."

I lifted my gaze, knowing the look on my face would give Claude the answer he was seeking. "I was tired," I lied. More lies. They kept coming, more and more often.

"Did you drink too much last night, Charlie?"

"I had a few drinks. It wasn't a big deal. It wasn't the reason I spoke to that man." But, it was.

"You are on a path of destruction," Claude accused me. "I can't have you destroying our lives too. Do you see what you're doing? You're pulling us down with you."

That was probably the most hurtful conversation I had with Claude. Hearing the "we" and "us" in every conversation made me feel a little smaller and a little more insignificant to his life. "What more can I do other than apologize?"

"You'll have to find us a new place to live now, ja?"

I took my coat from the hook set behind Claude's back. "I will find a new apartment, and I will be responsible for moving our belongings. Stay indoors and keep Juliette safe."

Claude didn't argue with my propositions. He stood back and allowed me to walk out the door. I took the stairs two at a time, feeling the anger work up inside of me, knowing I would have to fight through the crowd without getting attacked.

If Amelia was to have walked by, I could only imagine the panic she would feel, seeing the signs, assuming a Nazi was living within the building.

I was a Nazi. She might have felt that way about me.

"That's him," a voice shouted, and a finger pointed in my direction.

"Get out of our building, you murderer!" another yelled. "We don't want your kind."

"I am not a murderer," I fought back. My argument was useless. What reason would they have to believe me?

"Are you a Nazi?" I didn't know who was asking the questions. There were so many people lining the sidewalk, all staring at me with hatred in their eyes.

"I was once considered a Nazi, but I do not hate any kind. I was raised to be—"

"He's a Nazi!" The shouts were endless. "Get out of here you Jew killer!"

I deserved this too.

A hand tugged on the bottom of my coat. It was a little girl, and she was staring up at me with bright hazel eyes. "Did you hurt people?" she asked sweetly. "Are you a bad man?"

"Tatiana," a woman yelled. "Tatiana!" A woman, who I assumed to be the little girl's mother, lunged at her daughter, pulling her away from me. "What did I tell you about talking to strangers?"

Tatiana dropped her teddy bear at my feet. I glanced down at the worn fuzzy animal remembering the night we were pushing the Jews onto a train when the little girl dropped her doll and I tried to help, but the fear in the mother's eyes from that night was the same as the fear in this mother's eyes today.

I will forever be seen as a killer.

I lifted the bear and reached out with it. "Madame, your daughter dropped her—"

The woman turned on her heels, ran toward me and snatched the stuffed animal from my hand. "Go back to where you came from," she said, spitting on me.

I walked away with my heart thumping in my stomach. The pain—it was back, but for a different reason this time.

Finding a new apartment for three was not going to be a simple task, mainly because I didn't know where to start looking. Street after street felt like a ten-mile uphill march by the time I fell against a wall in between two shops. I glanced around, spotting a pub that looked to be settled underground. It was hardly noon, but pubs closed late and opened early in the city. Therefore, they wouldn't think much of my patronage.

Before I knew it, I was seated at the bar, ordering the poison that made my world start spinning out of control the night before.

CHAPTER 33

1948—NEW YORK CITY, NY

It had been three months since we moved into our new apartment. The space was smaller, and we were more cramped, but Claude and Juliette were hardly home with as much as they were both working.

I didn't complain about the quiet or loneliness, but the dark thoughts were eating me alive. Even the time of day was beginning to escape me. It was common that I would be sitting on the sofa in our living room until Juliette or Claude were to come home for the night.

The lights would flicker to life, and if it were Juliette, she would sigh, remove her keys from the lock and toss her coat onto the rack.

That night was no different.

"Have you been drinking all night again, Charlie?"

"Not all night," I answered.

I lied.

"Did you have any luck finding a new job today?" I wanted to tell her to stop hounding me, but instead, I stared down into my glass full of amber liquid and swirled the contents.

"No," I answered.

Juliette walked in front of me and leaned forward with her finger pointed in my direction. "I am calling your mother."

I may not have been entirely inebriated at that moment, but Juliette's words pulled me from my lazy trance. "There is no need to worry my mother," I told her.

"Bullcrap. You have a serious problem, Charlie. You have been let go from two jobs in the past three months, and you can't sit on the sofa all day and feed off our income. You are not our child or our responsibility, and this isn't fair to us. Charlie, were you aware that Claude and I want to start a family?"

I was stone sober at that moment. "A family?"

"Yes, Charlie. Claude and I want to have a baby, but I can't fathom bringing a child into this world where you are sharing our space and drinking yourself to sleep every night. You know Claude still suffers from the thought of drinking? Yet here you are filling the apartment with bottles of liquor every day."

"He works in a damn bar, Juliette!"

The argument was going nowhere fast, and I knew better than to argue with her. Juliette was headstrong and stubborn like I was.

"If you don't clean up your act, I am calling your mother, Charlie. Maybe she will get through to you."

I placed my glass down on the side table and stood with a wobbly stance. "I'll find my own place to live. How about that?" I told Juliette as I made my way down to my bedroom.

"That's just fine, Charlie. You can make this out to be our fault, but it is you who has the problem."

Our fault.

After putting my anger aside within the confines of my bedroom, I realized that my stupor led me to the solution—a solution fit for Claude and Juliette. If they wanted to start a family, it shouldn't be while I'm living with them.

* * *

When morning came after a restless night of sleep, I sat at the small kitchen table and waited for Claude and Juliette to wake up so I could tell them with a clear head what my plan was.

It was Sunday morning, the only day neither of them had to work, so they both slept in a bit later. Claude was awake first and dragged his heavy feet down the hall toward the kitchen inlet. In silence, he sat down at the table across from me. His hair was a mess, and he looked exhausted. "Brother, talk to me."

"What is there to talk about?" I was quick to respond. Though, I wasn't sure what else he was expecting me to say.

He leaned forward, resting on his elbows and framed his hands around his face. "Your drinking is out of control. Take it from a man with experience. I know we have already spoken about this several times, but it is affecting your life, Charlie."

"I have decided to move out so you and Juliette can have your own space, and so you won't have to worry about me any longer. She told me you two were thinking about starting a family, and I don't want to interrupt those plans."

"She said that?" Claude sounded like the information was news to him rather than a conversation they had.

"Last night when she came home from work," I added. "Claude, I understand her point of view. It is natural to want to share a home with just your spouse, and I'm becoming nothing more than a nuisance around here.

"You are not a bother, Charlie, but I am worried about you."

I am worried... not, we are worried.

"I don't want to be something or someone you have to worry about, Claude."

"Juliette and I briefly talked about moving to Connecticut, to a suburb. She has mentioned wanting children a couple of times, but it was never a conversation. I didn't know she was thinking about it so intently."

I felt confused hearing what he was saying. "What about her career?"

"She has talked about cutting back on the shows to three nights a week. She can take the train in for that."

I could tell they had been discussing this move more than he was leading me to believe. It only meant that they were, in fact, sticking around for me, or so it seemed. "I think that would be a good change for the two of you," I told him.

Claude nodded his head. "Sure, but I'm not leaving you until you are well, Charlie. So, if that is motivation for you to try and help yourself, so be it."

"I don't need you to stick around and watch over me," I told him.

"Fine. Prove it and throw away the bottles, Charlie. Get a new job. When you can do all that, I will reconsider the move."

"Juliette must hate me right now," I said.

"She's frustrated," he said.

I stood from my seat and tended to the bottles lined up on the kitchen counter. With a scoop of my arm, I brought them to the sink where I poured the contents of each bottle out, one by one until they were all empty.

Claude's gaze dropped to the table as I returned, and he released a heavy breath. "Thank you, Charlie."

"She threatened to call my mother," I told him.

Claude's eyebrows sewed together and he tilted his head to the side. "She said she was going to call your mother?"

"Ja, brother," I responded.

Claude and I both had a good laugh. "Juliette wouldn't dare."

"To be honest, she seemed angry enough last night that I wouldn't put it past her."

"I guess we shouldn't test her," Claude said with another snicker.

"I'll start looking for a new job today," I told Claude.

"You know, I saw a hiring sign on the window of the art gallery across the street. That might be something."

I don't know why I hadn't thought of working in an art gallery. It was a brilliant idea. Amelia said she had a passion for art, so she would naturally be drawn to a gallery. "I will stop over there and see if I can charm them into hiring me."

"Nothing a clean shave and freshly laundered clothes can't fix." I had let my hygiene fall behind after I was let go from the last job. It has been a couple of weeks since I had shaved or gone to the laundromat.

"Thank you for the subtle hint," I told Claude.

"Anytime."

* * *

The day was full of tasks I hadn't tended to in the previous weeks and included stopping by the window of the art gallery Claude mentioned.

I noticed the hiring sign first, but then some of the show-cased pieces in the window caught my attention.

The colors were vivid—pinks, purples, and blues brighter than the sky. The landscape looked familiar, and after a moment, I recognized the bridge—the Charles Bridge from Prague. The scene was set in the springtime when the meadows were full of life. My memory of Prague was much different, since I was there in the dead of winter when the people and villages had been overtaken by the gloom of the war.

I squinted toward the signature at the bottom of the painting. I then blinked several times because I was sure my eyes were playing tricks on me. Without realizing what I was doing, my hand and forehead were pressed against the glass window, trying to get closer to the painting.

The name written—it was Amelia B.

"Amelia," I spoke out as if she could hear me.

Could it be?

I needed to see every painting in the gallery, and I needed to know if the owner knew the artist. If it was Amelia, my Amelia, she went and became an artist and had a showcased piece of work. I prayed that her dream had come true.

It was a sign, and I had to take it as such. Maybe I was not intended to be with Amelia in this lifetime, but that one painting, full of life and beauty made me realize what I had been doing to myself. What if she had seen or known about my current state? I would have been a great disappointment

The light flickered from within the gallery even though I wasn't expecting anyone to be inside. Most shops were not open on Sundays, and art galleries were no exception. A woman appeared inside, dusting some of the fixtures. She noticed me almost immediately and came to the door. It took her a moment to unlock the gallery, but she stepped outside and looked me up and down as if she needed to piece me together. "Is there something I can help you with, sir?"

She looked stern and a bit rigid by the way she stood, the fine lines of makeup painted along her face and there was a sheen bouncing off the top of her slicked hair, finished with an elegant knot on the top of her head. For a Sunday, she was dressed as if she was ready to host an art show.

"I was fascinated by the painting in your window," I told her.

She looked pleased by my response. "Oh, yes, that is one of our finest pieces. The artist is a rare gem, or that's what we call her, anyway."

"Amelia, you know her well?"

"Not exactly, but it sounds like you might?"

It wasn't the answer I was hoping to hear. "I'm not sure. Is the artist Amelia Baylin?"

"Yes, sir, that is what the B stands for."

She was alive. It was her.

"Do you know anything about her?" I asked again, even though she didn't seem to know much the first time I asked.

"I do believe she's local here in the city, but that's all I know."

"We were once friends," I explained. "It's been a while since I have seen her." Friends, lovers, or the love of my life. I could refer to her in so many ways, but after the length of time we had been apart, I couldn't refer to her as much more than an old friend.

"I see, well you are lucky to have known her," she said. "Are you big into the arts?"

"Oh yes," I lied. "It is my passion in life."

"Is it now?" she asked, folding her arms over her high-collared white blouse.

"Very much so, and I happened to notice your hiring sign. Is there a position still available?"

The woman glanced across the show window at the sign. "Hold on just a moment," she said, pointing her finger up in the air. She stepped back into the gallery and returned, holding the sign in her hand. "Any old friend of Amelia Baylin's would make for a fine employee here."

"Just like that?" I asked, surprised that she was so willing to hire me after just speaking for a few moments.

"A person needs to have a passion for art to work here, and I would be lying if I said the applicant list was a mile long. In truth, we have not had one applicant since I hung the sign last week."

"I would feel honored," I told her while trying to be subtle about glancing past her to Amelia's painting.

"That's wonderful. And your name?"

"Charlie Crane, ma'am," I reached my hand out to shake hers.

"I am Elizabeth Monterey," she replied. "And I imagine you must have quite a story about your other arm." Her gaze fell to my left shoulder. "I'm looking forward to getting to know you more, Charlie Crane. Does nine o'clock tomorrow morning work for you?"

I smiled and dipped my head. "Yes, ma'am. I will be here."

I wasn't a fool to think my problems could disappear overnight, but something told me I was in the right place at the right time for a change.

CHAPTER 34

PRESENT DAY

"Wow," Emma says, her elbows pressed into her knees, and her head propped up on her fists, staring at me with intent.

"Charlie," Amelia croaks. "My heart—you were in so much pain because of me."

"I couldn't give up. I couldn't," I tell her.

"And that's why I'm still here, too," Amelia says.

"So, did Claude end up moving out after you got the new job?" Emma inquires.

I smooth out a crease on my pants and let the memories roll back. "It wasn't without hours of convincing, but my friend needed a life of his own with his wife."

"What about you?" Emma asks.

"I needed to learn how to be on my own. I needed to find myself." I reach down for the next envelope in the stack I have tied together inside of my briefcase. "The day Claude and Juliette moved away, I sat down inside of my new apartment and wrote you another letter."

Amelia reaches over to the rolling table where the remnants of her dinner wait to be picked up. She takes a tissue and presses it to her nose. "Go on, read it, please."

I focus my attention and study the first words as I find the breath needed to read.

Dear Amelia,

Today marks the three-year date of when I saw you last. When I close my eyes at night, I can still see you running with Lucie cradled in your arms as you turned back to see if I was all right. Your face was filled with worry, hope, and pain. I couldn't be with you, but I still wanted to make you feel better. I wanted to give you the motivation to run faster and harder, even though I knew you were surviving through skin and bones. Your eyebrows were downcast, angling in toward your nose, and your eyes were wide as if you were struggling with every thought racing through your mind. I watched you until you were out of sight. I don't know why the guards took mercy on you that day, but I considered it a miracle that they were more concerned with my wrongdoings than yours.

I have asked myself if there was something I could have done differently, but no matter how many times I replay that day in my head, I can't think of a different path or potential outcome. I just haven't been able to convince myself that our fates were not aligned.

Today starts a new chapter in my life; it seemed like an appropriate day to do so. Within the last couple of months, I have taken a job at an art gallery after I noticed your painting in the window. I later found out there were a dozen paintings with your name signed elegantly on the bottom right corner. The time I have spent in the gallery has consisted of hours staring at every stroke and wisp you painted. It wasn't hard to imagine you sitting in an art studio, listening to violins and pianos that might inspire your ever mark. The paintings were full of emotion and life, and this is being assumed by a man who has never so much as given a second glance to a piece of art. That has changed for me now. I crave the time I spend analyzing each hue of color, the pressure of a brushstroke, and the textures of paint. I feel connected to you in a sense, being the observer of your masterpieces.

I have done my best to get well these last couple of months. I put the liquor bottles aside and began taking walks and baking, as well as tending to the gallery. I needed to prove to Claude that I was capable of caring for myself, so he and his bride could move to a small Connecticut town so they could start their family.

It was the least I could do for my friend.

As they were saying their goodbyes today, Juliette took my hand and placed it on her stomach. She smiled sweetly and her cheeks blushed. That's when she told me they were expecting their first child.

I was so pleased for them, but like all the milestones I have been bearing witness to with Claude and Juliette, there was a nagging pain in my chest. I wish I could have been a father to Lucie. She deserves a papa. I wish we could have had our own children too, and I could watch your belly grow with life inside. It's a silly dream in the grand scheme of life, but I want a family someday.

When Claude and Juliette decided it was time to move, I found a new apartment—one much smaller than the place we were living. I didn't need the extra bedroom, and downsizing would make the rent much more affordable. The place is quaint, on a quiet corner near Midtown. I have a small galley kitchen, a television room, a decent size bathroom, and a bedroom. The bedroom is a bit smaller than I would like, but I only plan to sleep there. There are closets though, and that's the best part. I can keep the apartment neat without clutter.

This morning as I was unpacking my belongings, I realized I needed some furniture for the television room. There is no use having a room as such without furniture, right?

I went to a small furniture shop down the street and spotted the most wonderful set-up right in the window show-case. There were two plush leather chairs, with a small circular table that would fit neatly between the two. The pieces spoke to me. I purchased them right away, and one of the men who worked in the shop was kind enough to help me move the furniture two blocks and up to my apartment unit.

Now, I have his and hers chairs in front of the television. It might sound absurd, but in case we find each other, I wanted you to have your own chair. The furniture makes the apartment feel homier. I can see myself staying put for a while now.

Amelia, I must confess though, I am beginning to feel like I'm in a relationship with an invisible woman. If anyone were to know the truth, I might be sent to a hospital to have my head examined. Maybe I have lost my mind, Amelia. I am not entirely sure. Holding on to hope is all I have, and if I didn't feed that hope, the chances of seeing you again would be gone.

For now, my love, I hope you are doing well.

Love Always,

Charlie

Amelia is smiling proudly as she brushes a loose strand of her hair behind her ear. "You saw my paintings?"

"I was and am in love with those paintings, darling."

"I was very fortunate to have sold my paintings. With two small children at home, I didn't have the ability to do much else. It was as if my life was pre-planned. Each direction I took was because of where I was standing. One thing led to another, and my dreams began to come true—well, most of my dreams."

"That gave me the motivation to do the same, Amelia," I tell her.

"How so?"

CHAPTER 35

1958—NEW YORK CITY, NY

TEN YEARS LATER

It may have taken years, but an epiphany is what I called the moment when I realized there was a way I could offer my peace to the world. I planned to go from school to school, pitching my proposition. About half of the school administrators were interested to hear what I had to say.

"Welcome, Mr. Crane. What is it we can do for you today?" The conversations all started the same. "Please have a seat."

I removed my fedora and reached my good hand out for a handshake before taking a seat on the blue-tweed cushion in front of a gray metal teacher's desk. Certifications and college degrees lined the walls, and filing cabinets stole every free inch of space aside from two chairs and the principal's desk. The area was small and I felt cramped, as I normally did before beginning my spiel.

"My only request is that you hear me out before you make a decision," I said. I found that by asking the administrators to listen, I wouldn't be asked to leave before explaining my true reason for being there.

"Go on," this administrator said. She looked young for her position, but stern at the same time. Mrs. Fox had a habit of checking her watch every thirty seconds, which caused my nerves to flare.

"I am a former Nazi," I began.

Mrs. Fox stood from her chair and pressed her red painted fingertips to the top of her desk. "Please leave my office," she said. Her nostrils flared with anger, but I had to continue speaking.

"I witnessed every act of hate this world has seen. I watched countries crumble in suit. I was bred to a monster, but inside, I wanted to save every innocent person. I came here, and I have visited many other schools to teach about the repercussions of hate crimes."

"Mr. Crane," Mrs. Fox tried to interrupt.

"I am not here to condone my life as a Nazi, but to teach of the way life once was, with the hope that this world never sees another era as such. I believe in the good of humanity, and I never hurt a soul. In fact, I was imprisoned for helping two Jewish people escape. That is what I'm most proud of."

"Mr. Crane, please allow me to speak," she said, still staring down at me with a scowl screwed into her lips.

"Very well," I responded.

"This world has seen a very ugly time, and though I was taken aback by your initial comment, I respect your desire to make things right in the world. Our children must know the truth of what war causes, so that they can grow up and make better decisions."

"Precisely, ma'am."

Mrs. Fox sat back down in her chair and drew her finger down a straight line on her desk calendar. "How does next Tuesday at ten a.m. sound? I can have the school assembled in the cafeteria where you can give your presentation."

"That will work perfectly, Mrs. Fox."

"Mr. Crane," she spoke firmly. "Please know we cannot offer you any form of compensation for your time."

I placed my hand over my heart. "I have never conducted my presentations in exchange for anything more than time, Mrs. Fox."

"We will have a police officer present," she added. That was a typical response. In their heart, the educators knew it was a good lesson to teach. However, I was still known as a former Nazi, and they needed to keep their pupils safe.

"Of course. I do understand."

I was escorted out of the school with sidelong glances from faculty in the hallways. I didn't have a familiar face, but they couldn't have known my background. I had spent years assuming people could take one look at me and see what I had done, or what I was a part of for so long. In truth, all anyone saw was a man with fear etched into his face in the form of aging lines and sad eyes.

Though the looks I received made me want to crawl into a hole as if no time had passed, I managed to keep my chin up, knowing I was doing something of good nature.

I tried my best to allow the positive thoughts to drown out the bad, and typically by the time I made my long walk back to my apartment after one of those meetings, I had convinced myself that acts of kindness would lead to better in the world.

Not that day, though.

I made my way up the five flights of stairs to my small apartment. As I slid the key into the lock, I heard the chiming of my phone echoing between the walls inside. The only people to phone me were Claude, Juliette, Mama, or the art gallery if someone called out sick.

I struggled to make my way inside, pushing through the stickiness of my door, nearly tripping on the area rug set in front of the circular table where I kept my phone.

"This is Charlie," I answered.

"This is an international collect call from Kinder Hospital in Munich. Do you accept these charges?"

Mama. "Yes, of course. Please connect the call."

It felt like an eternity had passed when I heard Mama's voice wheeze into the phone. "Charlie, are you there, my sohn?"

"Mama, why are you at the hospital?"

The sound of a cough filtered through the receiver. "I am ill, Charlie."

"With what, Mama? You sound terrible."

Another cough—heavier this time. "Oh, I don't know, Charlie. They said I might have a tumor growing in my lungs, but I don't think these doctors know what they are doing. I was sure it was just a cold, but after what happened to your papa, I came right in to make sure it wasn't influenza, which it is not. They can only assume the worst."

"Mama," I exhaled with pain. "What are they going to do to help you?"

Mama sighed. "They're not. They said they could not do much for me. I could die in a few months or a few years. It's hard to tell, but it is important that I tell you, sohn."

I began wrapping the cord of the telephone around my neck, feeling the coils cut off some of my circulation. "Mama, I am sending for you. The doctors in New York will be better. We can see about getting you care here."

"I simply can't put you through that, Charlie."

"Mama, it is my turn to care for you. Do you understand?"

I heard a sniffle followed by, "Charlie, I don't know what I did to deserve you as a sohn. I am truly blessed. I am also very scared right now." I could hear the cries hitching in her throat. She didn't have to tell me she was scared. I knew the sound of her voice well. "I will acquire you a green card. I need you to stay strong, Mama, but I will get you here safely, ja?"

"Ich liebe dich, Charlie," she uttered with a sigh.

"I love you too, Mama."

As the call disconnected and I unwound the cord from

around my neck, I dropped down into my leather chair, staring over at the other chair—Amelia's chair.

"I should have been a better son, Amelia. Mama, she's terrified, and I'm over here in America chasing a dream, while she's alone in a German hospital. Shame on me. Just shame."

I closed my eyes, imagining what Amelia would say in return.

Maybe she would say something philosophical that would erase the selfish thoughts I felt, but I couldn't imagine what those words might be. I couldn't hear Amelia's voice at that moment. I couldn't hear anything more than my inner cries.

* * *

The process of helping Mama emigrate took longer than I would have liked, but I knew it would not be a simple task. I was thankful that through the months that had passed, Mama was still alive. She was becoming weaker but doing what she could to get by.

I arranged for air transportation. It was Mama's first time flying, and I imagine she must have been quite nervous, but knowing she would be here in the end got us both through the tough time. Her flight was due to arrive within the next couple of hours, and I spent that time pacing the airport, people watching as I enjoyed doing.

I planned to find a seat near the terminal Mama would fly up to, but there were large crowds of people that day, so I took my spot in between a payphone and a water fountain, watching the hustle and bustle.

I had been standing in one place for about an hour when something caught my eye. Across the way, there was a forest green leather padded bench where a woman sat patiently with a magazine in hand. Two young girls sat on the ground in front of her playing hand-clapping games. The family was a picture of pure happiness.

It had been years since I promised myself I would stop assuming every beguiling woman with dark hair and a little girl was Amelia. It took me a while to break my habit, but I knew I needed to stop looking for the purpose of my well-being.

However, the woman just across the way looked just how I imagined Amelia would look in her early thirties. Her auburn hair was in large barrel curls with fancy pins holding up the sides. She was wearing a green and white tweed day dress with matching heels. Pearls decorated her ears and neck, and her lips were the color of cherries. She was beautiful. More than beautiful—she was stunning. I was sure it was not her, however.

"Mama, could we go into the store for some candy?" one of the young girls asked the woman.

"It's up to your father," she replied. "He's coming back from the restroom right now." The woman pointed to a well-dressed man who was heading toward them.

"Daddy, could we please buy some candy," the girls continued. "Please, Daddy."

The man looked at the woman and smiled teasingly. "Amelia, darling, why are you always putting me up against these girls and their long batting eyelashes. You know I can't possibly say no."

Amelia.

It could be a coincidence, just as it was at that time in the jazz lounge. Amelia was a popular name.

The man reached into his pocket and retrieved some change for the girls. One of the daughters had long, blonde wavy hair, and the other had long dark curls. They were both adorable, but looked entirely different from one another.

I knew I should stop speculating.

If Amelia had two daughters, only one was likely to be

biologically hers. The other would mean she was happily married to that man the girls called "daddy."

It was not her.

I didn't want it to be her.

"Amelia Baylin," a man called out from across the terminal. "Are you Amelia Baylin?"

"Yes, sir. Can I help you?"

I closed my eyes. *It was her.*

"I was hoping for your autograph. I'm a big fan of your work. I recognized your face from the article in the magazine last month. Brava, miss. Brava." I forced my eyes back open. I needed to face the truth. Amelia held her hand over her chest and took the pen from the man before signing her name on the article in the magazine. I didn't know her face had made it to print. "My wife and I have several of your paintings hanging in our foyer. You are a true artist. Thank you for your time, Ms. Baylin."

"The pleasure is all mine," Amelia said, gracefully.

As the man walked away, I watched the interaction between her and the man who appeared to be her husband. He shook his head as a smile pressed into his lips. He then glanced back down at his magazine. "Unbelievable. You never cease to amaze me, Amelia. I never doubted this would be your future." The man leaned over and placed a quick kiss on Amelia's cheek.

My heart exploded, or so it felt.

The daughters were quick to return, jumping for joy, hugging and kissing their parents with gratitude. They were all so happy, just as she deserved.

I considered my options: I could approach her and pull her in for a hug as if no time had passed, even though thirteen years had passed. Or, I could walk away knowing that she was safe and happy—living out her dream.

I asked myself what love meant.

Love meant walking away.

If I chose to approach her, I would bring back those memories and all the nightmares. I would cause her more pain than she appeared to be carrying. I would be selfish.

After all this time...

Amelia and who I assumed to be her husband stood from their seats. Each took a daughter by the hand and walked away side by side. It was my last chance, but I stood there, frozen.

I don't know if it was a sound she heard or a feeling in her gut, but Amelia turned to look over her shoulder. Her focus skated over me, and for a brief moment, I wondered if she noticed me too.

"Charlie, sohn, you haven't said much," Mama said as I was helping her up the stairs to my apartment. I didn't consider how challenging it would be for her to walk this many steps in her condition.

"Mama, I am just so happy you are here in America," I told her.

"It is wonderful. The smells, sights, and sounds; it's everything I imagined it to be."

"It is very nice," I agreed.

Mama has aged dramatically since I had seen her thirteen years ago. Since we spoke weekly on the telephone, I imagined nothing more had changed, but she looked much older than fifty years old.

Mama took me by the wrist and pulled me to face her as she sat down on a wooden chair at my small dining table. "There is much sadness in your eyes, Charlie. Something is not right with you. Talk to me, please." She released my hand, and I pulled out a chair on the other side of the table.

"Claude, Juliette, and their little girl, Penny, are bringing supper over tonight," I told her.

"Charlie, do not change the subject. I already knew about our dinner plans." Mama sweeps her hand along the table, finding a speck of dust I must have missed while cleaning the night before.

"I—I saw Amelia at the airport just before your airplane landed."

Mama's eyes grew wide as if she were full of questions. "Your Amelia? The Amelia you haven't seen in more than a decade?" I couldn't tell if Mama was about to call me crazy or if she was as surprised as I was.

"Yes. She was with a man and two little girls," I told her.

"Well obviously, you talked to her," Mama said, her brows furrowing with confusion.

"No, Mama. She was happy. I couldn't interrupt that after what she had been through. I knew it was best to walk away."

Mama's eyes closed and she brought her folded hands up to her lips. "My sohn. Wise beyond your years, you are. Let me tell you something very important: If two people are meant to be together, the universe will not stand in the way."

"She was with a man, Mama. She was most likely happily married."

"You don't know that, Charlie. You don't know her story, and you don't know his." I listened to what Mama said, but in my heart and my head, I was sure of what I saw.

"I suppose," I said to appease her thoughts.

"Charlie, not everything is as it seems. I believe if you want to be with someone, you pave the way for that to happen, and if they are meant to be with you too, the rest will come at its own time. You see, the universe does not follow a clock. Life is full of lessons one must learn and conquer before the reward of receiving what we want."

"What about you?" I questioned. "You are dying, ja?"

Mama smiled and reached across the table to place her hand on my cheek. "I am dying, Charlie. I am dying to be reunited with your papa again. I have accomplished everything in this life, and soon, it will be time to move on."

Mama's words stuck with me. I dissected the meaning and once again tried to understand that forever was a defined period.

Maybe I should have approached Amelia. It was my one chance, but I followed my heart, just as I have always done.

"How old is Penny now?" Mama asked.

I glance up at the tiled ceiling in thought. "She turned nine a few months ago," I said.

"Claude's mother is crazy about that little girl. There are photographs all over her house. It makes me think of grand-children..."

"I know. A family would be nice to have."

* * *

Juliette would never allow for an opportunity of tardiness. If there was one thing I could depend on, it was that they would always arrive on time whenever we had plans. Though typically, I would take a train to Connecticut as it's a bit tricky for them to make it to the city with Penny in tow, they insisted on making the trip out to the city tonight for Mama's sake.

Mama jumped when the buzzer screamed through the apartment. "Ach du lieber Gott! *Oh my God.* What is that wretched sound?"

I had set up a cot for Mama in the television room so she could comfortably relax. However, she had made the bed look more like a couch after adding an array of throw blankets. She didn't want to appear sick as she thought it would frighten Penny.

"It's just the door buzzer," I told Mama. I kept forgetting how new everything in the city was for her. I was sure it would be quite an adjustment. "I'm going to let them in. I'll be right back."

I opened the front door for my friends, welcoming them with a smile. Penny was the first to throw herself at me, shouting, "Uncle Charlie!" I lifted my goddaughter and swung her around. "I missed you, little princess."

"I drew you a picture, Uncle Charlie," she said. Penny was in a daisy-yellow pleated dress. "Oh, and Mommy bought this pretty new dress for me to wear tonight. Do you like it, Uncle Charlie?"

"Oh, Penny, I think it is the most beautiful dress I have ever seen," I crooned.

Juliette placed her hand on my shoulder and pressed up on her toes to kiss me on the cheek. "Hi honey," she said.

Claude slapped me on the back and marched ahead for the stairs. "I can't believe Mama is here," he said.

I carried Penny up the stairs as she attempted to braid the short strands of my hair. "We brought a roast for dinner," she told me. Penny could talk my ear off for an hour straight without taking a break.

Mama had tears in her eyes when I walked inside with Penny hanging from my neck. "You are already such a big girl," Mama cooed.

Penny placed her head down on my shoulder, acting a bit shy in Mama's presence. "It's okay, sweetheart. This is Uncle Charlie's mommy," Juliette explained.

Claude has Mama wrapped up tightly in his arms, squeezing her so hard I'm not sure she can breathe. "It has been so long," he said. "I have missed you so much."

"Oh, darling. I have missed you too," Mama told him.

Juliette was next in line. She had gotten to know Mama a bit when she and Claude first met, so they weren't strangers.

I stood back, waiting for the hellos to commence, but while

Juliette was chatting with Mama, Claude went to sit down in one of the two empty leather chairs—*Amelia's chair*.

"Oh, why don't you sit in this one over here," I told him, pointing to my chair.

"What's wrong with this one?" he asked. I hadn't told Claude why I purchased two of the same chair. He might have thought it was for symmetry within the décor.

"Nothing, I just—"

"That is Amelia's chair," Mama paused her conversation to speak up.

"Brother, come on now."

"Charlie saw Amelia today," Mama continued.

Claude moved away from the chair. "You saw Amelia today?"

"I did. She was at the airport with her husband and two children." I didn't think the words would come out so easily.

Claude dropped his hands into his pants pockets and rolled back onto his heels. "Brother, I am—"

"It's fine," I told him.

"Well, what did she say when she saw you?"

My gaze dropped to the hardwoods below my feet. I shook my head. "I didn't approach her. She was happy, and it was enough for me to go on with."

Claude ran his hand up the side of his face. "I'm sorry, I am just in shock. I—I'm proud of you, brother."

"Yeah," I said, taking in a deep breath. "We should eat. I don't want the roast to get cold. Thank you both so very much for bringing dinner over."

Juliette cleared her throat and tended to the platter Claude carried upstairs. "I will just need a couple of minutes to prepare the plates," Juliette said. "Charlie, what cupboard is your China in?"

"The far-right cupboard. I'll come in and help you."

"No, no, I am more than capable of helping Juliette in the kitchen," Mama interrupted me.

"I'm going to help too," Penny said, following her mother into the small kitchen.

Claude walked up to me and slapped his hand against my cheek. "Charlie, maybe it's time we found you a nice woman. I hate to see you so lonely, brother."

We had had the same conversation many times over the years, but Claude didn't understand what I meant when I said that Amelia was 'the one' and always would be. If I couldn't have her, I didn't want to be with anyone, and it was a decision that made me feel comfortable. "I don't know, Claude. I am not alone now. Mama is here, ja?"

"Charlie," he said with a heavy sigh. "You know what I mean, brother. Even you have said before that you want a family of your own."

With Amelia, yes.

"I know, Claude. I just don't think it's in the cards for me."

CHAPTER 37

PRESENT DAY

I finally talked until Amelia fell asleep last night. Then, I persuaded Emma to get some sleep too, though I think she might have voluntarily listened to me talk for hours more. She has been at the hospital for days, lacking sleep. The hotel next to the hospital offered a good night's rest, but the moment visiting hours began this morning, I was right back where I need to be—at Amelia's side.

"You must be starving," Amelia says while staring down at her toast and eggs.

"I brought some muffins from the bakery down the street," I offer as I pull the bag out from behind my back.

"It's been less than two days, and you are already spoiling me again, Charlie Crane," Amelia says, pointing her fork at me.

"I don't know when you fell asleep last night, but—" I begin.

"The airport," she states. "Yes. I can't say I'm not upset that you didn't approach me in the airport, Charlie. I would have liked to have a say in the decision you made. But, with that said —" She pauses and it makes my heart skip a beat. "I can't fault you for loving me enough to put my happiness first. But, how did you know I was happily married?"

I place one of the muffins down on Amelia's plate. "Would you like some butter?"

"No, thank you," she says, peeling the paper away from the bread. "Charlie, don't avoid my question."

I snicker as I take a bite. "You looked quite smitten over one another."

"A woman can be that way with her best friend, right?"

Just a best friend? I would never have assumed.

"I suppose," I reply.

"Well, Max was a good man, and he gave me a good life, but we were companions at most. Now, it has been years since he has passed, and I have had the time to consider that I never allowed myself to care about another man as I care about you."

"I didn't think a day would come where I would hear you felt the same way about me that I have about you," I tell her honestly. It was a fact I had accepted long ago.

"Good morning," a voice startles us from the doorway. It's the doctor, the one who saved her heart.

"Oh hello, Dr. Beck," Amelia says while dabbing her lips with a small paper napkin. "What good news do you have for me this morning?"

"Well first, how are you feeling?"

"I'm a bit sore, but with all things considered, I feel quite well. Well enough to go home, in fact."

Dr. Beck walks further into the room, laughing gently at Amelia's suggestion. "Yes, I think you will be able to go home soon. We're going to keep you until tomorrow, and then I think you will be well enough to go home. However, we'll want to check on you next week."

"Of course," Amelia says. "I suppose I will have to make room in my life for such accommodations, but I'm sure I can work something out."

Dr. Beck merely raises an eyebrow at her sarcasm, but I

think he's learned enough about Amelia during these last few days to know she's toying with him. "Understood, Ms. Baylin."

After Dr. Beck checks Amelia's vitals, he leaves us to our privacy.

"Charlie, I want you to bring me to your apartment in New York," Amelia says. Her statement shocks me as I never imagined she would have a desire to travel those three hours just to see a small apartment.

In fact, I almost choke out my words. "Darling, do you think that is a good idea in your fragile state?"

Amelia crumples her napkin and tosses it down on to her table. "Charlie Crane. Do not confuse me for a weak person. I can take a train like any other person. I am capable of getting into a cab and walking up a couple of flights of stairs—"

"Sweetheart, you just had a stroke and heart surgery. We should be taking it easy."

"Charlie, do not tell me you don't feel like a ticking time bomb in your nineties. Today could be it for both of us, and if I'm going to die, I'm going to die doing what I want to do, and I want to see your apartment."

I clear my throat because I'm taken aback by the scolding. "Well, okay. You make a good point," I say.

"Fabulous. Then it's settled."

I have a strong suspicion that her family will reject this idea, but I'll leave that argument to them.

"Your mother sounded like a wonderful person," Amelia says. "And you were a good son. I think you should know that."

Amelia must have been listening to me talk longer than I thought she was yesterday. "I did what I could after being away from her for so long."

"Were the doctors in New York able to help her?"

My throat tightens at the question. "Oh... I wouldn't know."

"I'm proud of you, sohn," Mama said as I was leaving the apartment for another school lecture. More and more schools were agreeing to hear my presentation. Most instances went well.

"Thank you, Mama. Do not even think about cleaning my apartment again, please. Just take it easy while I'm gone."

"Yes, Charlie," she said, shooing me away. I wasn't sure how she had the energy to keep moving around the apartment, dusting and baking. I did my best to keep her rested, but she refused to comply. It had only been two weeks since she arrived in America, but she was happy being in New York.

I would bring meals home from nearby restaurants so that she could taste the local cuisine, and she would set a chair near the window to people watch. The way to Mama's heart was always food and fashion, though fashion took a back seat in her life as she became sick.

The school I was visiting was only a mile down the road, and I took to walking rather than the subway. Fresh air was the key to clearing my mind before a presentation. I found that my speeches were always clear and concise, but it was the questions

I received after that threw me for a loop. Children do not have much of a filter, and their curiosity sometimes got the best of me. Many of the children wanted to know what it was like to shoot a gun, or if I had killed someone. One child even asked what happens right after a person dies. Do their eyes close or stay open and stare back at the person who killed them?

While I knew my speeches were of good merit to teach about hate crimes, I was having more and more flashbacks and nightmares. It was my toll to pay.

This particular school had a different crowd of children. It was as if the administration wasn't as organized or strict as some of the other schools I visited. It was as if the children were running amok, taking over the school with their idea of rules. I had mostly visited junior high schools, but this was a high school. The questions would be more challenging, but I knew that walking inside.

I was set to speak in their auditorium at a podium with a microphone. There I stood, waiting for silence—silence that would never come. None of the children would quiet down, even when I tapped my finger against the black foam of the mic.

"Pardon me," I spoke up. "It will be difficult to speak over all of you."

A boy, one of the older looking boys, stood up and waved his arms at everyone. It appeared that he was trying to quiet the crowd down for me. "Everyone, shut your mouths. The Nazi wants to speak."

I hated being called a Nazi. It symbolized everything I didn't believe.

However, the word, Nazi, seemed to bring along a muttering hush throughout the room. "Yes, I was called a Nazi," I began.

"Jew killer," a student shouted. I wouldn't know where it came from as the words bounced off the walls.

"Go home, Nazi," another shout.

"Candyass!"

I tried to tune out the name-calling, but it was distracting. "It began back when I was a young child, much younger than all of you, in fact. I wasn't given a choice in the matter of following our vicious leader."

"Ring a ding, ding!" Yet, another student yelled.

I knew I wasn't going to get far with this lecture.

"I'm sorry, but I have a question." At least this student stood up to talk. I usually didn't take questions until the end of my presentation, but maybe it would help wrangle the others.

"Of course," I responded.

"So, someone told you killing Jews was a good idea, and you did it. Is that like someone telling you that everyone is jumping off a bridge and you should do it too, so you do it?"

A roar of laughter heckled through the auditorium.

"I'm Jewish. Do you want to kill me?" A girl spoke up. "Can I request a gas chamber though? I don't want my head blown to smithereens."

It was all I could take. I hadn't felt the urge to run away like I did that day, but I stepped away from the podium and walked right out of the auditorium, then out the front doors. I vomited in a trash barrel out in the front of the school and told myself I was through with the presentations.

The walk home felt much longer than the walk to the school. Images of gas chambers and executions were vivid in my mind's eye. I had seen it all and would do anything to forget everything. I was beginning to think no one would ever be able to understand why I was in that situation. I was put there. I was forced to be there. If I left, I would put my family in jeopardy. If I ran away, I would be imprisoned—like I had been.

My legs felt like heavy weights as I trudged up the stairs to my apartment. I opened the door and lamented, "I give up, Mama. No one wants to hear me out."

I tossed my briefcase by the coat hook and walked into the television room, finding Mama resting. I was thankful she listened for a change and decided to take a rest.

"Mama?" I walked over to the cot where she was resting comfortably. I *was* surprised to see her sleeping in the middle of the day. Naps were not her thing. I nudged her shoulder, shaking her subtly. "Mama." She didn't budge. I rested my hand on her cheek, feeling the dreaded ice-cold sensation. "Mama!" My mouth was numb, but I was yelling so loudly the neighbors must have heard. "Wake up, Mama. We have just a week left until your doctor's appointment. Mama!"

It was no use. I stared at my mother's lifeless body, wishing I was there with her when she took her last breath, but instead, I was trying to convince an auditorium that I was a good Nazi instead of being a good son. "I am so sorry, Mama. I should have been here."

I ran for the phone and called for Claude. Juliette answered: "The Taylor residence."

"Juliette," I groaned.

"Charlie, what is it? Are you all right?"

"Mama," was all I could manage to say.

"Oh, no, no, no. Charlie. Speak to me."

"She's gone, Juliette."

"But the doctor's appointment is next week," she cried.

"It's too late," I breathed into the phone, wrapping the cord tightly around my wrist.

"I'm going to go get Claude at work, and we will be there as soon as we can." I heard what Juliette was saying, but I couldn't find the words to speak. "Charlie?"

I glanced down and shook my head, trying to collect my thoughts. "I need to call the hospital. I don't know what to do—"

"Go on, call the hospital. We'll find you, Charlie. Be strong. We will be there as soon as we can. I love you."

Regret. So much regret. It's all I felt at that moment. I

pulled a kitchen chair up to her bedside and took Mama's heavy hand, holding it in mine. "I'm here, Mama. I'll always be with you." *Like I hadn't been.*

As I lowered my head to our entangled hands, I spotted a note tucked under a fold in the sheet. I gently placed Mama's hand back down and took the note.

My dearest Charlie,

Sometimes in life, we just know when it's time. Sometimes, we know when it's not the right time. I wish I had longer with you, but your Papa—he has been calling for me. I was tired, Charlie, and I have held onto this note since I arrived here in New York, thinking each time I rested might be the last time I would close my eyes. My sohn, you have been my greatest joy in life, and though the world was not a friendly place for many of our years together, I learned how great your heart and soul is and will forever be. You have taught me more about life than I could have imagined knowing.

In my left hand is the ring your father gave me when he asked for my hand in marriage. Charlie, take the ring and give it to the person who makes your world feel complete. I also ask that you never give up on your dream, because you deserve more than you give yourself credit for. A mother's intuition is stronger than most might think. Remember that. Therefore, I know there will be a time when your life will be exactly the way you want.

Tell Claude, Juliette, and Penny I love them dearly, and if you get the chance to be with your Amelia, please tell her I love her too.

My sohn, my greatest accomplishment, my world, my reason for life—I will always watch over you and I will be listening if you ever need me.

Es wird am ende in ordnung sein; It will all be all right in the end.

I will love you for always,

Mama

My heart raced as I placed the note down on top of the white sheets and reached for her left hand. The ring fell into my palm as soon as I lifted her wrist. The ring was all I had left of my family.

I placed a kiss on my Mama's cheek and made the call to the hospital. They were going to send help.

Though her time of death was called, and she was taken to the morgue, I felt the need to sit in the lobby of the hospital, needing that time to contemplate my life. It was hard to convince myself that Mama's death was not my fault. I should have pleaded with the doctor to see her sooner than the following week, but they did not give me that option. *I thought we had more time.*

It was dusk when Claude and Juliette arrived. They needed to find someone to watch Penny, and then make the trip out to the city from Connecticut. They both wrapped their arms around me and cried into my shoulders. The tears were still frozen within me. I realized I had not cried, and I wondered why I wasn't capable of that emotion. Then the possible explanation hit me; Mama was fortunate enough to die peacefully in her bed. With all the ways she could have died over the years, she was lucky to go the way she did, and it was a reason to feel grateful.

"She's with your papa now," Claude tried to comfort me.

"I'm all alone in the world, and everything I have struggled to find seems to be out of reach. Every decision I have made since the war has revolved around chasing love, and I left so much behind."

Claude pressed his hands into my shoulders, pushing me back. "Charlie, you can't summarize your life that way. You have accomplished so much and overcome many battles. It has been a journey full of challenges you were meant to fight through. There were lessons to be learned."

I heard Claude's words, but they were swimming above my head, because I was now drowning in sorrow.

CHAPTER 39

PRESENT DAY

Amelia rests her hand down on my knee as our train ride zooms through the trees.

Another train ride, another destination.

"Life can't be full of gains, or we would never learn appreciation from our losses," Amelia says.

"I would never compare my losses to yours," I tell her, needing her to know I don't expect sympathy.

"You don't have to explain yourself to me," she says, holding my hand.

Even though we have seventy-four years' worth of conversation to catch up on, I am content with the quiet between us as we take in the view from outside the window. I enjoy listening to Amelia breathe, as well as inhaling the sweet scent of the rose perfume she is wearing. "When is the last time you have been in New York?" I ask.

"Oh, goodness. Maxwell and I moved to Massachusetts back in the seventies, and I'm afraid I haven't been back since."

"Not much has changed," I assure her. "People are still in a rush, dressed in their finest, and the streets are filled with chatter and smells from nearby restaurants."

"Just how I liked it," she says, smiling widely at the unraveling city skyline.

The train ride flew by rather quickly, and before I know it, I am helping her up the stairs to my apartment.

I open the door and allow her to walk inside first. A smile pokes at her lips as her eyes gaze around with wonder. "My paintings," she says.

"Yes, I own every single one I could get my hands on, darling. Your paintings have made my apartment feel like home."

Amelia circles the small area, tracing her finger along the white walls. "I often imagined how a place of our own might appear. I realized I knew less than I wanted to know about you, and while I knew some of your passions in life, I didn't know what made you, you."

"Well, I have spent many years figuring that out for myself," I explain.

Amelia takes slow, cautious steps around the perimeter of the space. "Everything is so neat and tidy," she says as she spins around in the center of the room, stopping in front of the brown, leather chair. "Is this—"

I sweep a piece of dust from the leather and smooth my hand over the seat. "Amelia, this is your chair. No one has ever taken a seat on it before."

Amelia's lips press together, and she offers me her hand. "May I?"

I press my lips together, stopping my chin from trembling, and nod my head. "Please. I have waited a long time to see you rest in this chair," I tell her, helping her ease down into the seat.

"It's quite comfortable, she says, leaning her head back with a smile. You have fine taste in furniture, Charlie Crane."

I find myself gazing at her, losing myself in the moment. All those times I imagined talking to Amelia, while she sat in this very chair, they are all coming to life.

"I'm sorry you never found that person who could make your world complete as your mama wanted," she says. "I had hoped and prayed for your happiness so many times, Charlie."

I reach into my pocket and retrieve the little yellow envelope I have kept safe. I slip my fingers into the opening and pinch the gold band. "Amelia, there was never a time limit on finding the person who would complete my world, and I knew I had to be patient for my dream to come true. I have only ever listened to my heart, regardless of how crazy I thought I had been so many times throughout my life, but my heart—" I tap my fist on my chest. "It was right all along."

It is a struggle to bend down on my knee, but it is a struggle I will endure. "Amelia, I have wanted you to be my wife for seventy-four years. I know we're old and certainly not getting any younger, but finding you has been a challenge in my journey, and I was never going to give up. Will you—"

Tears stream down Amelia's cheeks as her hand cups over her mouth. "Charlie Crane, please be my husband," she pleads through a soft cry. "I have never stopped loving you. I knew someday we would find each other again."

The thought of us escaping Austria together plays out in my mind. The vision of us holding hands and running through the meadows that would lead us to Zurich, and the bed and breakfast where we should have been saving up money together so we could raise a family in America. New York should have offered us late-night strolls through Times Square and Central Park. We could have leaned on our elbows on a cafe table while being mesmerized at live jazz bands playing our favorite tunes. I would have been at the art galleries standing beside her as she blushed at the attention. We could have sung our children to sleep and curled up in our chairs while sharing a bowl of popcorn that sat on the small circular table between us. I would have kissed my love before bed every single night, thanking God for allowing me to have her all to myself.

Those were all dreams, but I would give up those dreams again to know I could spend the rest of my days with her now.

At the end of each journey, there is a reward for our accomplishments. I survived. Amelia survived. We beat the odds, and now we can enjoy the end.

EPILOGUE

"Clara, Annie, and Emma are going to be quite angry with us, Amelia," I tell her as our New York ferry docks in front of Ellis Island and the Statue of Liberty.

"This doesn't concern them," Amelia says, slapping her hand against the air. She has clearly thought this through. "We have our witnesses, and that's all that matters."

I glance over at Amelia, who is decked out in a beautiful white dress beneath her black overcoat. Her hair is up, held with dazzling pins, her lips are red, her cheeks are pink, and white gloves cover her hands. As the other travelers disembark the boat, I offer Amelia my hand to help her from the seat.

I focus on the way the white glove eases in my grip. "My darling, shall we?"

Our grips are tight as we slowly make our way into the building. It feels as though we are walking into an endless sunset together. Amelia's heels click and clack, and I notice people lining the walls, applauding us as we walk through the corridor.

"A true inspiration," I hear from a man as we pass by.

"We were assigned a small room just down there," I say as we continue walking forward.

I spot my best friends at the end of the hall, just in front of the courtroom doors. As Claude and I had always planned, we grew old together, but I still see the young versions of us all. Claude and Juliette, with their hands still intertwined, walk toward us. "I was wrong, brother. You were right, and I have wanted to say those words to you for so many years. I see now why you never gave up," Claude says in my ear.

"It is a pleasure to meet you finally," Juliette tells Amelia. "I have spent a lifetime hearing how wonderful you are. I am elated to share this day with you both."

"I feel as though I know you both," Amelia tells Claude and Juliette. "Charlie has shared the ups and downs of his story with me these past few months, and while I realize I still have more than seventy years to catch up on, you two have been his foundation, and I could never thank you enough for being his family when he had no one."

"You have been alive in his heart, Amelia. He has always had you," Claude tells her, placing a kiss on Amelia's cheek. "It is beyond a pleasure to meet you."

Claude and Juliette follow us toward the justice of the peace that has been waiting for us to arrive. The two take a seat, and I take my girl's hand, staring at her with gratitude.

"Your story is remarkable," the justice of the peace begins. "In a time where true love is hard to find, you two have proven what patience and perseverance are worth. We cannot change our past, but we can allow our past to mold our future. We spend our days working hard to earn money and respect—but not often do we see the hidden fruits of our labor. You two have worked harder than most to get here with your soulmate, and I wish you both a lifetime of love and happiness."

"I love you," I whisper to Amelia.

"I love you, Charlie Crane."

"Vows are meant to be used as promises for couples who are intending to commit themselves to one another. However, you both have proven the vow you have for each other throughout the last seventy-four years of your lives. Therefore, I ask of you, Charlie, do you take Amelia Baylin to be your lawfully wedded wife?"

Tears fill my eyes as I gaze into Amelia's. Her eyes show no sign of age, and I can still see forever as I once had. "I do."

"Amelia, do you take Charlie Crane to be your lawfully wedded husband?"

"I do," she says just before throwing her arms around my neck and pressing her lips to mine.

Nothing has changed. Not a day has passed.

"It is at this time that I now humbly pronounce you husband and wife."

A kiss behind prison walls.

A kiss in front of a guard's tower.

We left the dangers behind, but the love has forever been captured between us, and our unspoken words were the links that tied us together, keeping our memories alive—the connection forever intact.

Amelia pulls away just enough to look me in the eyes. Her lips smile, and she blinks slowly. "It was a battle we fought, Charlie, but it was a battle we won."

A LETTER FROM SHARI

Dear reader,

I hope you enjoyed reading *The Soldier's Letters*. If you enjoyed it, and want to keep up to date with all my latest releases, just sign up at the following link. Your email address will never be shared and you can unsubscribe at any time.

www.bookouture.com/shari-j-ryan

I know how raw, dark, and emotional the story came to be, and it wasn't without great difficulty that I portrayed a narrative from the "enemy's" point of view. My main purpose for writing this book was to gain a better depiction of how some German soldiers came to be. Though it pains me to understand how much hatred grew during the years leading up to World War II in Nazi Germany and how many wore cruelty as a badge of honor, I know there were still some beating hearts beneath all the darkness. I poured my heart and soul into this story, but it was a journey I couldn't take without the support from you and the other readers. Thank you.

I truly hope you enjoyed the book, and if so, I would be very appreciative if you could write a review. Since the feedback from readers helps me grow as a writer, I would love to hear what you think, and it makes such a difference helping new readers to discover one of my books for the first time.

There's no greater pleasure than hearing from my readers—

you can get in touch on my Facebook page, through Twitter, Goodreads or my website.

Thank you for reading!

xoxo

Shari

www.sharijryan.com

 facebook.com/authorsharijryan
twitter.com/sharijryan

ACKNOWLEDGMENTS

Thank you. The words are simple, but the support I have received for this series has been unbelievable.

Linda, thank you for being my friend, commandant, and publicist. Having you to hold my hand along the way makes the process feel seamless.

Julie, thank you for sticking by my side and picking up my pieces along the way. Our friendship means the world to me.

Samantha, thank you for the quality and passion you put into editing. I rest easy knowing my words are in your hands.

Shannon, thank you for proofreading and putting the finishing touches on the manuscript. Your attention to detail is much appreciated.

My alpha/beta readers: I couldn't have done this without you. You quite literally stood by my side throughout the entire writing process and gave me feedback along the way. You kept me motivated and encouraged along the way and I'm humbled by the friendship you offer.

The Scream Team, thank you for always jumping at the opportunity to receive an ARC copy of my books. Thank you, from the bottom of my heart.

To my readers, I love you all and I'm forever grateful that you have taken the time to read my words.

My family: Thank you for always supporting my dreams and sharing my passions with the world. I love you all.

My boys: Bryce and Brayden... I look at you and feel proud. You're my greatest joy and my highest achievement. I hope I make you proud like you make me proud. I love you both more than life.

Josh, I don't know how I got so lucky to have a partner in life like you, but when you promised to stick by my side through thick and thin, you didn't know part of that would include more than two dozen books. You have taken my joy on as your own and help me more than I could ever ask. Thank you for supporting my dream, loving me, and believing in me as much as you do. I love you.